THE
INFINITE
LIGHT
OF DUST

BOOKS BY ANNA TODD

THE
INFINITE
LIGHT
OF DUST

A BRIGHTEST STARS NOVEL

ANNA TODD

W **FRAYED**
wattpad **PAGES**
books

FRAYED PAGES
wattpad books

Copyright © 2024 Frayed Pages, Inc. All rights reserved.
www.frayedpagesmedia.com

Published in Canada by Wattpad WEBTOON Book Group,
a division of Wattpad WEBTOON Studios, Inc.

36 Wellington Street E., Toronto, ON M5E 1C7

www.wattpad.com

First Frayed Pages x Wattpad Books edition: July 2024

ISBN 978-1-99885-402-8 (Trade Paperback)
ISBN 978-1-99885-403-5 (eBook)

Library and Archives Canada Cataloguing in Publication and U.S. Library of
Congress Cataloging in Publication information is available upon request.

Printed and bound in Canada
1 3 5 7 9 10 8 6 4 2

Author photo by Hong Jinwook
Cover design by Lesley Worrell
Cover image © fukume via Shutterstock
Page design by Neil Erickson

To the reader holding this book, may you always find comfort within the inked pages of love stories. May you feel a little less lonely and a lot more understood. We each deserve our own love story, but never forget that your greatest love is yourself.

THE
INFINITE
LIGHT
OF DUST

PLAYLIST

FIRST TIME
Hozier

LOGICAL
Olivia Rodrigo

AMSTERDAM
Wild Rivers

HATE YOU
Jungkook

THE WORST OF YOU
Noah Cyrus and PJ Harding

STREETLIGHTS
C. James

TO SOMEONE FROM A WARM CLIMATE
Hozier

STALKER
10cm

IF IT'S THE BEACHES
The Avett Brothers

IN THE KITCHEN
Renée Rapp

YOU'RE LOSING ME
Taylor Swift

YES OR NO
Jungkook

READY FOR LOVE
India.Arie

BEFORE YOU
Benson Boone

FROM THE START (ACOUSTIC)
Matt Schuster

TOLERATE IT
Taylor Swift

SOLO
Myles Smith

LET ME HURT (ACOUSTIC)
Emily Rowed

FEELS LIKE
Gracie Abrams

RUN FOR THE HILLS
Tate McRae

MEET ME IN AMSTERDAM
RINI

SHATTERED
O.A.R

WALKED THROUGH HELL
Anson Seabra

우린 빛나고 있네
각자의 방 각자의 별에서
어떤 빛은 야망
어떤 빛은 방황
사람들의 불빛들
모두 소중한 하나
어두운 밤 (외로워 마)
별처럼 다 (우린 빛나)
사라지지 마

We're shining, in each of our rooms,
in each of our planets
One light is ambition
Some light is wandering
People's lights
All are precious
This dark night, don't be lonely
Like stars, we shine
Don't disappear
—BTS, "Mikrokosmos"

CHAPTER **ONE**

Karina

As the shock wore off, we watched Elodie's husband, Phillips, come up my walkway and toward the porch where Kael and I were standing. Kael gently pressed his hand against my back to hold me steady. I could feel his palm flinching, shaking a bit. What the hell was going on?

Could there be worse timing than this? How did Phillips even get here? And when?

"Stay here," Kael said under this breath, but loud enough for me to hear.

I stayed planted on the concrete porch, listening to him for once. Something about Kael's body language was off as I watched him step down to greet the man who was supposed to be his best friend. Something in the way Kael's jaw tensed and his hand shook made me pay even closer attention to both men. Phillips had gone from some mythical man I had only heard about and seen pictures of to a real-life person standing in the middle of my yard. He hugged Kael and an alarm went off in my head.

Maybe it was because of the way Phillips was with Elodie lately—how he'd spoken to her on their video calls and the sadness in her voice and eyes when it came to him, but I no longer looked forward to meeting him. Not to mention the photo on Kael's phone, Austin and Elodie embracing, kissing, having an affair. I hadn't been able to even process that yet and now her husband was here in the flesh.

"Surprised to see me?" he asked Kael. The morning air was still crisp and dewy, and a puff of breath came out of his mouth as he spoke.

"As hell. When did you get in?" Kael responded, patting his battle buddy on the shoulder.

I didn't know if I should go inside or keep standing there watching them, but before I could make up my mind, Phillips's attention turned to me. Suddenly I wondered how he'd gotten my address in the first place, if he'd known Kael would be here, or if he was looking for his wife.

"You must be the infamous Karina," he said in a tone that could easily be either playful or sinister. I didn't know him well enough to know which, and the pit in the bottom of my stomach grew as the seconds passed. He rubbed his hands together to warm them. The weather was typical for a Georgia fall, but I guessed after being in Afghanistan for so long he was used to extreme heat, and being stateside would take a while to get used to.

I lifted my hand to wave, and it didn't go unnoticed that Kael moved around him quickly and strode back up to the porch. Something in Kael's eyes shifted, and for once I couldn't read his mind. He stood on the bottom step, putting a barrier between Phillips and me.

"I am. And you must be the infamous Phillip Phillips." I faked a smile.

He nodded, bowing slightly. "I am."

Silence ticked by, like none of us knew what the hell to say or do.

"Where is my wife?" Phillips finally asked.

"The PX," I blurted. The sun was still rising, turning the sky an orange hue. I would usually take it in longer, but this wasn't the time.

"Ah. I was hoping to surprise her, not y'all. When will she be back? Hell, I don't even know what time it is and don't have a phone yet. But what the hell is she getting from the PX this early?" He sighed, annoyed maybe? Or maybe I was looking for reasons to feel uneasy. He had just arrived from Afghanistan to see his wife and she wasn't here. I would probably be annoyed too. And thank god he didn't have a phone yet; what the fuck were we going to do about the photo floating around? I needed to talk to Kael alone, ASAP. I also needed to warn Elodie that her husband was here and thought she was at the store, not having a sleepover with my brother.

"I don't know, but I can call her?" I offered, trying not to let the panic in my voice shine through.

"No." His tone was clipped.

Kael's back stiffened, and he turned to Phillips.

"We can go to my place and Karina can bring Elodie over when she's back," Kael suggested.

His idea would only work if Elodie and my brother could get out of Kael's place before Phillips got there. There weren't many places the two of them could be, so they had to be at Kael's, where Austin had been staying for a while now.

Phillips shook his head. "Fuck. How long ago did she leave?"

"It's only been . . . I don't know, actually."

It was true; from the time that Austin and Elodie had left, everything was a blur. It was obvious why they didn't come back last night, but that was of no help to me or to Kael, who had to cover for them. My palms were clammy, my heart racing.

Phillips's nearly black eyes stared at me. I could feel him trying to reach for something. Maybe he already knew about Austin and Elodie? There was something so uncomfortable, so accusatory about the way he was studying me. God, this was a disaster.

"How do you not know?" he accused me. I took a step forward, though fear was creeping inside of me.

"I'm—"

"Don't talk to her like that." Kael's voice was commanding, and I was starting to feel like there was something I was missing, as always.

Phillips's lips turned into a smile, and he shrugged his shoulders back in a slow movement, like he was trying to control himself. Was he always this volatile? How could Elodie be married to someone like him? My judgment was fast and harsh, but something was seriously off with him.

"Is something going on here?" Phillips turned to Kael, and the blood rose to the surface of my skin.

"Other than you showing up here without warning and getting pissed off at the wrong people, no."

Kael's response made Phillips step back a little. His shoulders slumped, and he didn't seem as threatening anymore, even though he had to be almost six feet tall. In my mind, soldiers always carry a certain level of strength and intimidation no matter their physical appearance. But Phillips's bearing didn't feel like someone who was fresh from a war zone. He was only an inch or so shorter than Kael but a lot less built. He was much thinner than I'd imagined, but I had only really seen photos of him in his uniform, which always makes people look bigger than they are.

Phillips raised his hand and rubbed his forehead. "Sorry, it's been a hell of a week and I flew twenty hours. Bad first impression, huh?"

He looked up at me on the porch and his expression changed to one of innocence. I tried to rationalize his emotions and see his side, but it was harder than it should have been. He was deployed until a day ago; I should have way more sympathy for him.

"It's not a great one, but understandable. Do you want something to eat? I made some sausage gravy and biscuits. Or a shower? I might have some beer?" I didn't know why I was offering such a moody man alcohol so early in the morning, and I could tell by Kael's expression that he didn't either.

"We should go to my place. You probably don't even have clothes on you," Kael suggested. Again, my pulse raced. Did Kael not realize that Austin and Elodie had to be at his place right now?

Phillips shook his head. "I have a change of clothes, and a beer and shower sounds fucking amazing right now."

Out of the corner of my eye, I caught my neighbor Bradley watching the three of us. I had practically spied on Bradley many times, but for some reason I felt like he was seeing something he shouldn't. I was also trying to avoid looking at Kael because he was looking at me like I'd suggested we murder someone. I really wished I had my phone on me so I could at least check my brother's location and give him a heads-up that Elodie's husband had literally shown up on my doorstep.

"All right then, let's go inside?" I rocked back on my heels awkwardly.

Again, I could feel Kael telepathically cursing me out, but he stayed quiet as he led Phillips into my house.

CHAPTER TWO

Karina

"What the hell are you thinking?" Kael whispered the moment we heard the water in the bathroom turn on.

We were in my room, standing near the window. The sun had completely filled the sky, bringing the heat with it, and Kael's stare burned a hole through me.

"What was I supposed to do? Have a picnic in the yard? Why the hell is he here? And what are we going to do about Austin and Elodie? Where the hell are they? They must have stayed together at your place."

I pressed my fingers against my temples and paced the room. Thank god my room was close to the bathroom so we could hear the shower turn on and off. I hoped that Phillips took his time, and didn't take two-minute showers like most soldiers, Kael included.

"*You* aren't going to do or say anything about Elodie and your brother," Kael said pointedly.

He caught my arm as I paced by him and pulled me closer. "Seriously, Karina. You have to stay out of it. Whatever the fuck it even is. I was trying to get him away from you so you could get a hold of Elodie or your brother and have them get their asses back here."

"Don't tell me what to do, Kael," I whispered forcefully. "This is really not good, and it involves the two people I care about the most in the world." I glared at him, yanking my arm away from his gentle grasp. "Two of the three, I mean."

Kael sat down on the edge of my bed and put his head between his knees without saying a word. The last thing either of us needed was to turn on one another right now. I moved forward to comfort him, touching his head; the freshly shaven strands gently poked at my palm.

"He doesn't seem to have any clue that anything is amiss, so as long as we both stay calm, it will be fine. For now, at least," Kael said.

"I'm going to grab my phone before he gets out and see where the hell they are and tell Elodie to come back, now."

He nodded under my touch, and I walked as fast as I could to the living room to get my phone. The screen normally lit up when touched but it stayed black, so I tapped it—still black. No fucking way was my phone dead right now. I heard the water stop running and more panic set in. I rushed back into my room and asked Kael for his phone.

"This isn't not getting involved, Karina." He groaned but placed the phone in my hand anyway.

I called my brother first and couldn't manage to stand still as it rang and rang. His annoying voice came through on his voicemail, and I wanted to break Kael's phone and my brother's neck at the same time. I scrolled and found Elodie's name and tried her.

After two rings her voice chimed in my ear. "Hi, birthday girl!"

"Elodie, where the heck are you guys? You never came back last night." I tried to be as quiet as possible, knowing my walls were paper-thin.

"We're pulling onto the street now. Sorry, we ended up staying at Kael's. I was so tired, and it was nice and quiet, so I asked Austin if I could stay over. Sorry if you were worried," she said. "Is something wrong?" she asked, knowing me well enough to catch on to my tone.

"Well . . ." I tried to respond through the hurt of her lying to me so easily.

Putting my own feelings aside, I didn't know if I should ruin the surprise—if she would even be happy to see Phillips—or if she would want to be warned given the fact that everyone in the friend group just found out that she's having an affair with my brother. Before I could think straight enough to decide, she spoke again.

"We're pulling up. I'm coming right in."

Kael sat up as I handed him back his phone.

"They're here."

"You should stay in here. We both should," he said, nodding at the door. "This isn't our business and Phillips doesn't know anything about Fischer and Elodie yet."

"Are you sure?" I perched on one of his knees. He wrapped his arms around me, but his body still felt stiff as a board.

"If he knew your brother was fucking his wife, your house wouldn't be standing, and that's a fact."

His words rattled me, but they had to be true. Austin and Elodie . . . When? How? What the hell were they thinking? Not only was I still shocked from seeing the photo and them clearly staying the night together, but now she was acting like nothing had happened, which I guess to her, nothing had. I swear my head was going to explode, and we only had seconds before they'd come prancing through the door, totally *not* expecting Elodie's husband to be here.

"As much as I want to stay out of it, I can't—we can't. What if they fight or something?" I asked Kael, grabbing his hand and pulling him toward my bedroom door. He planted his feet and grabbed his hoodie, and pressed it against my chest.

"Put this on, at least." He looked down my body to my short pajama shorts and thin top. The last thing I was thinking about was my outfit, but I tossed the oversized hoodie, which came to my knees, over my head. Kael led me down the hallway. We passed the bathroom as the door to it and the front door opened at the same time.

"Karina! What's going on?" Elodie's voice was full of concern, and her doe eyes fell into relief as she saw me hand in hand with Kael. "You scared me!" she said, holding up the plastic bag in her hand. "We got the baby monitor before it sold out yesterday! And Austin even got them to give me an extra ten dollars off because the box is open and—" Her voice halted abruptly and her blue eyes widened as she looked at the figure behind me.

Austin came barreling in behind her, smiling and tossing his shoes off his feet before looking up. "What's—"

"Phillip?" Elodie's voice was barely above a whisper as she said his name.

She didn't rush toward him and throw her arms around him like I had seen many wives welcoming home their husbands do. She stood still, her eyes frozen on him as he walked into the living room. It had never felt so small.

"El, that's not the reaction I expected," Phillips said to her.

There was a confusing mixture of warmth and iciness to his voice. His dark hair was still wet from the shower, a bit longer than the typical required buzz cut. He stood awkwardly, swaying his lower body slightly, as if they were meeting for the first time.

Elodie's face was frozen for a few seconds before she snapped out of it and broke into a smile. Phillips wrapped his arms around her waist and hugged her, lifting her feet off the ground. She yelped in pain, and he put her down.

"The baby," she said, gently pushing at her husband's chest to put some distance between them. "You have to be careful of the baby."

Her direction was calm, but it wasn't lost on me that the bottom of his jaw twitched as she took another step back, away from him.

My heart sank as I finally took in my brother. Austin looked like he was being burned alive. I couldn't imagine how he felt, despite the chaos the two of them had caused. There were so many questions, so much confusion, but right then all I felt was his pain. I could see it, as clear as a cloudless sky; he loved her.

My brother was in love with Elodie.

How did I, his twin, not see this until now? Everything he was feeling in that moment was written on his face; the worry and pain in his blue eyes, the longing in his hands stretched out toward her, the helplessness he felt as he dropped them to his sides.

"Sorry, sorry." Phillips's hands went to Elodie's stomach, and he rubbed it gently over her sweatshirt. Austin's face was turning a sick shade of green.

"Let's give them some privacy?" I suggested, and Elodie's eyes darted to me.

"Yeah, I need to—" My brother was struggling to find the words.

"I'll take you," Kael offered. Austin looked relieved, but as his twin I could tell he was in some form of shock. I'd never seen him so speechless. "And you"—Kael looked my way—"you're coming too."

I wanted to tell him to piss off, that I wasn't going to leave Elodie here with this man, but the man in question was her husband, so it didn't make any sense for me to be this worried. None of what was happening did, so I followed Kael's very direct demand and slid my shoes on, pushing my dead cell phone into the pocket of his hoodie. I'd have to charge it in Kael's truck or wherever we were going.

I wanted to ask Elodie if it was okay to leave, but I didn't want to make things worse or more tense between her and Phillips. Neither of them had moved, like they didn't know what to do around one another, which was also pretty normal when a soldier came home after being gone awhile, and I'm sure having an audience wasn't helping.

"I'll be back home tonight, text me if you need anything," I told Elodie as we made our way out the front door.

Kael said the same to Phillips and gently pushed Austin's back, forcing him to follow us out onto the porch. The three of us were silent as we made our way down the grass. Kael opened the passenger door for me, and there was a lurching sound followed by the splash of liquid on the concrete. I looked back to see my brother hunched over, vomiting on the street. Kael patted my brother's back, and he was saying something that I couldn't hear.

Kael must have felt so conflicted between his best friend and my brother. We were all in the middle of a spiderweb and there was no way for all of it to fall into place peacefully. Someone was bound to get bitten.

"Breathe . . . try to breathe." Kael continued to rub his hand across my brother's back.

"This is so fucked up," Austin mumbled, his voice broken as he wiped his sleeve across his chin.

I wondered if he was going to elaborate, but it wasn't the time to push him. Not yet.

After Austin was done being sick, we drove with only the loud rumble of Kael's truck. I hadn't even brushed my teeth, and it was late in the morning. Austin was staring out the window in a void, his lids heavy, his head slumped. It didn't feel right to start grilling my brother about Elodie right now, but we also had to warn him that people knew about the two of them, and now that Phillips was back things were even more complicated. My head ached and I only realized I was crying when Kael reached over and wiped my cheek. I wasn't sure if it was for my brother, or because of the stress of all of it, or for my best friend, who didn't seem to recognize her own husband.

CHAPTER **THREE**

Kael

Damn it all to hell. The list of problems and potential solutions ran through my head as we drove to my place. My hands were going numb because of how hard I was gripping the steering wheel. There were a whole lot more problems than solutions coming to mind. How the fuck had Phillips gotten home when he still had months of deployment left? The possible answers to that were all but good. Something was fucking up; not only did he look like a shell of the man I knew and there was no way he would have flown home without telling me, but how did he know where Karina lived?

I rolled my neck, trying to release some of the tension. I looked into the rearview mirror at Fischer, who was a sickly shade of green, and then to Karina at my side. My instincts told me that their father was involved somehow. I had no reason necessarily to come to that conclusion, but I simply knew it. He was too involved in every problem in our lives, from covering up innocent deaths in Afghanistan to trying to break Karina and me apart; why would this time be any different?

Karina sniffled next to me, and I could feel her anxiety rippling off her in waves. It was so strong that it was hard to focus while driving. She was shockingly quiet until we pulled onto my street.

She hadn't been to my duplex before and this was not the way I wanted to show it to her, but I had to get them out of that house before Karina let something slip out of nervousness or Fischer lost his shit. I could see it on his face—if Phillips touched Elodie again, he would snap. I knew that look too well.

I pulled into the driveway and Karina looked over at me. "This is your house?" She looked forward. The yard was neat, recently mowed, but there were materials scattered at the front of the house. Wooden planks, metal fasteners, a bucket of paint that had to be dried out by now, hammers, a drill—everything needed for all the DIY I had going on lately.

"Yeah. I wanted to show you it when it was done, but here we are." I shrugged, feeling oddly nervous for her to see it in such an undone state.

"Here we are," she repeated, her voice tight. I wanted to hug her; I could only imagine how much tension she was holding right now, even though not one bit of it was her fault, and this was how she was spending her birthday. What a fucking mess.

I reached up and grazed her cheek again; this time it was slightly more dry. She closed her eyes and leaned into my palm. Her skin was cold even though the heat was on in the truck.

"Let's go inside," I said.

Fischer climbed out of the back without making a peep and Karina watched her brother closely as we walked to the front door.

"Do you think they're okay?" she asked as I typed the passcode into my automatic lock. She examined it like she had never seen one before, and if we weren't in the middle of such a fucked-up situation, I would tell her I could install one at her house, too, so she doesn't have to worry about losing her keys or getting locked out.

"Yeah. They'll be fine. It will take a little while to get used to each other." I tried to keep my voice as steady as possible. I didn't know for sure if I was lying or not, but it felt like I was.

"Elodie seemed so . . . uneasy, scared?" Karina said as I flicked the living room and porch lights on.

Fischer pushed past us and went to the bathroom, slamming the door behind him, and the violent sounds of him puking made Karina shudder.

"Austin—" She followed the path her brother had taken, stepping over boards and boxes, and opened the bathroom door down the hall. This was far from how I had envisioned showing her the work I had put into this place. As soon as she closed the door behind her, I pulled my phone out of my pocket and called Mendoza. He answered on the second ring.

He picked up with a casual "Yo."

"Phillips is back," I told him, walking to the kitchen area and the back door.

"Huh?"

"Phillips. He showed up at Karina's house this morning." I kept my voice as low as I could, but Mendoza didn't do the same.

"What the fuck you mean he showed up at Karina's house?" I heard the familiar screen door creak open followed by the noise of a car honking, letting me know he had stepped outside, away from the kids.

"What I said, he showed up here in his ACUs, fresh off the goddamn plane, looking for his wife."

"Fuuuuck. Fuck, fuck, fuck. Did he see the picture? Does he know about Fischer and her?"

I wanted to slam my fist through the screen door and feel the aluminum mesh cut through the flesh on my hand.

"So far it doesn't seem like has a clue, but we know that won't last for long. I don't know what to do, man. Karina's losing it, and we should be fucking up Fischer for touching our friend's wife, but—" I said.

"But we can't. And we know damn fucking well we won't. Fischer can't keep himself out of trouble. I'll try to handle it on my side and keep the shit from reaching Phillips for now, but it's only a matter of time." Mendoza added, "Fischer's leaving soon for basic, if we can keep them separate until then."

"And Elodie? I wouldn't have considered this before but I'm telling you, something is really fucking off with Phillips, he seems even worse than before. You don't think he would hurt her, right?" I was surprised by my own question, given I was usually the handler of all the shit, not the one asking questions on next steps.

"He's been fucked up. I told you that, and I wouldn't put it past him. Don't forget what he did to Nielson and that Afghani woman he fell in love with. Phillips is the one who told the command where Nielson was hiding, and they were supposed to be friends."

My stomach turned. "If he does anything to Elodie, I will kill him myself."

"Correction, bro. *We* will kill him. Let's play it cool for now— you take care of Karina and Fischer and I'll try to keep Phillips busy and find out how the fuck he got home so early."

I didn't tell Mendoza about my suspicion about Fischer's dad being involved because of all the shit that would bring up. The guilt that Mendoza struggled with daily, the lie Karina's father had created and forced us all to not only be a part of but to keep our mouths shut about—those wounds would be torn open again and they hadn't even properly healed yet. None of us had healed, and maybe we never would. I hated that he was responsible for one of the many open wounds inside of me, and that I couldn't escape him, not the way I needed to. I would be haunted for the rest of my life by what he had caused, all while Karina and Fischer's dad was sitting pretty as a retired high-ranking officer. I used to dream of retiring the honorable way, not a fucking medical retirement. I knew I'd needed and deserved it, but deep down it felt like a cop-out. The line between shame and dignity was as thin as ever.

"Does he have a phone yet?" Mendoza asked.

"Nah, not yet. But I'm sure he'll get it turned back on tomorrow."

"This is really not fucking good." Mendoza sounded exasperated, and a lot of his concern must be for Fischer—whom we'd all taken in. Mendoza was the kind of man who would do everything he could for the people he loved, and now Fischer was one of them. Mendoza and Phillips had already drifted apart during our deployment, the latter using his adrenaline and anger as an excuse to shoot his gun many more times than needed. It wore on Mendoza, who was the most righteous of us all.

"Yeah, really not fucking good. I brought Karina and him to my place for now, and we can come up with a plan or try to navigate this tomorrow? Thanks for answering, man."

"I've got you. You always do everything for all of us. I'll do what I can. We all will." I could tell Mendoza hadn't been drinking by his calm, rational thinking. I hoped this wouldn't make him go inside and pick up the bottle, but knew it probably would.

"All right, talk tomorrow. Call me if anything happens," I said, hanging up the phone.

When I turned back around Karina was standing in the front of the kitchen, and the look on her face fucking ripped me apart. I have always been able to stand everything that happened to me— having bullets graze and tear at my body, getting shrapnel stuck inside my neck only a fraction of an inch away from an artery, having my leg mutilated—but seeing Karina in pain nearly brought me to my knees. She didn't say anything, so I walked toward her, reaching my arms out to grab her as her shoulders collapsed.

"How is he?" I asked her, stroking her hair softly with one hand and holding her tightly against me with the other.

"He finally ran out of things to vomit. He hasn't said a word. He doesn't know we know, and I don't know how to approach that. What they did was fucked up, and I should be pissed at him for hiding this from me, but I feel bad for him, for both of them."

She looked up at me, her green eyes full of small red veins. "And I'm sorry for you too. I know Phillips is your best friend . . . this puts you in such an awkward position."

"I can go." Fischer's voice came from behind us. Karina turned around and I looked over at him, shaking my head.

"You're not going anywhere," I told him, meaning it. I'd tie his ass to a chair before I let him go right now, and he didn't have anywhere to go anyway.

"And neither are you," I told Karina, pulling her even closer to me. "It's your birthday, both of you. We can at least order some food or something? Nothing is going to happen this afternoon or even tonight, so let's try to have some fun, then go to bed and come up with a solution tomorrow."

"A solution," Fischer repeated, then slumped his way to the couch.

I was sure if he were able to think clearly he would have caught on that we knew why he was having such an intense reaction to Phillips's sudden return. Neither of us were saying it, but it was taking up so much air that we could barely breathe.

"I'm not hungry," Fischer and Karina both said at once.

"I don't care. You're not going to starve today of all days, and you can nap after you eat something." I pulled out my phone and walked into my room to order Chinese takeout. I knew what both of them liked, and I asked the woman on the line if they had any desserts and candles, offering to pay extra. She said she would see what she could do.

By the time the food arrived the silence was nearly driving me fucking mad. I was torn between wanting to tell Fischer to come clean about everything right fucking now and leaving him alone in his misery. Both seemed like the right and the wrong answer. Instead, I turned the TV on and searched for *Twilight* to comfort and distract Karina. I offered to play *Call of Duty* with Fischer, but he sat there, uninterested. The food arrived and they picked at it, barely eating, and the lady who'd said she would see what she could do about a birthday dessert failed me by sending one blob of what looked like melted ice cream on a brown square, so I tossed it and called in reinforcements.

Gloria and Mendoza showed up at my back door less than an hour after I texted them. Gloria handed me a small store-bought cake with a monster truck painted in blue icing on it.

"It was all they had." She shrugged, pulling out a pack of candles.

"Where are they?" Mendoza glanced around me.

"They're hibernating on the couch. I forced them to eat something but they're doing this twin silent suffering thing and it's driving me fucking crazy."

"We gotta snap them out of it, especially him." Mendoza pulled a lighter from his pocket and Gloria pushed the thin colorful candles in all over the cake. It didn't look like twenty-one, but at this point the number of candles was the least of any of our concerns.

"Let's go out there before they hear us and come in here," I suggested, waving to the living room.

Gloria started singing and we followed. Karina's face went from colorless to alive when her eyes landed on Gloria. Fischer wasn't as affected—more surprised, but not as reactive.

"You really didn't have to have a second birthday cake for us."

Karina looked at Gloria after she blew out the candles. "But I do love monster trucks."

She laughed lightly, and it was music to my goddamn ears.

"Fischer, what's up with you?" Mendoza asked, as if he didn't already know. He went to sit next to him and wrapped an arm around him, pulling him closer.

"I'm just—" I could see the struggle in Fischer's eyes, hear it in his voice. "I don't want to talk about it, but thank you for being here."

Mendoza squeezed Fischer then patted him on the head. "I'm always here, man. No matter what."

Fischer began to cry, and Mendoza brought him in for a full-on hug, covering his shaking shoulders. I turned the volume up on the TV, and Gloria turned her attention to distracting Karina, who was slumped over with a plate of cake in front of her, watching her brother's breakdown.

"*Twilight*, huh?" Gloria pointed at the screen. "I haven't seen it in forever, but I'm team Charlie. Poor guy."

Karina's mouth twitched at the corners, pulling up the tiniest of bits. On the screen, the two main characters were flying around the trees. It was completely ridiculous, but was seeming to work to keep Karina from breaking down too.

"Imagine the story from Charlie's point of view," Gloria continued, reaching to pull Karina to sit by her on the floor, so the couch was behind their backs. "It's a horror movie. His moody daughter comes to live with him after her mother runs off with some athlete, then she's a hermit, finally gets a boyfriend, and he's this creepy pale white boy whose family all look like dolls and have tons of money, then bam, she's in the hospital, he leaves her, she becomes depressed, he comes back, and suddenly she's married, pregnant, and turns into a freaking vampire."

Karina laughed, her body rocking with real laughter. "Well, I've never thought about it like that. You summed up the story in thirty seconds and it's so much funnier from Charlie's point of view."

"I bet he doesn't think it's funny." Gloria wiped her eyes, laughing tears at the corners. "Then his only grandchild grows at a freakish pace, and Jacob turns into a werewolf in front of him then ends up with his granddaughter. Talk about family trauma."

Even I'm trying not to laugh at this point. Calling the Mendozas over was the right move. I might not be the best at comforting or distracting because I tend to stay in my pain and deal with the suffering myself, but having Gloria here was a breath of fresh air. She suffered, too, but handled it better than the rest of us.

After a while, we all picked at the now-cold Chinese takeout, and Gloria picked most of the icing off the cake. Fischer and Mendoza played Xbox for what felt like days, and Karina and Gloria talked and talked and fucking talked. I zoned out, not because I didn't care what they were saying, but because I wanted to give them privacy without leaving Karina's side. Eventually, the Mendozas had to go back to get their kids from the neighbors, and Karina's eyes were barely staying open as she leaned against the back of the couch.

"Bed?" I whispered in her ear from where I sat behind her.

She nodded and I helped her to her feet. Fischer was asleep on the couch and Karina covered him with a blanket before following me.

I led Karina to my room and opened the door. It wasn't much at the moment, but at least the floors were finished and my bed frame was almost done. I'd been focused on the renovations, not decorations, so the room looked empty and sterile, but I doubted Karina would even think about that tonight.

"I'm finally staying over," she said, standing in the center of the room, in front of the mattress on the floor. "We left in such a hurry. I don't have anything, not even a toothbrush."

"I have an extra. And you're not a hostage—well, maybe for tonight you are, but tomorrow we can go back. Think about it like camping." I tried to lighten the mood a bit.

"So, this is your room," she said, looking around. "I love the paint and the flooring, the fixtures." She pointed to the matte-black handle on the door to the en suite bathroom. "Is that a connected bathroom?"

I nodded.

"What a dream."

"I have a bathtub too. I installed it a week ago, but if you want to use it? Your tub is so small," I said.

She jutted her hip to one side and placed her hand on it. "Do you think this is the time to insult my tub?" She smiled, and a huge feeling of relief opened in my chest.

"No time like the present," I responded, and sat down on the edge of the bed, rubbing my hand over my leg. I couldn't focus on the pain—I was out of pain meds and had forgotten to pick up my prescription this morning.

"You don't even want to see it?" I asked Karina, knowing curiosity was going to get the best of her, no matter how stressed she was.

She stared at the door then nodded, pulling her bottom lip between her teeth. I stood up and winced in pain, trying to dull it with my mind, but Karina noticed it before I could hide it.

I opened the door to the bathroom and watched her eyes go wide, and the way I could tell she was impressed made me feel like I had won a medal.

"The inside of this place is much flashier than the exterior," she told me with a smile.

It was fucking wild that approval from her felt so intense and important when I'd spent my life not giving a fuck about what people thought about me outside of my ma and my sister.

I would be lying if I said the bathtub being in the center of the room hadn't been influenced a bit by getting to know Karina. I had imagined her in the porcelain tub many times, lying in the bubbly water and letting the anxieties of her day melt away. Even during the uncertainty of what was going to happen with us, the idea of it had made me move a lot faster to get it done. Just in case.

"Maybe I do want to use it . . . do you know what a luxury it is to have a bathtub that a grown woman can fit in?" she told me, turning to face me.

"I do, actually. That's why I put this here, so whoever buys it can have a place to relax and not be sitting in a shallow cube of a bathtub."

"That's pretty thoughtful."

"What can I say, I'm a planner."

"Do you think Austin is—" she began to ask me. Lifting my index finger to her lips, I pressed it against her mouth.

"He's as okay as he can be. And I don't have any alcohol in the house, so he'll probably play Xbox again if he wakes up. There's nothing you can do for him right now except take care of yourself."

She sighed, acknowledging that I was right. "Should I at least text Elodie?" She pulled her cell phone out of the pocket of my hoodie.

I gently took it from her, shaking my head. "I'm going to charge this more, and you're going to take a bath."

She looked too tired to argue. When I came back from plugging her phone in by my bed, she was holding a copy of a book in her hand. Fuck me.

"What's this?" Karina's face had gotten some of its color back, and she grinned from ear to ear as she waved the novel in her hand at me.

My hand went to the back of my neck. "It's . . . I wanted to see what you love about it so much, so I started reading it during my breaks while finishing up in here." I pointed to the dust from construction in the corner; there wasn't much left to do, but there was an open light fixture I was waiting to install, so wires were sticking out. Aside from that, it was damn near perfect.

"And?"

I shrugged, staring at the hands holding a a bright-red apple on the book cover. "I'm only five chapters in, so not sure yet. But when my schedule clears, I'll read more."

She looked so pleased. "Can I borrow it for the bath?"

I leaned across her and turned the faucets on, the water rushing out. I nodded and walked over to the vanity and opened a cabinet door. "Lavender or eucalyptus?" I held two bottles of bubble bath up and she laughed.

"Should I be worried that you have a fully stocked bathroom in a mostly empty place?" She cocked an eyebrow. "Who else has used this bathtub?" Her voice turned a bit serious, and I held my hands up.

"No one. I got these for you. See? They aren't even open yet." I twisted the caps off and showed her the silver stickers covering the tops of the bottles as proof.

"For me?" she repeated quietly, smug and clearly extremely pleased with my response. "Lavender, please."

"You're such a brat." I laughed, pulled the sticker off, and squeezed the bottle over the tub. Bubbles instantly began to rise in the low water. "More?" I asked, and she nodded, watching the foamy bubbles grow.

"Yes, please." Her hands went to the bottom of the hoodie and she pulled it over her head, along with her T-shirt. Her shorts dropped to the floor, then her panties, pooling at her feet. Stepping out of them, she dipped the tip of her fingers into the warm water, testing the temperature.

"Too hot? Too cold?" I asked, trying not to stare at her naked body but finding it impossible not to.

"It's perfect," she replied, climbing into the freestanding tub and sitting down.

The tub was only halfway full but with the bubbles, nearly her entire body was covered. I could see the slight outline of her breasts, her pink nipples poking through the white foam. Now wasn't the time to be thinking of how soft her tits were in my mouth, how hard her nipples would be if I gently sucked and bit at them, but that was all I could think about.

"Does this luxury spa happen to have any candles?" Karina asked, distracting me for a few seconds.

"Yes, we do." I opened the other vanity drawer and pulled out three candles. Fuck, I had it so bad. I had never in my life owned a candle until I met this woman.

"Let me go grab a lighter, stay put," I told her, stealing one last glance at her perfect body as the bubbles and the water rose.

My cock was hard as I walked down the hallway to the kitchen to grab a lighter from the drawer. Fischer was passed out on the couch, his arm dangling over the edge. I grabbed the lighter and a glass of water, adjusting my pants before entering the bathroom again. Karina watched me as I lit the candles and placed one on the vanity counter and the other two on the windowsill behind her. I flicked the light off and looked at her, glowing in the soft candlelight. The water was now up to her shoulders, and the bubbles would have looked comically out of control if she didn't look so striking, so magnetic. Every time I looked at this woman all the noise in my head went on mute.

I stood there, entranced by her, taking in the sense of calm she brought me and noticing the way her shoulders dropped away from her ears and her eyes relaxed, falling into a calm and curious stare. Despite all the times I've imagined her in my place, in my bed, in my kitchen talking at the table with her mouth full—and even though I had changed my bathroom renovation around in case she happened to come here sometime—the imaginary scenarios never fully felt real.

The lavender scent filled the room and a few more seconds passed and neither of us could look away. It had been such a long day, in both a good and a bad way.

"Do you want some privacy?" She slowly shook her head. "Do you want me to read to you?"

Her eyes moved to the book on the ledge of the window. "Really?"

"Yeah, I have to know what becomes of the old vampire man in a teenage body and the teenager who thinks it's a good idea to date him, and you said the book is better," I teased.

"It's the love story of a lifetime. So much *Twilight* slander in this house today. So stop talking shit about it and get to reading." She smiled, closed her eyes, and leaned her head over the edge of the tub.

I grabbed the book and sat on the floor next to her. Thank god I had perfect vision because it was pretty dark in the bathroom. I began to read out loud, something I had always hated doing, but for her, I would do anything. That was becoming more solidified every day.

After a few minutes, I thought she was asleep, but she surprised me by rising to her knees and reaching her wet hand out to close the book.

"Come in with me?" she asked, her voice a bit shaky. I put the book down and stood up.

I lifted my shirt over my head and her eyes, hungry in the glow of the room, focused on my chest.

CHAPTER **FOUR**

Karina

Kael climbed into the tub and slid his body behind mine. His muscled chest felt solid against my back, and I rested my head against his chest. His arms stretched out in front of my body, one resting on my hip and one dipping into the water, taking a puff of bubbles and running fingers along my chest. Only a few minutes ago I was drifting in and out of consciousness, exhausted from the whirlwind of the day, and listening to Kael's deep voice was exactly what I needed. This was the type of intimacy I craved, and I'd never felt closer to another person in my life.

"What an insane day. This, though"—I leaned deeper into his embrace—"is heaven in the middle of hell," I whispered.

"That's what you are to me, Karina. Heaven in the middle of a constant hell."

I turned around to face him, the bubbly water splashing around us. I tucked my legs under his lifted ones and reached for his face.

"I'm serious, Karina. For years, so much darkness has taken over my mind. Since I met you, when I feel those shadows creeping in, I think of you, and I'm able to push them back. No therapy or mind-numbing medication can help the way you have, and I know it's not your responsibility to fix me, but I really fucking appreciate it."

"I love you, you know that, right?" I said. The vulnerability in my voice left me feeling as if I was being cracked open and splayed out. The fight-or-flight instinct in me that usually came with any intense feelings wasn't present; there was only Kael and his sparkling yet tormented eyes in the dim bathroom.

I brushed my thumb across the scar on his eyebrow and his eyes fluttered closed. "I love you, Karina," he said.

The way he pushed the words out as if they pained him didn't send me into an anxiety-filled tailspin the way it usually would have. Instead, I tried to understand his turmoil, the confusion and chaos around us, inside of his mind and out.

I leaned in to kiss him, startling when he gripped my ass, pulling me to straddle him and pressing our bodies so tightly together that I could barely breathe. His mouth was hungry, starving, as if I was his last meal. He adjusted my hips to lower onto his cock, fitting tightly and opening me from such an intense angle that he used one of his hands to cover my mouth and the other to pull at my hair, yanking it hard enough to make my eyes water and my core tighten so deeply I arched my back as I began to ride him. His eyes poured into mine every second of our contact, never looking away, never ashamed, only fully lost in one another. I braced myself with my hands on his shoulders, then his thighs, as his hips lifted to meet each of my movements.

"Fuck, Karina. You feel so good. I needed this, I needed you."

I nodded, all I could do as I came, my legs going still and my fingers digging into his broad shoulders as he lifted up, pounding into me to take me over the edge completely. I faintly heard the water splashing as he groaned, releasing himself into me. We both slowed our movements, catching our breath, and his hand moved from my mouth to my cheek, gently brushing my skin.

We stayed silent, only our breathing filling the bathroom, until I began to doze off in the lukewarm water. I faintly remembered Kael lifting me up, gently toweling my hair dry, and taking me to his bed.

CHAPTER **FIVE**

Karina

My brother was wide awake and sitting on Kael's couch staring at the wall when I walked into the living room the next morning. He didn't even look up or over at me, just sat there still as stone. I almost walked back into the bedroom to drag Kael out with me, but decided against it. I'd known my brother since the moment we were born, and I could usually navigate him in a way that no one else could, but I had never dealt with him being heartbroken . . . if that's what this was. I still wasn't sure, but I saw the way he looked at Elodie as Phillips hugged her, and it sure looked that way to me.

"Hey," I said, leaning into the couch next to him.

He looked at me for a second, then looked away, back at the wall.

Austin let out a sigh. "Hey."

"You okay?" I asked, knowing he obviously wasn't.

"Why wouldn't I be?" With a shrug, he attempted to sit up straight.

Oh, Austin. My idiotic, loving, always-getting-himself-in-a-mess-but-has-good-intentions twin brother.

"Because of Phillips coming home?"

Austin jutted out his jaw like he did when he was caught stealing liquor from our parents' cabinet. "What does that have to do with me?"

The sourness and hurt in his voice was hard to swallow. I didn't know where to start, but it was impossible to ignore everything happening around us. "This is the worst timing, but this picture is floating around," I said.

I opened the photo on my phone of Austin and Elodie kissing against her car and showed it to my brother. They were in their clothes from the day before yesterday, the same sky-blue hoodie Austin was still wearing. His already pale face lost the last little bit of color it had, and he jerked my phone from my hand and shot to his feet. He nearly ran into the low-set coffee table in front of the couch as he paced.

"What the fuck? How the—" He ran his fingers through his tousled hair and pinched the screen to zoom in on the photo. "Who sent this to you?"

"Mendoza sent it to Kael, but we don't know who sent it to him. It's going around the group and everyone agreed to not tell Phillips . . . but now he's here, so I don't know what is going to happen."

"I need to call her," he said, then realization hit him again. "Ugh, fuck, I can't even call her. Does she know about this?" He looked panicked.

"I don't think so. I haven't been able to ask her because he showed up before you guys even got home."

"Have you heard from her?"

I shook my head. "When did this start, Austin? And what are you guys . . . like, are you just sleeping together? This could ruin her marriage," I reminded him. I was trying so hard not to judge them, but man was it hard, especially without any context.

I wanted the best for them both and couldn't wrap my head around them having an affair.

"It's not like that—no, it is, but we aren't sleeping together." His voice was strained and he was on the verge of tears. "We haven't slept together, honest to god, but Kare, my feelings for Elodie are so much more than that, more than some girl to fool around with. I love her." He sat down, slumping in defeat.

I sat there for a moment, letting his confession sink in. How had I been so blind? I was around them all the time. Maybe I was so consumed with Kael that I hadn't even realized my brother and my best friend were falling in love?

"Does she love you?" I asked him, knowing the answer, but wanting to see how he'd react to my question.

He nodded. "I know she does. And now she's trapped in your house with a man she barely knows. How can I protect her, Kare? I don't trust him. This is making me crazy. To hell with what anyone thinks, she's not safe with him."

Him—being her husband.

"Austin, how did this . . . How did you guys . . ." I didn't know how to ask, but needed some sort of understanding.

"I don't know when it started, I think the moment I met her. I ignored it at first, that feeling that kept popping up when I saw her, the way I couldn't stop staring at her when she moved her hair out of her face, the way her laugh made me feel like life made some sense. The more time I spent with her, the more I needed her. I tried to stop it, Kare, I really fucking did, but it was impossible."

"Austin." I leaned over to touch his shoulder.

"I know, it's fucked up. She's married and I'm not in the place to take care of her and the baby, but I really love her, Kare, and will do anything for her."

The situation was so mixed up, messy, but somehow, I believed my brother's words and could feel his fear and care for Elodie. It wasn't possession—it was genuine. I had never witnessed Austin caring about another person with this depth before. I wanted to jump in the car and go to my house to check on her. Instead, I texted her and stared at my phone, waiting for those little bubbles to show up.

Nothing.

Thirty minutes. That was how long I'd wait before going home. It was my house, after all. Austin's knee shook; his leg never stopped moving for the entire half hour. We mostly sat in silence, staring at the phone. And when my eyes weren't glued to the screen, I spent the time looking around Kael's mostly bare living room, memorizing every detail. It was styled in a minimal and thoughtful way. There were coffee table books, all about home design and décor; their covers and spines were all the same brown-and-beige color scheme. The low, grayish wooden table was decorated with an abstract vase with no flowers in it and a bare light-gray, almost white tree branch laid on its side. I touched it to see if it was real and it was. The walls were mostly empty; only one painting hung between the kitchen and living room. At first glance it looked like someone had simply painted a white canvas brown, but the closer I got, the more detail I noticed. It was textured, the same dark brown, but the paint was thick and had brushstrokes all over, in all different sizes and going in different directions. Simple, yet defined and complicated. That seemed to be the theme around here.

Finally Kael came out, shirtless and wearing baggy sweatpants, with a deep-purple mark under his collarbone. I flushed, wondering if my brother would notice. Kael took one look at the two of us and immediately noticed our distress.

"What happened?" He moved toward me like he was being yanked by a string, quickly but not as smoothly as his usual movements.

"We're waiting five more minutes before we go to my house and check on Elodie," I explained.

"You're not going alone," Kael stated, with no room to argue. "And you—" He pointed at Austin. "You're staying here. If I were you, I'd keep my distance until we assess the situation and find out what he knows, and see what kind of headspace Phillips is in."

Austin immediately protested. "I am not staying here, Martin. I can't."

"He can't stay here, look at him." I pointed to my brother's panic, which was clear as day on his face. My brother's desperation made my stomach hurt.

Kael sighed, rubbing the back of his neck with one hand. "You two are going to be the death of me." He paused, rolling his head in one smooth circle. "Let's go," he finally said.

I wore a pair of Kael's gym shorts and a T-shirt that hit below my knees. Kael put a shirt on, and Austin wore the same clothes from yesterday, even though he had most of his clothes and belongings at Kael's. It wasn't the time to bother him about his choice of outfit.

CHAPTER **SIX**

Kael

When we pulled up to Karina's house, my instincts were going haywire before we even stepped out of the car. Not knowing what kind of situation we would be walking into had my mind creating every possible scenario, and none of them were good. Nothing on the exterior of the familiar house had changed, but a wave of alert went straight up my spine as we got out of the car. I told Karina to stay there, but obviously she didn't comply. Fischer moved faster than I did, so I had to catch up as we approached the porch.

Karina pulled out her keys to open the door, but I stepped ahead of her and turned the doorknob. I had a feeling it would be unlocked, which was an example of the mental state Phillips was in—he hadn't even locked the front door with his pregnant wife inside. When we stepped in, I wasn't surprised to see the state of the room, but Karina's gasp let me know she was.

Phillips was between lying and leaning on the couch, his back stretched along the cushioned surface and his long legs dangling over the arms. His eyes were glassy, and the coffee table was littered with empty beer bottles, unidentifiable trash, and enough take-out containers to have fed all of us for days. It looked like we had been gone a week, not one night.

"Where is Elodie?" Karina asked.

Fischer's eyes darted around the room while he waited for a response. I could tell he was trying not to react, but he was dying to know where she was and if she was okay. To distract himself and make it less obvious, he immediately began to collect the mess on the table, but Phillips's arm shot out, gripping his wrist. "What're you doing?" Phillips's words were slurred.

"Are you drunk? It's eight in the fucking morning." I grabbed his arm, making him let go of Fischer, who was shaking. Not out of fear, but out of barely controlled anger.

"Drunk? Me?" Phillips laughed, and the small gap between his front teeth seemed more menacing than before. "I may be." His laughter grew.

Karina's voice was louder now. "Where is Elodie!"

Phillips looked at Karina with an expression that made me want to snap his neck in half. "She's around here somewhere."

Fischer rushed down the hallway, calling Elodie's name, with his sister on his heels.

"What the fuck are you doing, bro? You haven't even been home twenty-four hours, and your wife—who you haven't seen in months—is pregnant. Did you even sleep last night, or did you just drink yourself into a stupor?"

Phillips searched the table for something else to drink, and I smacked the beer bottle he found out of his hand. It flew across the room and shattered against the baseboard near the kitchen. He stood as if to challenge me, even though he definitely fucking knew better.

"What's your problem? I'm home. I should celebrate." He shrugged his thin shoulders. He had lost a considerable amount of weight, especially muscle, since I had seen him last, and something about him was drastically different, even beyond his physical appearance.

"Celebrate being home with your wife and unborn child, yeah. Not by trashing Karina's place. How did you get home in the first place? You had months left."

Phillips eyed me in a way I'd only seen him do in a war setting. If I was anyone else, I would probably be intimidated by his behavior.

"Wouldn't you like to know? Now isn't the time to get so technical. You've gotten awfully close to the Fischer family, what the fuck is up with that? Curious what made you switch sides and if it has to do with the hot—"

"Do not fucking finish that sentence. Watch your mouth," I interrupted him before he said something that could risk his life.

He raised his hands, grinning again. "I'm joking, bro. Don't be so sensitive. She is hot, though."

I gritted my teeth, keeping my balled fists at my sides and trying to keep the shaking to a minimum.

"I got home exactly like you did." He tapped his finger against his right temple. "For being too fucked up to stay." Phillips stood up, swaying a bit, and made a move to clean up. "You're not being very hospitable, Martin. You're not even happy to see me," he said, confusion on his drunk face.

"Because when you're wasted, you're not you."

When I finished the sentence, he closed his eyes and began to laugh. I have never been afraid of a motherfucker in my entire life, but I'd be lying if I didn't admit that a chill went down my spine at the sound he made mixed with the look on his face. He felt like a stranger, like something in him had cracked in the months since I saw him last. He was never perfect, but he'd tried to do his best by me, by our platoon. But he wasn't the same man who'd pulled me out of a burning tank or who'd sung old country songs to distract us during our long treks through the desert.

"And you're not you. How could we be? Now come sit with me and celebrate that we're both back and alive." Phillips dropped back down on the couch and patted the empty seat next to him. "For now." He smiled.

His humor had always been dark, but now it felt too real. I couldn't get a grip on how to handle him, and that was what I was usually the best at, handling people. I'd known Phillips longer than Karina and Fischer, but it didn't seem that way right now. He was like a stranger to me. And that felt dangerous.

I glanced down the hall but didn't hear anything coming from Karina's room, where Elodie, Karina, and Fischer were, so I assumed they were okay. If anything had happened Karina would have gotten me by now. I sat down next to Phillips and pressed my elbows on my knees to stop them from bouncing.

"Let's get some air before you clean this mess up."

I tugged on his arm and gently pulled him from the couch.

"Did something happen with you and Elodie?" I asked him, another attempt to gauge what he knew and didn't.

He sighed as we sat on the edge of the half-demolished porch. His eyes were small compared to the strong bones of his face, and his cheeks were more sunken in than they had been the last time I saw him. His pupils were blown out from the alcohol and thin red veins filled the usual white of his eyes.

"Something's been happening . . . lots of shit. But now I'm here and I thought we could figure it out together. She's different now. I don't know what changed, she used to be so happy and carefree but now she's full of stress and always worried about shit. Instead of me, she's focusing on work, the baby—"

I stopped him. "She *should* be worried about the baby, and so should you. Instead of coming home and getting drunk you should be spending time with your wife and figuring this shit out together."

"She wouldn't even fuck me, man. She's acting like she doesn't know me."

I dropped my head into my hands. He couldn't be fucking serious.

"Let me get this straight, you came home"—I looked into his eyes, forcing him to keep eye contact with me—"and immediately tried to have sex with your pregnant wife who hasn't seen you in months, and from what it seemed like, you guys hadn't been on good terms—"

"What do you know about that? What did she tell you?"

"Nothing, you just did." No way in hell was I going to tell him a word about what Karina had told me about the two of them fighting on Skype lately.

"Hmph," he said.

"You know damn well that most people don't get home and rush right to the fucking bed. Especially in this situation—it's fucked up that you put that pressure on her."

"She's my wife." He defended himself with a snarl.

"Exactly. So why the fuck aren't you respecting her?"

Phillips sat on my words for a few seconds before he spoke. "I don't know? I just wanted to touch my wife and she freaked out, not getting why I got pissed, and acting like I'm a goddamn alien or some shit."

"Give her time," I told him, ignoring the fact that his wife was clearly in love with another man and we would all have to figure out what the fuck was going to happen with that.

He closed his eyes again and tilted his head to the porch ceiling.

"This time feels so different, Martin. This was my third time coming back but it feels at odds this time, and not from the booze. My head is all over the place, like I don't know where I am or who anyone is anymore. Even you."

This was more like the man I knew and cared deeply about. Being over there and then coming home is like being in a car wreck. One minute you know exactly what you're doing, where you're headed, and then you're suddenly back and everything is upside down, body mangled, thoughts scattered like a broken windshield, mental scars for the rest of your life.

"That's normal—well, not fucking normal for regular people, but for us, it's normal. You've barely been back for twenty-four hours, and no matter how many times we go, it doesn't become normal. It never will. A little bit of us dies each time. I've tried to accept that, and it's made it easier, but give yourself and your wife some grace." I bent the truth—nothing made it easier except Karina, but that wasn't what he needed to hear right now.

"On top of that, you didn't have a family or any responsibilities except keeping yourself alive before. Life is different now, you're different now, we all are."

Phillips's shoulders began to shake, and he started to dry heave. He was crying hysterically within seconds, and I did my best to comfort the man I once knew.

It took a few minutes to convince him, but he eventually agreed to let me take him to my place so he could get some real rest and give Elodie some space. He fell asleep on the way there, and I practically carried him into the house. He mumbled something about bloody hands as I helped him lie down on my couch. I waited a few minutes until he was snoring to make my way back to Karina's.

CHAPTER SEVEN

Karina

Elodie's body curled into a ball on my bed made me instantly burst into tears. I didn't know what—if anything—had happened, but my nerves were so tight and Phillips was obviously drunk as hell, so it couldn't have gone well.

"Hey." I went to her side as my brother moved past me, getting to her first. He lifted her up, pulling her onto his lap. Their physical contact didn't bother me, maybe because of the stress we were all under, but it didn't feel as weird to see it as I had imagined it would. She wrapped her arms around his neck and buried her face in his hoodie, her entire body shaking with silent sobs.

"Did he hurt you?" my brother asked her.

I held my breath.

"No. I'm okay."

I sighed in relief as she replied.

My brother held her closely but was inspecting her body—her cheeks, her wrists, all the go-to spots for bruising. He seemed to accept her answer as the truth, and rubbed her back as she slowly calmed down.

"I'm so sorry," Elodie gasped into Austin's neck.

She turned to look at me. "And Karina, I'm so sorry. This mess is my fault."

I moved over to sit by them on the bed and ran my hand over the back of her hair.

"This isn't your fault. This is . . . well, it's a mess, but there's no point in blaming yourself right now. No one knew he was going to come home like this. You didn't have time to figure out what you were going to do or to prepare." I looked at Austin so he would know I was speaking to them both.

After a few more minutes, Elodie gained enough strength to sit up on her own, but she stayed close to my brother. The sleeve and neck on her shirt were stretched out, like someone had yanked on them.

"What happened to your shirt?" I asked, alarming my brother.

She awkwardly tugged the fabric lightly, fingering the loose hem of the neckline first. "It's nothing, I just—" She fumbled with a lie, her eyes darting back and forth between me and my brother. I wanted to ask him to leave and give us a second, but after last night, I realize they are closer than I imagined, closer than her and me.

Cupping her face gently like she was made of porcelain, Austin said her name slowly.

"He thought we were going to . . . he wanted to . . . you know." She winced and my brother's eyes nearly blew out of their sockets. He clutched my bedding with a tight fist but managed to keep his face and voice calm for Elodie.

There was a world of difference between trying to sleep with someone and getting rejected and pulling at their clothing. Did Phillips assault her? The thought made me nauseous. We should have never left her alone with him. It took everything in me not to march into the living room and knock his damn teeth out.

I could call the cops?

But what good would that do?

I hesitated, because not only had Elodie not asked me to, but they were married and this was the South; I wasn't naïve enough to not know there was still a disgusting stigma and injustice around what terms like "rape" or "sexual assault" within a marriage looked like.

"Did he force you?" my brother asked, lips tight, jaw twitching.

"No." Elodie shook her head. "He stopped before. He drank way too much and hasn't been home long enough to have any sense. After he rests and sobers up, I'm going to figure out what's next."

There was so much weight to that, to all of the unanswered questions and chaos, but for now, I was simply going to be there for her, no matter what.

CHAPTER EIGHT

Kael

The familiar smell of Phillips's ACU wouldn't leave my mind as I quietly walked down the hallway to Karina's bedroom. Flashes of bullets blasting from the barrel of an assault rifle, the screams of people on the street as guns and IEDs blasted around them, the sound of flesh being ripped apart nearly knocked me to my knees. A few more steps and I would see her face, and the memories would fade.

With a shaking hand I opened the bedroom door and the three of them stiffened, immediately locking their eyes on me. Fischer moved between the bed and the door, then relaxed as he realized it was me and not Phillips. Elodie lay back against the headboard, her face red and blotchy, her eyes nearly swollen shut.

"Can I come in?" I asked, still in the doorway. Elodie and Karina nodded in unison and Fischer sat down, notably still blocking Elodie from the doorway.

"I took Phillips to my place," I explained. No one said anything, but the relief among them was palpable.

My mind quieted as I moved toward Karina. I sat next to her on the edge of the bed and she nearly collapsed into me, leaning her entire body against me. Her hand found mine and I squeezed it.

"You should sleep while he does," Karina advised Elodie.

"We're not ever leaving her alone with him," Fischer said, his chest out and the most serious look I'd ever seen in his usually carefree eyes.

"What's the plan? Technically, he doesn't have anywhere to go. They're still on the waiting list for housing. Is it possible for him to go to a barracks room for now even though he's married?" Karina asked me.

I shook my head. "We would have to have a really good reason, one that would likely get him in trouble, for them to give him a barracks room alone. It's complicated, and unless he did something that you want to report"—I looked at Elodie, who was clearly miserable beyond words—"then there's nothing we can do unless he wants to go somewhere."

"Whose side are you on?" Karina snapped at me, ripping her hand from mine. "He can't stay at my house! I didn't even invite him here, he showed up, basically tried to rape her—"

Fischer stood up and Elodie winced. "I think we should report him for attempted assault. Call the MPs and get him out of here."

"It's not that simple. Elodie, what do you want to do? Do you feel safe with him? If not, I will do whatever you need to protect you, but I also need to tell you guys that realistically the MPs might not do shit, and then he will be even more out of control and angry."

Karina looked at me with a disgusted expression. I knew that she understood that I was being realistic, and the last thing she wanted right now was to deal with the reality of how fucked up the system was, so I tried not to even look at her. She could take her anger out on me after we found some sort of solution.

"I don't know what I want," Elodie said. "I can't even think about it."

"Phillips is at your place today and then what?" Karina urged. I knew her anxiety had to be through the roof right now.

"Then we take it a day at a time. Unless anyone else has a plan?" I tried not to take my frustration out on any of them, but that was easier said than done.

"But Austin lives with you. Can you handle them both there at the same time?" I wasn't sure if Karina was asking me or her brother, but I answered first.

"I can handle it," I assured her, slightly annoyed by her question.

"As long as he's not with Elodie," Fischer responded, his voice low but serious.

This situation was so beyond fucked. Elodie was Phillips's wife. Whether Fischer was in love with her or not, he couldn't really think he could keep them separated, right? Or did we all need to do that? If Phillips was as aggressive with Elodie as Karina had expressed, he was a danger to all of us, but most importantly, to Elodie and the baby. I ran through scenarios in my head about who in our chain of command I could call about this, but none of them were viable. If someone tried to put him in a barracks room, Phillips would either lose his shit and escalate the situation to a point of no return or, the most likely scenario, no one would give a shit and Elodie would still be stuck with him.

"Do you want him to be kept away from you?" I asked Elodie. This was her choice after all, and she hadn't spoken much as we talked around her, about her. She looked at Karina, then at Fischer, and I tried to guide her eyes back to mine. "Don't think about what they want, think about what you want and what's best for your safety, physically and mentally."

Karina made a noise and gave me a look that I could easily read as *Fuck you, Kael.*

"I don't know. This all happened so fast. I haven't had time to think about it," Elodie said in a whisper. "We're safe as long as he doesn't drink. But where will everyone be? I don't want you all worrying about me like this, but I'm afraid—"

"That's all I needed to hear," I told her. I almost reached for her hand to comfort her, but I wasn't sure that being touched by anyone was what she wanted right now, so I put my hand on my own thigh.

"The other half of the duplex needs about a week before it's livable, but if we bust our asses we can get it done. Then Phillips can stay there, and Elodie, you can take your time. Figure out what you want. Right, Fischer?"

He nodded. His cheeks were red with suppressed emotion and he was still pacing around the small bedroom. His phone vibrated on Karina's bed, next to Elodie's knee, and the letter *M* was on the screen. The area code wasn't the same as Mendoza's, whom I thought of first. Fischer grabbed the phone as if it was on fire and flipped it over. Elodie shot him a look that I couldn't interpret. Karina didn't notice, but the two of them glanced at her, then back at each other. Mentally, I filed it away for later. Just how many secrets were these two hiding?

CHAPTER **NINE**

Kael

"Let's get some food in you," I told Phillips as he plopped down on my couch. He hadn't eaten since he'd arrived two days ago. Lots of sleep—well, if you counted waking up in hot sweats and screams every two hours or so as sleep.

I microwaved a bit of lasagna that Karina had dropped off before she went to work, knowing that we wouldn't see each other much for at least a few more days. With everything still left unsettled with Phillips and Elodie, and me trying to keep Elodie's husband from the group for as long as possible in hopes of avoiding him finding out about his wife and Fischer, and Karina taking care of Elodie while trying to manage her brother's shit, we were both booked and cooked emotionally.

But still, Karina had thought of me and had brought me a sheet pan full of lasagna. It didn't have meat in it, eggplant instead, which I had never in my life had, but it was fucking good and even cold I shoveled it down my throat. As I heated some up for Phillips, I closed my eyes for a second, remembering how sexy she'd looked when she stopped by. She was in her normal work clothes, too tight for her to wear around anyone but me, but I couldn't say that without her cussing me out, so I quietly watched the sway of her

ANNA TODD

thick ass and the brightness in her eyes, even though I knew she had to be so damned tired, and the way she looked at me made me feel starved for her touch.

She was at my house for less than five minutes and we were outside the whole time, but I managed to kiss her as many times as humanly fucking possible, and kept her in my arms as long as I could. I was fully addicted to her now, and the comfort she brought by simply being around me. The smell of her hair instantly brought my heart rate down, the sound of her voice silenced the screaming ones in my head, and the thump of her heart beating against mine when I hugged her close made the pain in my throbbing leg fade.

When I asked her how Elodie was, she told me she was okay, that the two of them were working double shifts to keep themselves busy until everything settled. Problem was, neither of us knew when or how any of this would be settled, but there we were, hugging and kissing goodbye as if we wouldn't see each other for at least a month.

The microwave beeped, bringing me back to the kitchen and away from Karina. I plopped the square of lasagna onto a plate, grabbed a fork, and carried it into the living room.

"Thanks, bro." Phillips's eyes were a bit lighter, a little more life to them. He blew on the steaming food and took a bite.

Inspecting the plate as he chewed, he looked pleased. A touch of color came back into his cheeks as he scarfed down the whole thing. I offered him more, and he followed me into the kitchen.

"You seem to be feeling better?"

"I feel okay, then not, then okay again. There's a sense of . . . panic?" He seemed like he wasn't sure of the exact emotion, but I could relate all too well.

"Yeah, that's understandable. Your body is used to being on

guard, your mind, too, and now it's like, what am I supposed to be doing?"

"That's exactly it. I don't know what the fuck I'm supposed to be doing? And not just about the fact that my wife hates me now, but I *literally* don't have a clue what the fuck I'm supposed to be doing? Like even now, I'm eating . . . then what? I don't have to report to the company until tomorrow, what am I supposed to do all day?" He scratched at his head and stared at the numbers counting down on the microwave.

"You're going to help me and Fischer today. If you want to have a place to live, you've got to help us finish the flooring next door. If we bust our asses we can get everything done in a week."

"If she even wants to live with me anymore. You should have seen the way she was looking at me, like I was some fucking psychopath, like she had never met me before."

"She hasn't met this version of you before. And you need to think about how she must feel. That makes it easier to process, if you try to put yourself in her shoes. The man she married didn't come home, you were drunk off your ass. Did you really try to force her to have sex with you? Just because she's your wife does not mean you can sexually assault her." I felt my anger bubbling but tried to keep it at bay, knowing it wouldn't be helpful right now.

He shook his head. "I didn't assault her, but I was way out of line. I've sent her so many apologies but she still doesn't want to see me. I was wrong, that's for damn sure, but I don't know how to get her to forgive me and make her understand that nothing like that will ever happen again."

"Can you guarantee that?"

He nodded, his eyes dead set on mine. "Yes. I fucking missed her, and you know it's been a while."

I clenched the countertop. "That's not an excuse for what you did."

"I know, I know." He threw his arms up in defense. "That's not what I meant. But it will never, ever happen again."

"I'll kill you myself if it does, and if I'm gone, I'll turn you in and have someone else do the job for me."

The microwave interrupted the tension for a second. "I fucked up, I know. I'm going to be on my best behavior from now on, and I'm not going to drink again."

"And give her space and the time she needs," I added.

We were both quiet as the food whirled around in the microwave between us.

"Martin?" He said my name in a whisper and his gaze was far away. "Do you ever want to go back?"

"Back where?"

"Over there." Phillips jerked his head toward the front of the house, but I knew where he meant.

"To be honest, yeah, sometimes. I feel a bit lost here, trying to figure out who I am without the uniform, what my purpose in life is without the guise of fighting for freedom that will never come." I leaned my arms against the island.

"I keep thinking I should have stayed. When I got called into the tent, I said yes right off the bat. But now I think I might regret it. It might be because it's so new, but at least there I knew what I was supposed to be doing."

"Who called you in?" I asked, even though I knew who'd orchestrated the entire thing; all roads led back to Karina's dad. No one else cared about a low-level PFC coming home early. The question was why? You don't just happen to get called into your commander's tent with orders to leave early from a goddamn war.

"Our commander. I didn't get a lot of information and I didn't ask, I was just ready to get the fuck out of there at the earliest possible time. I hopped on a plane and here I am. But now I'm supposed to be a husband, and a father soon." The pure panic in his eyes was very clear. Truthfully, even if I didn't know about Elodie and Fischer, I would be utterly terrified.

"Let's focus on one thing at a time. Today we get the shit done next door. Fischer will be here soon to help. He's gotten damn good, he's nearly faster than me at all this."

"Speaking of Fischer, he's so different now. I didn't know him much before, but I met him at Mendoza's right before we left last time, and he was just a kid. Now he's . . . I don't know. Not to sound like a whiny bitch, but I swear he doesn't like me."

I considered asking Phillips more about Karina's father and if they'd spoken directly, or if my paranoia was making him more of a game maker in our lives than he was, but decided not to yet.

"You sound like a whiny bitch, one hundred percent." I laughed a little, not because it was funny, but because all our lives were so fucked up right now.

"And you're fucking his sister. How does that work with you two being so buddy-buddy?"

"I'm not fucking his sister, I'm in love with her. We're together, not only fucking. So it doesn't matter what her brother thinks about it, or what anyone thinks."

Phillips began to talk with his mouthful of food. "I'm not judging or saying shit. I'm curious because you've never even looked at a woman, even Turner, who wanted to rip your clothes off many, many times. What made you fall for the Fischer girl?"

"Karina," I corrected him. "Her name is Karina, so call her that and only that. And everything. Everything about her made me love her and makes me love her more every day. So keep that in mind when you mention her name in front of or behind me. Now stop asking me about my love life and eat so we can get shit done."

CHAPTER TEN

Karina

"My relationship with Austin started slowly. I know it's wrong—" Elodie sat on the edge of the massage bed in my workroom with her legs dangling over the edge.

We were both between clients and had about twenty minutes until our next ones.

"I'm sorry for keeping it from you. This was the last thing I thought would happen."

"You don't need to apologize to me. I'm not judging your character."

"I don't know where to start." She sighed, worry etching her beautiful face.

"You know you don't need to explain or defend yourself to me, El. I only need to know what I can do to help you, both of you."

I put my hand on her shoulder, and she squeezed it gently with her own.

"I can't believe I didn't realize what was going on. I always say how perceptive I am but looking back, even at the camping trip, it was so obvious. But . . ." I tried to bring my thoughts back to the issue at hand. "This isn't about me, the important decision you need to make is what do *you* want? Do you want to try to make things work with your husband or be with my brother?" The sentence felt so ridiculous that I lit another candle to try to make myself feel a little calmer.

I had spent the last forty minutes moving things around on my shelves and making sure my new mood light from Walmart worked effectively. It cast either pastel or stormy colors on the ceilings and walls. I was definitely in a stormy mood, so I set it to that.

"I know what I want, but I don't want to ruin Austin's life. This is bigger than what I want, and he's leaving soon, so I can't expect him to change his whole life. And I'm having a baby. Phillip's baby." She pressed her hand against her round belly. In tumultuous moments like this it was somehow easy to forget that soon there would be another person, a newborn baby, here to add to the equation.

"I'm sure my brother doesn't see this as life ruining. He's not the most responsible person."

Elodie winced at my words. I wasn't helping but was trying.

"But even though I was blind, I can tell he is different with you." I explained, "I've never seen him take care of anyone but himself, but he's been trying with you." I put my hands in my hair, pulling the rubber band out and redoing my ponytail to distract myself. "This is coming out wrong, I'm sorry. You should ask Austin what he wants before assuming you'll be ruining anything for him."

"This is such a mess that I didn't mean to make. *Je n'arrive pas à me décider.* Maybe I should go back to my parents? Maybe they were right the whole time."

I stayed quiet while she processed her emotions in real time. She went back and forth from French to English. I couldn't relate to her stress level and I didn't have a solution to offer her, so it was best to let her vent.

"I can't be with Phillip anymore. For so many reasons. Not only because I had an affair and betrayed him." She looked around the small room, her eyes landing on the cloudy ceiling. "But I love someone else. Not just an affair, I love Austin more than I knew was possible. I have never felt so much for anyone, except my child."

Austin was so lucky to be loved by someone with a heart like Elodie's. I wanted to say that, but she continued.

"I'm never going to feel safe with Phillip again. If he even wants to stay married, that is. I don't know if my baby will be safe here either." Her shoulders shook.

I reached for her hand and squeezed it. I couldn't imagine the complexity of what she was feeling, trying to tie right and wrong together, trying to balance what she "should" do and what she wanted to do.

"Would you be happy if you went back to France? Is that really viable?" I asked her, doubting that she would make that choice.

"I'm not going to be happy anyway. I will never be happy, Karina. I need to accept that." She whispered under her breath, *"Je ne me sens plus chez moi en France."*

"What does that mean?" I asked.

"I'm no longer at home there, I feel so much more at home with you."

"I love having you. You know that. But what makes you say that you'll never be happy? You're so young, you have your whole life ahead of you. Sure, you're going to struggle, we all do. That's our rite of passage as human beings, but what on earth makes you so sure that you'll never be happy again?"

"Because, Karina, I know how it feels to be in love now, and to be loved. Now that it's been taken from me, I'll only know the bitterness of regret and remorse. This is the punishment I must accept for the actions of my heart," she explained, sadness overcasting her words.

I was speechless for once, not knowing what to say or how to react. I also now knew how it felt to be loved and to love another, and if that was taken away from me suddenly, without warning, I would feel the same. I usually had some sort of advice, something to add or offer, but I was blank.

"Is it awful that I wish I would have had a little bit more time? Just another week, another day, or even another hour with Austin, in that bubble of happiness? That's all I keep thinking. I know it's wrong, but I was so happy. For the first time in my life I felt like I wasn't lost anymore. Like I was capable of being happy and a good mom, like I wasn't completely crazy for moving here. It felt like things made sense, and now I'm scared again and miserable and can't believe I'm bringing a baby into this situation. I never thought I was a bad person, but I am."

I moved to hug her, petting her soft hair with one of my hands. Her stomach, as full as ever, pressed between us. "You are not a bad person, Elodie. Life is complicated and uncontrollable. I know your guilt is crushing you right now, but you are not a bad person."

"I'm sorry for everything. I didn't mean for this to happen. Thank you for being here for me." She hugged me tighter and I felt the warmth of tears touch my neck.

"I'm always going to be here for you. No matter what. You're not alone and never will be, this will take a bit to figure out, but I'll be here every step of the way," I promised her. "*Je t'aime.* That's how you say it right?"

Elodie laughed. "Yes, that's perfect. *Je t'aime toi aussi.*"

I closed my stinging eyes, finding myself wishing that she and my brother could run away together and raise the baby and live happily ever after. I knew that was so far from reality, that there was no possible way this could end well, but still I daydreamed about it for a moment. When I thought about the futures of Elodie, my brother, Kael, and Phillips, I had a pit in my stomach. Whether it was my anxiety or not, I couldn't shake the feeling that this was only the beginning of something bigger, something really bad, for all of us.

We closed our shift with three more clients, an unusually busy day, but we both needed the distraction, to say the least. I smiled down at my phone, staring at the selfies Kael had sent me throughout the day. I felt silly holding my phone up and giggling at my reflection on the screen. After ten attempts, I made a silly face and sent it before I could change my mind.

He responded immediately:

Wow, my first selfie from you. I'm honored.

Shush, I'm trying.

As I said, I'm honored. How was work? Are you home yet?

I looked around the messy lobby. I still needed to vacuum, wipe the counters down, move my bedding from the washer to the dryer, wait for it to dry, restock and fold the towels, do the bookkeeping for the day, check the schedule for the next day, and shut down the computer. I would be at the spa for at least another hour and a half minimum, and it was already eight. My eyes burned and I yawned while I responded to his text.

I have to clean up. Elodie's gone home.

Do you want help?

No, you're already so busy. I appreciate you offering, but I'm going to put my phone away and do it all as fast as I can. I'll text you when I'm home, okay?

He didn't respond as fast as he had been, so I put my distracting phone away and got to work. As I was wiping the front glass with a towel, I nearly jumped out of my skin when someone appeared through the little dots of cleaner I'd sprayed. My heart rate dropped when I realized it was Kael. I quickly unlocked the door and let him in.

"What are you doing here? I said I didn't need help," I said, though I was so damn glad to see him.

"No." He kissed my forehead, hugging me with one arm, and then kissed the top of my head. "You said you didn't *want* help, not that you didn't need it."

"You're annoying." I smiled, hugging him tighter.

"Thank you." He laughed, his chest gently shaking against my body.

Kael took the towel from my hand and gently turned my shoulders toward the hall that led to the treatment rooms. "You take that side, and I got this side. Deal?" he offered, his beautiful face and warm voice rushing over me.

I nodded as he locked the door, deciding that instead of arguing with him or trying to do it all myself, I would accept his help without a fight, for once. We finished all the closing duties in less than thirty minutes and the shop had never been cleaner or more organized.

"Two is always better than one," he said as he wound up the cord on the vacuum.

"You must be so exhausted." I pointed to the paint, dirt, and unrecognizable matter covering his clothes.

He was dressed in a black T-shirt and sweats, but they were so covered in stuff that they looked like a designer outfit that was made to look that way.

"So do you," he countered. "How's Elodie feeling?"

"Her feet are really swollen, and I couldn't stand the idea of her being on them any longer today. Plus Austin is at my house, so I figured I would give them some time."

Kael rolled the vacuum past me and I followed him down the hall to put it back in the closet.

"He's been practically withering away at my place the last few days without seeing her."

"Are we accomplices in this whole thing? Like we both know this is wrong, but we're basically aiding and abetting an affair." I leaned against the wall.

"It's not so black and white," he said.

"I never thought I would be okay with an affair, under any circumstance, but I feel so bad for them. Phillips, too, to a point, but honestly, I hate him, so I don't feel that bad for him. But does that make me just as guilty?"

Kael stepped toward me, cupping my face with his hands. "You're not guilty of anything. They're adults and they make their own choices. As people who care about them, all we can do is hope for the best and mind our business."

I couldn't help but laugh. "You make it sound so easy. Mind my business, as if I'm capable of that."

His espresso-colored eyes shone at me, humor in them despite the intensity of the topic. "You're capable . . . when you're distracted." The air between us shifted and chills ran over me as he put his arms on either side of me, practically pinning me against the wall.

"Distraction sounds nice." I gulped.

"It does." His mouth moved to my chin, slowly kissing across my jawline.

He lifted me up, my thighs wrapped around his waist, and we moved into my treatment room, never breaking at the mouth. His kiss was wild, more desperate than expected, but I mimicked it, letting my built-up longing crackle and burst between us as he laid me on the bed. I never in a million years would have imagined myself as the type to do something like this at my workplace, but my house and Kael's were full, and we both deserved the distraction, the connection that would drown out the rest of the world.

CHAPTER ELEVEN

Karina

"A cookout? All of us? Do we think that's a good idea?" I asked Kael, leaning up a little so my chin rested on his bare chest.

It felt like we had barely spent time together in the past week even though we had found tiny ways to spend even ten minutes together. Him helping me at work, me bringing food by his place; he even sat with me while I got an oil change and tire rotation during the break between his discharge meetings. We still hadn't had a full conversation about what was going to happen to us in the very, very near future, but that was a future Karina problem. Right now, the idea of losing him, even to a city in the same state, made me want to curl into a ball and scream until my throat burst.

"I'm not saying it's the best idea. But it's happening anyway, and we can either go or not go, but I probably have to go to make sure everyone survives," he said in a low voice, with a touch of humor.

"It would be funny if it wasn't reality." I sighed, closing my eyes as he brushed my hair to tuck it behind my ear. His fingers played with my earlobe, an extremely relaxing touch. "I wish you weren't the designated babysitter, but thank god there is one, I guess?"

"I'm tired of being the babysitter too. Trust me. But, Karina, if you don't want to go, you really don't have to."

I shook my head. "Anywhere you go, I go."

"Hmm, I love the sound of that." He grinned. My heart ached as it sang.

"So, when is it?"

"Tomorrow night." He smiled bigger to counteract my eye roll.

"Of course it is. I do miss Gloria. I haven't seen her in a week and a bit. I feel like we've been in a vortex."

"We have. You've been working your ass off and I've been trying to get that damn place done so I don't have two idiots who hate each other but love the same woman staying in my house."

"Do you think Phillips really loves her?" I asked Kael. He squeezed me to him, kissing my forehead.

"I'm not sure. For sure he thinks he does, but that doesn't mean he loves her the way he should."

"We all have our own versions of love, and that's hard for me to understand. It seems so easy. You love someone and respect them, protect them, make their lives easier. Simple. But he doesn't do any of those things for her. Maybe he did before, but they hardly knew each other when they got married."

Kael agreed. "But your brother . . . he loves her. He's doing everything he can do to protect her even though it's hurting him. So, he loves her in a different way."

"In a better way," I added.

"I wouldn't be able to be in the same room as Phillips if that was you. I would have killed him the moment he even thought about touching a single hair on your head," Kael said.

The threat came out casually but I could feel it was genuine. I was so proud of Elodie for standing her ground and putting herself and the baby first. The road ahead for her was going to be bumpy as hell to say the least, but as a group or a family, it didn't seem as terrifying. I was relieved that we all had each other, and someone like Kael to watch over and handle all of us.

The next night I couldn't decide what to wear and my room was a tornado of every item of clothing I owned. I stood in front of the mirror in a loose-fitting black dress with thin straps and buttons at the top, and an oversized tan cardigan around my shoulders. I debated whether to wear the leg warmers I'd gotten at a garage sale last year after I saw someone on Pinterest wearing them but pulled them over my legs anyway. Elodie came into my room as I scrunched the tops down a bit.

"You look so cute! I love this outfit, very autumn," she gushed, a genuine smile on her face and light in her eyes. *"Très chic!"*

She was wearing jeans and a long sweater, tight at the stomach but loose everywhere else, and her hair was tied low against her neck with a few loose strands by her ears.

"You look so cute too. Are the leg warmers weird?" I asked, doing a half twirl in the mirror.

"No, I love them," she said, gently untucking some of my hair from under my cardigan. "And I love when you have your hair like this." She fluffed my wild hair. I'd let it air-dry and the universe was on my side today, the waves falling in the right place for once.

"Thank you." I leaned against her a little and stared at our reflections. Two women trying their hardest to figure out life and where we fit into it—a beautiful and terrifying thing.

"We're okay, right?" she asked, her eyes dropping a little in the mirror.

I nodded, still leaning against her. "Yes. We're okay. We will figure all of this out together, so don't you worry about me.

"Are you sure you want to come?" I asked her for the third time today.

Nodding, she assured me. "I'll be fine. Phillip isn't coming, and if he does, he will behave himself. I'm going to drive in case I want to leave early. Don't worry." She kissed my cheek and reached for the lip gloss pile on the top of my dresser.

Opening the top of one, she stepped closer and swiped the soft applicator across my lips. It was such an intimate thing to do, such a best friend thing to do. In the middle of all the things I could worry about happening tonight, instead I found myself grateful to have her in my life.

I rode with Elodie to Mendoza's, where Kael and my brother were meeting us. Kael wanted to drive me, but it didn't make sense to have him go out of the way and come off post to get me. He eventually agreed and asked me to text him when we were leaving so we could arrive at the same time. I could hear the roar of his truck bellowing in the distance as we pulled up. What meticulous timing on his end. Elodie's entire demeanor changed when my brother stepped out of Kael's truck, and Austin practically ran to the door to open it for her. Kael was a bit slower, but I waited to have him open the door for me, thinking about what it would be like if Elodie wasn't pregnant and married and my brother could love her without complications, but of course life wasn't fair like that.

Kael hugged me as if he hadn't seen me in weeks, and I relaxed into the warmth of his body. He was wearing an oatmeal-colored cotton sweatshirt and matching joggers, stark-white sneakers as usual. My favorite type of outfit of his. He smelled so good, so clean and comforting.

"You look fucking adorable," he told me, gently lifting the

delicate moon-shaped necklace off my neck. His eyes traveled from the top of my wavy hair to the bottom of my loafers.

"Thank you." I smiled up at him, hugging him again, wishing we were going to my house alone instead of to a crowded cookout, but I was happy to have time with him either way.

Both of us purposely avoided looking at my brother and Elodie as we made our way to Mendoza's front door. Before we even knocked, Gloria opened the door and grabbed me into a hug.

"Karina! I'm so glad you came!" She squeezed me.

She smelled like a feminine floral perfume and shampoo. Her long black hair was as silky as ever, straight and parted in the middle, and she was dressed casually in a black crop top with long sleeves and low-rise jeans with wide legs. She always looked so effortlessly cool; her makeup was light, her skin glowing, and she didn't look as exhausted as she usually did. That made me so happy. Things must be better with Mendoza.

"Everyone's in the back. How have you been?" She wrapped her arm around me and looked back to wave at Kael, my brother, and Elodie.

"Good. Just, you know, there's a lot going on." I glanced back at the distance my brother and Elodie were putting between themselves, trying not to draw attention to the obvious.

"Yeah. I'd fucking say." Gloria smiled but I couldn't tell how she felt about the whole thing.

I knew she liked Austin and Elodie, but I wondered if she was judging them—rightfully so, but I wished no one would. She didn't seem like the judgmental type at all, though, so I ignored my own paranoia.

"No one is going to bring up the picture," she whispered to me, as if she could read my mind. "I've warned them all, and if they do, I'll beat their ass."

I had nearly forgotten that photo of them floating around, and we'd never figured out who'd sent it or why, or if Phillips had seen it yet, but I mentally crossed my fingers that everyone could keep their promise to Gloria and not say anything to my brother and Elodie tonight.

The pit in my stomach grew, and I couldn't tell if my body was going to its usual anxious place or if it was trying to warn me. I would find out soon enough.

CHAPTER **TWELVE**

Kael

Gloria had stolen Karina from me by sitting in the chair next to her and pulling the two seats close together, leaving no room for me. I was glad to see them bonding, so I wasn't going to sulk, but the more people who showed up, the more I kept my eyes on Karina. She hadn't moved from that chair since we'd gotten here about an hour ago, and she was on her third drink. Not that I was counting. I was still on my first beer, knowing I'd be driving and not knowing what the fuck the night would bring, so feeling that I needed to stay as alert as possible.

No one had pestered Fischer or Elodie yet, but there were more than a few glances their way when Fischer sat next to her and Toni. Noticeably, Fischer was drinking a Coke from the can instead of alcohol, and had declined Mendoza's finest tequila.

"So, you're out next week? What are you gonna do?" Mendoza asked me as we stared at our women, who were cracking up over something. Seeing Karina relax enough to laugh felt so good.

"I have no fucking clue. I thought I knew what I was going to do, I have that place in Atlanta, but I'm not sure what I want to do anymore."

"I know damn well what you want to do, and involves that one." He tipped the bottle of tequila in his hand toward Karina.

"She won't go with me, and I can't leave her here. But I already bought the house and will lose money on it if I sell it right away. For the first time, I don't have a plan."

"Why don't you get married?"

I laughed at that, taking a swig of my beer. "Yeah, getting married will solve everything."

"That's the Army way." He joined me in laughter and took a drink straight from the bottle. "Why won't she come with you? If I were her, I would get the fuck out of here."

"She has her house here and her dad—even though she hates him. It's complicated. I think she's afraid of depending on me." I surprised myself with my honesty.

"But you're the most dependable motherfucker in the world."

I shook my head. "I haven't been to her."

As I watched her hold her cup as Gloria poured vodka into it, I allowed myself to wonder what life would be like if Karina and I got married, if she didn't have so many ties to this place, and if I wasn't so desperate to cut mine with it.

The sun had gone down and a few of the younger privates had gone, leaving a smaller group of us. Only Toni, her husband, Tharpe, Lawson, Mendoza, Gloria, Elodie, and Fischer were left. We were all sitting around the firepit; Karina was on my lap now, sitting sideways with her legs dangling. Her shoes were off but the high sock things she was wearing were keeping her legs warm. She was relaxed, drunk, and definitely giggly. She wrapped her arms around my neck. Her public displays of affection were surprising and welcomed.

Mendoza was offering shots again, and Karina accepted. "You've been drinking vodka, if you mix your liquor, you're going to get sick, baby," I told her quietly, knowing there was about a 10 percent chance she would listen to me.

"Baby?" She winked at me. I laughed at her and she kissed my cheek. "Baby sounds nice. How about you take it for me, then, and I'll drink vodka?"

"I have to drive."

"Give it to me." Tharpe reached for the bottle and Karina went to hand it to him but stopped right before he could reach it.

"You can at least ask nicely," she said.

He looked at me, then Karina, clearly pissed at being called out.

"Yeah, don't be a dick." Gloria backed Karina up.

Tharpe seemed to be deciding if he wanted to go up against the two of them, but after one look back at me, he simply smiled and rephrased his sentence.

"Can I have it, please?" The words were pulled out of him, but Karina smiled happily and handed the bottle to him.

Toni started talking about some upcoming FRG meeting and how much planning she had to do. Elodie offered to help her, and I zoned out as they talked about tablecloths and Mendoza and Fischer talked about some football game that I couldn't give a fuck about.

I buried my head in Karina's neck. This was the first time I had ever been publicly affectionate with a woman in front of my guys.

"Wanna go soon?" I asked her, gently placing a kiss on her neck. She nodded.

"Definitely. Five minutes?" she asked, and I nodded.

The conversation moved around us, and Karina teased me, softly running her fingertips over my neck and adjusting her body on my lap enough to make me hard.

"If you don't stop, I'll take you to my truck right now and we won't make it home," I said against her ear.

She shivered and lifted her shoulder to her ear, cheeks beyond flushed, glowing in the light of the fire.

"Sounds good to me." She rocked her ass against me again and I couldn't take it anymore.

"We're leav—" I began to announce as someone walked out of the back door, heading toward us. I immediately recognized Phillips's physique.

"My invite must have gotten lost in the mail."

Everyone's reactions rippled, Elodie and Fischer moved identically, both stiffening. Karina took the longest to realize who was there, and once she did, she turned her body to face him but stayed on my lap. The entire group's energy changed.

"Yo, glad you came." Mendoza stood up to hug him, being the first to break the ice.

"Really? Since I wasn't invited, I didn't think you'd be glad to see me." Phillips's voice was off. He was impaired.

"It was a last-minute thing, not a big deal," Mendoza said, pointing to an empty chair a few feet away from me and Karina. I wrapped my arms around her waist and pulled her even closer. No way in hell were we leaving now.

"How's it going? It's been a while." Tharpe patted Phillips's back as he passed.

"Been better. But still breathing," he replied, his eyes on Elodie.

She smiled at him but anyone with eyes could see that she was beyond uncomfortable and surprised to say the least. The worry on her face made the hair on the back of my neck stand up. I didn't think Fischer realized it, but he had turned his body to face her, creating a small barrier between her and Phillips.

"Breathing is good," Gloria added awkwardly.

Phillips sat down on the plastic chair and put his elbows on his knees, staring from one of us to the next. It was so fucking awkward and tense that it made me want to tell everyone it was time to wrap it up and go home. I watched him.

"What's there to drink? Is no one going to offer me a drink?" He smiled; the fire reflecting on his face made him look menacing.

"Phillip, I don't think you should—" Elodie began to say, but he held up a hand to cut her off.

"Honey," he said in the least affectionate tone I'd ever fucking heard. "I don't think you should tell me what I should and shouldn't be doing."

Karina tensed and turned to him. "Don't talk to her like that."

I groaned, knowing she was right but wishing she wasn't as drunk as she was, because I could see exactly what was going to happen if this escalated. And it wasn't going to be good at fucking all. I lifted Karina a little and held her at her waist, watching Phillips as he glared at her before speaking.

"Sorry, but what do you have to do with me talking to my wife?"

"Phillips," I warned him.

Karina attempted to move her body but I held on to her, so she didn't go far. I pulled her back onto my lap and she leaned her torso toward him.

"Because she's my friend and you're being an asshole and embarrassing her. And yourself." Karina's words seem to crackle with the fire. My body was in full preparation mode now; I planted my feet in the grass and scanned the group, my eyes landing on Phillips as he laughed.

"I'm embarrassing her?" He smiled, pulling at his mouth and thin lips with one hand.

"Stop it. Both of you," Elodie pleaded.

Fischer looked like he was one second away from exploding. He was visibly shaking.

"No, no. I want to know how I'm embarrassing you. Do you feel embarrassed, El?"

Elodie put her face in her hands and shook her head gently. "I'm going to go."

"But I just got here," Phillips retorted. "And someone needs to tell me how I'm embarrassing my wife by being here. This is my unit, not hers, or yours." He pointed at Karina and my adrenaline began to spike. "They're the ones who don't belong."

"Enough!" Fischer yelled. Karina jerked in my lap. "I can smell the whiskey on you from here. You need to shut the fuck up or leave," Fischer hissed, leaning up like he was ready to pounce at any moment.

I rearranged Karina again so I could move between them if I needed to. It was clear that no one knew what to do, or what Phillips would do.

"And I can smell my fucking wife on you from here. Speaking of embarrassing, the two of you"—he pointed at Fischer and then Elodie—"are the ones who should be embarrassed."

"Okay, okay. This is a party and you're fucking up the vibes," Mendoza interrupted. "Either chill the fuck out or leave my house."

"Whoa, really, dude? You're taking the drug addict's side over your battle buddy? He's been fucking my wife but I'm the bad guy?" Phillips seethed.

He stood up and kicked the chair he'd been sitting in, knocking it to the ground.

Fischer was on his feet now, and I put Karina on the chair and stood up, moving between them. Karina and Elodie looked like they were going into shock as everything from the night sky to the fire, to the chairs, to the faces around me began to spin slowly, moving out of focus. I was back in Afghanistan, the smell of tar and dirt filling my nose. The sound of round after round of bullets sweeping next to my ears—so close the heat pulsed from them onto my skin. I felt my hands hitting against my ears in the present, but I couldn't bring my mind back to it with my body.

"Kael!" I could hear Karina's voice but could only see crumbling buildings, the devastating looks on the faces of nearly starving children, whose only crime was being born in the wrong country.

I shook my head, trying to find her, and felt her arms wrap around my back, squeezing my torso. I blinked; bits of reality began to shimmer through in waves. Mendoza was between Fischer and Phillips, and Karina screamed. The sound pulled me fully into the present and without thinking, I moved as soon as I saw the black gun in Phillips's hand. It was pointed directly at Fischer.

Karina's and Elodie's voices melted together into a swirl of agony, and I felt the metal of his pistol dig into my hip as I tackled Phillips to the ground. I reached between us and gripped the pistol, pushing it out of his reach. There were too many voices to know who was saying what, but all I cared about was that Phillips was pinned beneath me, unable to move. He thrashed, and I dug his wrists into the ground with all my body weight on his thighs.

"Call the MPs!" Toni screeched. "Call them right now!"

"Get off of me!" Phillips yelled, still trying to move.

In my mind, I was gripping his throat until his eyes went blank, moving my hand to his chin and snapping his neck—but in reality, I let him live but limited his air supply enough to weaken his liquor-fueled body. My mind felt like a vast body of water, a murky lake with no bottom, only mud and endless darkness, waves and silence, waves and silence.

"I'm not going to hurt anyone! I'm fucking around," Phillips tried to explain, his voice so strained I could barely understand him.

I couldn't gauge how hard I was squeezing, and I didn't care. He was the enemy now.

I had never wanted to hurt anyone, even while at war and having to, but the thought of ending Phillips's life was overwhelming. I felt out of touch with my body as I let go of my grip, and he coughed, just catching his breath in time for my fist to collide with his cheekbone. I felt first a rush of warm blood on my hands, then splatter against my face. Hands pulled at my arms, my back, tugging at my sweatshirt, but I couldn't stop. I didn't want to.

Finally I was ripped off him and pinned to the ground. Mendoza, Tharpe, and Lawson were holding me down like I was a rabid animal. I didn't fight, just lay there catching my breath, trying to get out of the dark water and back to the world, back to Karina. Where was she? It had been a while since I'd had this kind of loss of control and succumbed to the volcano inside of me, but I couldn't find it in me to feel bad, or to feel anything, really. I had kept it dormant long enough and now that it had erupted, I was numb. The sound of sirens rang through the air, and I could barely recognize Karina as my eyes met hers. She was standing above me as they let me sit up, looking at me like I was someone she had never met. Her face disappeared as I tried to hold on to the memory of it, of her, but the past took over the present.

CHAPTER **THIRTEEN**

Karina

I had never driven drunk in my life. I wasn't sure if I was even still buzzed after the insanity, but I had spent my whole life proudly never, ever, drinking and driving. But there I was, opening the driver's-side door of Kael's massive truck. I hadn't even started the engine yet but was already so anxious. I was hoping that Kael would come back to me, to this realm of reality. It sucked, sure as hell, but I didn't want to face it alone, and I didn't know what to do with the man standing at the passenger side. I waited for Kael to open the door before I started the truck. When the door didn't open, I climbed back out and walked around to him. He stood there, still as stone, eyes nearly as dark as the sky. It was so quiet, even as everyone scrambled before the MPs could arrive. We needed to go, and fast. I had already witnessed what could happen if the MPs and Kael crossed paths again, and this time, I knew it would be much, much worse.

His wide chest moved up and down in waves, his facial features not moving at all. Wet dots of blood on his cheek reflected the moonlight. A thick chill ran over me, and my fight-or-flight instinct kicked in, but I forced it down, needing to put Kael first.

"Kael." I quietly said his name. "Kael, we need to go." I stood in front of him, leaning up on my tippy-toes so my eyes would meet his. He was still blank, no one and nothing in his eyes. He blinked, confusion blurring his features.

"Who are you?" he asked me.

I lost my breath. I had never dealt firsthand with someone in the middle of an episode of PTSD. I had heard many of stories from my clients, but this was entirely different. I loved Kael and he was lost; I didn't know where to go or what to say to find him. My heart had never been so broken.

"Martin." I cleared my throat. His attention snapped to me. "Martin," I repeated as a tiny, tiny bit of life came back to him. "Sergeant, we need to evacuate. Immediately."

I had no fucking idea what I was saying but it worked, something clicked inside of him, and he moved so quickly to get into the passenger seat that he nearly knocked me over. The sirens wailed through the air as I rushed to the driver's side and turned the key. Kael's seatbelt was already on, and his eyes were tracking inside of the vehicle and out the windshield in quick little movements. I couldn't comprehend what was happening inside of him, but I knew I had to get him out of there.

"I'm going to drive now," I said in the most neutral, flat, soldier-like voice I could manage.

"Got it."

I drove away from the Mendozas' house and got off the post as fast as I possibly could. The heat of my own uncontrollable tears covered my face and flowed down my neck. Not wanting to make any sudden movements, I let them fall. I left the radio off, and time dragged and dragged, making it feel like it took an hour to get to my house. I parked in the driveway even though Kael usually left his truck on the street. Bradley, my neighbor, was walking into his house, so I waved and waited for him to go in, hoping he wouldn't be able to see the difference in Kael from a distance. The last thing I needed was Bradley, or anyone, getting involved and escalating the situation.

Fear coursed through me as I prepared to look over at Kael and speak to him.

"Martin." I spread my voice like butter, trying not to alarm him.

His brows drew down his forehead, eyes confused and lips frowning. "Martin?"

Was Kael back?

If so, was he aware that he had blanked out?

My hands were slightly shaking, my heart pounding, as I turned my body to him.

"Kael?"

"Yeah?" He responded as if nothing had happened, as if I had asked him if he wanted pizza for dinner.

"We're home," I told him, looking at my yard and house. The porch light was on and the materials for the deck were all over the place.

His eyes met mine and he studied me. I could feel him assessing me. I pulled my gaze away first and climbed out of the truck. Kael met me on the driver's side at a pace that made me jump. He stood in front of me, his body towering over mine, his jaw ticking as if he had a million things to say but the words were caught, unable to escape.

I reached my hand out, unsure what would happen. Before my fingertips touched him he fell to his knees in front of me, sobs violently overtaking his body. He pressed his head against my torso and his muffled screams shook my body. We stayed like that until he was dry of tears. I rubbed his head, telling him it would be okay, that everything would be okay. I knew I was lying, but I repeated it anyway.

"Where did you go?" I asked Kael as I turned the cold water for the bathroom sink on and let it run over his hands.

He didn't so much as flinch as the water touched his open wounds. He was seated on the closed toilet seat, and I stood over him.

"What do you mean?" he asked, his voice low, eyes not meeting mine.

"You *know* what I mean," I tactfully responded.

I wasn't intending on opening his emotional wounds after what he had just gone through, but I couldn't pretend like nothing had happened. His soul had disappeared in front of my own eyes. A chill ran over my entire body as I recalled the uncontrollable difference in him and the release of it on my lawn. Of course I knew he would never lay a finger on me, or anyone except a lunatic holding a gun, but deep down, I wasn't sure if I believed that after what had happened less than an hour ago. My hands shook as I poured peroxide over his skin and dabbed it with a clean towel. His skin was ripped, and I took a pair of nail clippers from the drawer and disinfected them before cutting the dangling skin.

I went to press a bandage gently over the wounds, and Kael reached for my hands, clasping them in his.

"Are you afraid of me right now? Is that why you're shaking like that?" His voice was so low, and misery and shame filled his eyes.

My heart sank; the pain was nearly indescribable. "No." I tried to even out my voice.

"Yeah, you are." He let go of my hands and dropped his head.

ANNA TODD

My eyes burned as I attempted to stop tears from pouring out.

"I'm not. I'm . . . Tonight was terrifying. He had a gun. An actual gun, and I was so scared you were going to kill him." My shoulders shuddered, and my entire body reacted.

As I said it, I realized how big of a deal it was, how badly things could have gone, and a million scenarios ran through my mind, from bad to worse, to bodies lying on the ground—mine included. It was suddenly freezing in the bathroom. I could barely hold myself up, and I held on to the edge of my sink. When I looked into the mirror, my lips were purple and my skin was pale.

Kael stood up and I didn't move—I couldn't. He turned the shower on, and the steam filled the small, poorly ventilated bathroom.

"Can I?" He lifted his battered hands toward me.

I nodded, words not coming.

He reached for the bottom of my dress and lifted it up over my head. I felt like I was in a plastic bubble, not quite touching reality but still aware of what was going on. He kneeled in front of me and pulled my leg warmers off one by one.

I put my hands on his shoulders to steady myself and he turned his face up to look at me. "You're freezing. Get in the shower," he instructed. His voice softened as he added, "Please."

I followed his lead and held on to his hand as I stepped over the tub's edge to stand under the warm water. As the drops hit my bare skin, they burned because of how cold I was, but after a minute or so my body warmed up. My shoulders finally stopped shaking and my breath was coming out more evenly as I closed my eyes and let the water attempt to wash away the traumatic experience we'd just had.

I had no idea how much time had passed, but the air was so thick with steam when I opened my eyes that I could barely see the curtain. I pulled it back and saw the outline of Kael's silhouette leaning against the wall, his head lifted and resting against it.

"Kael," I said, reaching my arm out of the curtain and toward him.

He turned his head quickly, stepping toward me, foggy steam swirling around him.

"Come in?" I asked, needing to be close to him. Now that a little bit of the shock had worn off, I desperately wanted him to be close to me.

Silently, he undressed and stepped into the shower. He stood behind me, still not saying a word. I turned around to face him and cupped his face. His eyes dropped closed, and I brushed my fingers over his skin. I felt guilty for making him feel like a monster, but I didn't know how to say that without taking away from the seriousness of what had gone down. On top of that, there was the Elodie and Austin situation—were they okay? I reminded myself there was nothing to be done about them in this moment, so I allowed myself to have a moment of peace with Kael; we both needed it.

"Turn around," he said, eyes still closed.

My heart sank. "Kael, I'm not—" I began to explain myself, but he interrupted me.

"I'm going to wash your hair," he said, and leaned down to grab my shampoo from the edge of the bath.

I turned around and put my face in the water. His hands clumsily rubbed my scalp, but after a few seconds it became more natural. The smell of my shampoo filled my senses; the scent of the lather was incredibly relaxing. Circling my neck, I let my shoulders relax into the sensation. All the worries of the night washed away, rolling down my wet, warm skin as he unhooked the showerhead and rinsed the suds from my strands. It felt so, so good. His hands moved my soaking hair to the front of my shoulder, and he massaged my neck. As a licensed therapist, I was surprised how good he was, hitting all the right pressure points and pressing and kneading exactly where I needed relief.

"Thank you, that feels so good," I said, as the water rushed over my face.

Kael's hands moved down to my shoulders and he continued to show me a deep level of intimacy that I couldn't have fathomed had existed before knowing him. It wasn't the first time he'd done this, but it still felt so new to me. Was this our new thing? How would I ever be able to bathe or shower alone after being so pampered by him?

"My pleasure," Kael said, pressing his lips against the spot between my shoulder blades.

I hesitated to say it, but he knew how religious I was about my shower routine. "Can you do the conditioner too? Otherwise my hair will be a tangly mess. I can also do it myself, I appreciate you even—" From behind me his hand clasped my mouth before I could finish.

I laughed against it, and he grabbed the conditioner bottle, reading the label to make sure it was the right one. Once it was rinsed out, he ran the loofah filled with body wash across my entire body. I held on to his shoulders as he washed my thighs, my calves, and even my feet. I felt like crying again. I really needed to get a handle on my emotions, but tonight had just been too much. Once he was finished he tried to hand me a towel from the rack outside the shower curtain, but I pulled at his hand, taking the towel gently and tossing it onto the floor. Confusion filled his face and I waved my finger for him to switch spots with me.

"It's your turn," I said, kissing him softly on his bare chest.

He didn't say anything or try to refuse; he just moved around me to stand under the water, and I squeezed the body wash onto the loofah and rubbed it across his wide chest, down and under each arm. He was surprisingly ticklish and kept moving, which made both of us laugh. The trauma of the evening felt like it had happened a month ago. I bent down on my knees to wash Kael's legs and he jerked back, hitting his head on the metal part of my showerhead.

"What happened?" I looked up, my heart racing.

"I don't . . . I don't want you to touch my leg. Or even see it . . ."

Huh?

"What are you talking about? I've seen your legs a hundred times," I told him, looking at the bottoms of his legs in front of me.

What in the . . . ?

"See—" He groaned, not looking at me.

I raced through all the times we had been undressed in front of one another, all of the time we'd spent in bed, all of the massages, and it all clicked in my head. This was why he always hid himself.

"I can't see anything." I closed my eyes. "Now let me wash you, it's only fair since you did me."

My heart raced, aching and ripping apart all at once. The burned skin, the healed but still inflamed skin, the idea of him suffering nearly made me sick on the spot, but I refused to show him that. I refused to make him feel like he had anything to be ashamed of, like every part of him wasn't absolutely, unquestionably exquisite.

I knew he had an injury but he kept it shielded from me, so I guess my mind had filed it away and I hadn't thought much about the appearance of it. I didn't care how it looked; I only cared if he was in pain. And I wanted to kill whoever had done this to him. As I swirled the bubbly soap around his skin and down to his feet, I remembered back to our first meeting, that fateful massage when he wore sweatpants and I just thought he was uncomfortable, to the party at my dad's and how he was about to reveal that part of himself to me but we were interrupted.

"You have nothing to be ashamed of. Not with me." I looked up at him and his eyes were blazing, intense yet careful, as he watched me.

I leaned in a bit and kissed his scarred skin, making him gasp, and stood back up to face him.

"You're perfect," I assured him, meaning it to my core.

CHAPTER FOURTEEN

Kael

When we woke up in the morning, I had four missed calls from Phillips. Assuming he hadn't been arrested, I wondered what the fuck had happened to him, and where he'd slept. No matter how hard I tried to recall, I couldn't remember leaving Mendoza's last night. I remembered glimpses of the fight, of the gun, of my memories taking me back to deployment, the way Karina had looked at me like I terrified her, but I blanked on the end of the party. Next thing I knew, I was in Karina's bathroom with her and now in her bedroom, her body wrapped around me, hugging me from the side.

"Hmmph," she murmured in her sleep, a noise that usually meant she'd wake up soon.

Without moving her an inch, I carefully reached for my phone on the nightstand and texted Fischer, making sure he and Elodie had gotten home safely.

After a few minutes, he responded.

We're in the living room. Elodie is still asleep. How's my sister?

She was really shaken up, but she's okay.

I sent it, then typed, **I think.**

Elodie, too, she was really fucked up after what happened.

Did Phillips get picked up by the MPs?

No. They never came.

I didn't know if I was relieved or pissed. The MPs were usually slap happy to come enforce the little bit of power they held over the rest of us, but I guessed it was Phillips's lucky night.

I put my phone down as Karina stirred awake. Her eyelids were swollen as she blinked them open, her bloodshot eyes full of lingering anxiety as I watched her come to.

"Where's my brother?" she asked, voice strained. "I had a dream that he—" She didn't finish the sentence, but she didn't need to.

My phone buzzed next to me. I gently picked it up with the hand that wasn't brushing Karina's cheek. I lifted it behind her head and read the message.

The MPs are here, banging on the door.

What?

What do you mean the MPs are there? At my house?

The texting bubbles popped up and I held my breath. They disappeared before a message came through. *Fuck.*

"Everything okay?" Karina tilted her chin to looked into my eyes.

I considered lying, but what good would that do? She could read me like a damn book, and by now I'd learned my lesson when it came to keeping the truth from such an aware woman as Karina.

"Not sure. Fischer said the MPs are at my place."

She sat up and reached for my phone.

Her eyes scanned the screen, reading the texts between her brother and me. She wasted no time calling him. Her eyes closed when his voicemail came on.

"We should go." She climbed off the bed, flung open her dresser drawers, and began tossing clothes onto the floor.

The level of panic she felt was contagious. I tried Fischer again while picking up the clothes she was flinging around and putting them on her bed. After pulling a sweatshirt over her head, she hobbled on one leg, then the other, and slid socks onto each of her feet. I got dressed as fast as I could, and Karina called for Elodie.

"Babe, she's at my place."

Her key chain shook in her hand. "Oh god. Yeah, I forgot."

"I'm driving." I gently cupped her hands and removed the keys. No way in hell was I going to let her drive.

It seemed to take a fucking lifetime to get to my place even though it was only a few miles. When we pulled up, the place looked vacated. Elodie's car was gone and the front door was closed but not locked. We searched the duplex, calling Fischer's and Elodie's names, but no one replied. The kitchen and bathroom lights were on and there was a fresh glass of ice water on the coffee table. It seemed as if they had left unexpectedly, and given the MPs coming, it made sense. Fischer needed to stay off their radar or his enlistment would be totally fucked. As it was, he'd already gotten in trouble too many times.

Karina called Elodie over and over, but she didn't pick up on her cell either.

"I shouldn't have gotten so drunk last night," Karina groaned as we got back into my truck.

"There's nothing you could have done, and we don't know why they came. Maybe they were looking for Phillips?" I tried to comfort her but my gut told me something was wrong, beyond the obvious of the shitshow that last night had been.

"Hopefully. But I need to see my brother." Her lips quivered as she spoke.

I put the truck in Drive and headed to the closest MP station. My busted knuckles gripped the steering wheel until they turned white.

After two stops, we finally found Elodie's car parked outside the third station. Karina got out of the truck before I turned the ignition off. When we got inside, soldiers in ACUs were sitting behind their desks and two of them were standing, arms crossed in front of a hysterical Elodie.

"You're not listening!" she cried, covering her face with her hands.

Karina moved next to her and flung her arms around her as I approached the soldiers.

"What's going on, Private?" I asked the one with a clipboard in his hands.

He eyed me up and down before responding.

"What's your name, soldier?" the young private asked me. The other one tapped his shoulder and said something in his ear. Having been in combat had given me the ability to easily read lips. As he whispered my name, they both looked at me.

"Sergeant Martin, right?" the private with the clipboard asked me.

I nodded, my skin prickling.

"You need to come with us."

Karina immediately began to panic. "What are you talking about? Why would he—"

I held my hand up between her and the soldiers. I didn't want her temper to get her in trouble when these boys were so fucking obviously eager for escalation. I could tell by the way the shorter one had a fucking smug smirk drawn across his ratlike face. I could sense an instigator from a damn mile away. The patches on their ACUs let me know they had never been in combat, so of course they were thirsty for action . . . and for blood.

"You two should go home," I calmly told Elodie and Karina. I knew damned well that my girl wasn't going to listen, but I hoped her friend would convince her.

"No fucking way am I leaving! What do you need to talk to him about? And where is my brother?" Karina's voice traveled through the quiet station.

"They arrested him," Elodie sobbed.

"Arrested him for what?" Karina shouted.

One of the MPs stepped toward her, and every bit of my self-control flew out of the tiny station. I blocked him from getting so much as an inch closer.

"Give me some info. What grounds did you arrest him on? What are the charges, if any, that have been filed? Why hasn't he been able to call his next of kin yet?"

The two of them squirmed where they stood, looking at one another for guidance, then to the clock. "We brought him in for complaints of assault. We need to drug test him before we even start the discussion of release."

"Drug test him? He's not a soldier yet. You have zero authority to piss test him. Who's your commander?"

"He's almost here. You need to wait. Sergeant or not, you're not our boss."

I held my breath, taming the growing fire inside of me. Karina and Elodie's stress felt like it was blasting off them and through me. It was so hard to not react to the smug assholes, who from their point of view were just doing their jobs. But arresting Fischer didn't make any sense. He hadn't done a damn thing. The tiny bit of rational thought I had kept me quiet.

"Dad! What's going on?" Karina rushed toward her father as he strode into the room where we all waited. He was wearing his ACUs and boots. I couldn't remember the last time I'd seen that man in his uniform outside the Middle East.

"They said Austin's been detained but wouldn't tell us why." Her voice was frantic, but her father's face stayed as still as stone.

"Calm down, Karina," he said. Elodie's shoulders shook with a sob. She was wearing the same clothes as last night. "You two—" Her dad pointed at the two soldiers and wagged his finger for them to follow him. "With me."

"Dad!" Karina shrieked, but was ignored.

I went to her, whispering for her to try to calm down a little. I hated that her feelings were valid, but if she continued to show emotion, whatever the hell was going on was only going to get worse.

The two soldiers and Lieutenant Fischer huddled for a minute or two before Karina's father approached us.

"Your brother will be fine. We got a report that he was high, so once we drug test him he will be free to go. That is"—he eyed Elodie, then me, then his daughter. There was a tiny flicker of menace in his gaze, more so than the usual asshole he was—"if he passes."

"But he's not in the Army, how can they arrest him on post? And why are you here? He didn't do anything! If anyone should be arrested, it's Phillips, he had a gun, Dad—"

Lt. Fischer held his hand up to stop Karina from continuing. "Enough. You keep getting yourself involved in situations that you shouldn't. We also got a report of an assault."

His beady eyes homed in on my busted hands. I tucked them into the pockets of my sweats and kept my expression flat.

"But fortunately, the victim doesn't want to press charges." He kept his eyes on me. "So I suggest you take my daughter home and keep her there. I will deal with *my* son how I see fit."

"Sir." Elodie finally spoke. Instinctually, I tried to shield her from getting close to Karina's dad. "He—"

Karina had told me her father was fond of Elodie, but the way he was looking at her told me otherwise.

"Austin doesn't do drugs and he barely drinks anymore. He is trying really hard to do right in his service," Elodie explained to him, her hands at her chest like a prayer.

"Martin." He didn't acknowledge her and spoke directly to me. "Take them home."

In my head, I told him to fuck off, to for once in his pathetic life give his daughter the attention and love she needed, to stop being such a fuckhead to his son, who was trying to do his best. In reality, I did exactly as I was told.

"It's best if we go." I put my arm around Karina and watched as her father's eyes burned a hole in me. "I know you don't want to, and I'm sorry for pushing this, but—" I lowered my voice. "You know your dad better than anyone, and the best thing we can do is go home."

"I can't." Elodie shook her head. "This is because of me. I know it."

"Unless you want to trade places with him," Lt. Fischer threatened me as I tried to coerce the girls to leave with me.

"Are you threatening him right now? Seriously?" Karina snapped at her father. I gently gripped her tighter and watched the resolve slowly wash over her.

The look on his face told me that he had a lot to say, but he kept his thin lips in a harsh line.

"I fucking hate him," she told me as she held Elodie's hand, leading her out of the building. "God, I fucking hate him."

Since she was in no position to drive, Elodie left her car parked in the lot of the MP station and I drove the two of them back to Karina's house. When we pulled up, Elodie and Karina were speaking so rapidly that I zoned out while we walked up the grass, onto the porch, and I unlocked the door, leading them inside. They sat down on the couch, instantly embracing each other, and Karina called off of work for the day. Elodie was already scheduled to be off, but Karina explained to Mali that she was dealing with a family emergency. I didn't want to urge Karina to work while all of this was going on, but I did worry about her cutting her hours because of how tight she'd mentioned money had been lately.

I knew better than to offer to help her, but, damn, I wanted to. There was no way in hell she would take my money, or even borrow it, and I wanted to keep my body parts intact, so I kept my mouth shut whenever she groaned at her electric or water bill. The struggle between respecting her independence and wanting to make her life easier wasn't an easy one. In fact, I fucking hated it. Maybe I could accidently drop a couple hundred bucks in her purse and play dumb when she found it? Or leave it in an old purse of hers in the closet and hope she came across it? If she wasn't so in tune with me and the expressions I make when trying to lie, I would.

To give Karina and Elodie a little bit of privacy, I moved to the kitchen and pulled out my phone. I texted Mendoza to see if he knew what the hell had happened. My finger hovered over Phillips's name, contemplating whether it would make shit worse if I called him. The scabs on my knuckles were raw and dry, and as my mind traveled back to last night, I could taste the faint metal of Phillips's blood as it splattered across my face and mouth. I licked my lips and dropped my phone onto the counter. While I waited for Mendoza to reply, I opened Karina's fridge to see what I could throw together to feed them. She had to be hungover as hell and in need of some damn food. And Elodie was pregnant— she needed to keep her strength up.

Karina didn't have much, some green bell peppers, half an onion, some ground beef. I opened her small pantry and got out a box of instant rice and thanked god she had some seasonings outside of salt and pepper. As the beef browned and sizzled with the onions in the pan, I poured in a carton of chicken stock and checked my phone again. Two missed calls from Mendoza. I tried him back and he picked up on the first ring.

"What the fuck is going on, man?" he asked.

I glanced into the living room, turned the element down on the stovetop, and stepped toward the back door to shield at least some of my voice from the girls.

"I don't fucking know. Fischer is being held at the MP station on Wold Avenue. They picked him up from my place this morning but no one will tell me a fucking thing. And Lt. Fischer showed up there. Fischer's not even at basic yet—something's up and Phillips is at the center of it, that much is clear."

"Did he stay with you?" I asked.

"Nah. I don't know when he left or with who. Shit went crazy and everyone left before the police got there. I don't know where his ass slithered off to. You haven't heard from him?"

"Not a fucking word."

Mendoza let out a sigh. "Maybe he's dead and we can all go back to our regularly scheduled programming."

I laughed, kind of wishing it was true.

"But for real, what are going to do about Fischer? We can't just leave him there. Did his shitbag sperm donor say he was going to at least get him out?"

"If he passes a drug test." My response came out more unsure than I meant it to.

"He will. I mean it, bro. He's been clean as a goddamn whistle lately. No way in hell he's failing a drug test right now."

"You're sure?" I hated to doubt Fischer, but I wasn't a fucking idiot and I had seen him higher than a cloud on many occasions.

"Yep. Positive. The last time he smoked was weeks ago. Since he's become all domestic with Elodie, he's gotten his shit together. I wouldn't be surprised if his old man tries to rig it, though."

"The test?" I asked, knowing exactly what Mendoza meant but not wanting to acknowledge that as a possibility.

"Fuck. Let me call my old platoon leader and see if he can get me an update. But we know what their father is capable of." His deep voice shook on the other line, and I swallowed.

We both knew that better than anyone, and Mendoza not using his name wasn't lost on me.

I put my phone into my pocket and made sure the ringer was on while I finished making something that resembled dirty rice. I filled two bowls all the way to the top and shoved a spoon into each. My appetite was nowhere to be found, but it smelled good as fuck. I knew Karina's tastebuds enough by now to know she would love it, and the look on her face when I handed her the bowl proved me right.

"Any update?" Karina asked me as soon as I stepped into the living room.

I shook my head.

"I don't want to hear that you're not hungry. Both of you eat, now," I insisted. "Please," I added with a fake smile to make my command more of a suggestion, but if they didn't, I would spoon-feed the two of them myself.

"Thank you." Elodie's voice was quiet but she pushed a spoonful into her mouth and closed her eyes as she chewed. "I was so hungry but didn't notice."

Karina's eyes were tired, but the way she looked at me made me forget, just for a moment, the massive shitshow we were all in the middle of.

Thank you, she mouthed soundlessly and began to eat.

My phone rang in my pocket. "I need to take this."

I left the room before either of them could question me and stepped out the front door and walked down the porch. It was hard to believe it was barely fucking noon. The sun was just about over the clouds and the air had a bite to it. Karina's nosy-ass neighbor was by his truck, dragging a mattress by a rope into the bed of it.

"What did you find out?"

"Word is he failed. But I'm telling you, he fucking didn't."

"What the hell?" My mind raced with potential solutions, potential reasons this was happening. Was Karina's father trying to keep his son from leaving for basic training?

"What are we gonna do, Martin?" Mendoza asked me.

"I—" I paused, thinking about Karina and how she would be absolutely thrown deeper into hell if she knew what was happening right now, and that her father was not only not helping, but was potentially the cause of all this mess. My phone went off, the noise when someone was calling, and I had to blink to make sure I was reading the name correctly. It was Karina's father.

"Let me call you right back," I said as Mendoza called my name.

"Sergeant Martin." I answered in the flattest tone I could manage. My heart was racing and that pissed me off beyond words. This measly little man should have zero power over me, but instead he could play puppeteer with two of the people I cared the most about in the world.

"Come to the station, Sergeant," he instructed, calling me by my rank for the first time that I could remember.

"Why?" I dropped all formality.

"Because my son needs a ride home if they let him go, and you and I need to talk."

"A ride home? So he passed the test?"

Mendoza told me less than thirty seconds ago that he hadn't, so what the actual fuck was going on?

"Come to the station, Sergeant," he repeated.

Fuck it. If he wanted to play games with me, then let's fucking play.

CHAPTER FIFTEEN

Kael

Karina called me before I even made it to the stop sign. She must have heard my truck rev up and pull away from the curb. I hadn't even told them I was leaving. I'd hung up the call from Karina's dad and walked straight to my truck. If Elodie or Karina had said anything to try to stop me, I hadn't heard them.

My mind roiled as I drove myself into a situation that had less than a 1 percent probability of ending well for me. On the phone she begged me to turn around, to take her with me, but I pleaded with her, told her to keep herself and Elodie home. There was nothing either of them could do right now, and seeing her distraught would only make me act irrationally. I was so used to calling in backup, to radioing my platoon to come save my ass, but this time it was just me. Though I had been on death's door many a time, the stakes somehow felt higher in that moment driving away from her house.

For the first time in my life, I realized I would genuinely choose another person's well-being over my own. Not in an "every soldier has each other's backs" kind of way, but in an "I would burn this entire post down, I would go against every moral I had, I would do fucked-up, unspeakable things to anyone and everyone I had ever met for her" way.

"I'll bring your brother home," I said. "You keep Elodie calm and don't answer the door for anyone, I mean anyone, in case Phillips shows up there."

The thought chilled me to the bone. I would finish what I'd started the night before if he so much as came within a hundred feet of Karina.

"I don't like it, Kael," she said.

"You don't have to like it, but listen, please."

She said okay, and we hung up. As I pulled into the parking lot, I spotted Lt. Fischer standing against his truck with his arms crossed. I parked beside him and climbed out of mine. My leg was still sore from last night, but I'd be damned if I showed any weakness in front of him. I straightened my back and stared directly into his eyes as I approached him.

"That was quick," he said, indicating the space behind me.

"It's important."

He nodded as if that mattered to him.

"Come sit in my truck, Martin." He craned his neck; the blue veins were a grayish color under his slightly yellow skin.

"Does our conversation need to be that private?" I asked, knowing my rebellious questioning would piss him off.

"Yes. Yes, it does. If you care about my family the way I have the impression you do, then you'll do what I say."

The urge to tell him to fuck right off was strong but both of us knew I wouldn't do that. He knew as well as I did that I would do exactly what he said if it meant that Karina and Fischer would be okay. We got into his truck, and I couldn't help but scoff at the small photo of Karina and Fischer stuck inside his dashboard near the speedometer. They looked about ten in the photo; Karina's hair was to her waist and she was hanging on to her brother's back. He had a goofy-ass smile on his face, and it gave me the tiniest ounce

ANNA TODD

of peace to know that at some point their home life was decent enough to have caused those smiles.

"That photo was taken when the twins were about eleven. We were camping outside of Houston." He handed me the old photograph. It was cut around the left edge and I realized someone was cut out of it. Their mother.

"Funny that you have such sentiment about it, yet your son is being held without reason and your daughter is losing her mind over it, and you don't seem to give a shit."

All pretense and manners were gone. He didn't deserve my respect, and now that my discharge was right around the corner, there was nothing he could do to stop it.

"You know, the one thing I like about you is how decided and direct your opinions are. It's refreshing to have someone speak to me like they're my superior," he told me, a half smile lifting the right side of his face.

I didn't know how to respond to that. I thumbed the picture, looking at the cut edge.

"Anything else you like about me? Or are we just going to hang out in your truck while your children suffer?"

He laughed a bit. "Suffer? My children don't have a clue what suffering is."

In a way, he had a point. They'd grown up in a warm house with an officer's income, flat-screen TVs, hot meals, clean water. But human suffering came in a magnitude of forms. It wasn't as simple as saying someone hadn't suffered because they'd had necessities. Karina had been so emotionally neglected since her mother left, and that had taken a toll on her. Her father's coldness, along with being abandoned, was suffering. Fischer's attempts at being someone his dad respected while drinking and getting high to take away the pain he wasn't comfortable feeling was fucking suffering. Me

98

watching my mother work herself sick and never having a support system, listening to my sister cry when the kids at her private school full of upper-middle-class white kids made comments about her dirty uniform and sneakers was absolutely fucking suffering. I'd watched children die in front of me; I'd seen a man get his head blown off his fucking body as his wife screamed for help that wasn't coming.

"If you're too arrogant to consider that your children are going through the pain they're in because of you, I don't have anything to say to you. You and I both know the impossibility of putting a measure on what it means to suffer. We've seen it all, you even more than me, and if you can't separate being a soldier in the middle of war and being a father, you're useless anyway," I told him, not editing my words.

I wasn't talking to my lieutenant. I was talking to Karina's father.

"Look," I continued, turning my body to fully face him in the passenger seat and sighing. "I don't know why you called me here, but I'm done pretending that I don't hate you. Every breath you take feels unfair and unjust. Stop with the vague bullshit and tell me what you want."

I'd seen this man in the middle of a rocket attack, in a sandy tornado of shells, bullets, and explosions. I'd seen him watch innocent people die. I'd seen him ruin my battle buddy's sanity for the sake of his own reputation. I'd seen him with blood on his hands in every sense of the word, but I had never seen him speechless. He stared at me, and seconds felt like minutes before he finally spoke. Light rain began to tap against the truck, filling the windshield with tiny drops. I watched as they slid into one another, being immediately replaced by another. It felt metaphorical.

"I need you to get my daughter out of Fort Benning," he finally said. I cocked my head, not sure if I'd heard him correctly.

"What?"

"I need my daughter to leave this post, Martin. There's something bigger going on here, and despite what you think I feel for my children, I'd like them safe. I will do something in return for you—I'll get Mendoza the help he needs, I'll even help him get medically discharged if that's what he wants. I already made sure you got your ninety-percent disability so you can still work when you get to Atlanta. I tried to keep Phillips in Afghanistan as long as I could but—"

My head was spinning from each statement he made. Did he really have something to do with my discharge going so smoothly? Would he try to make up for what he'd done to Mendoza?

I asked my last question out loud. "Why would you want to keep Phillips deployed?"

He stared at me. The interior of the truck was so humid that the windows were fogging, and he had a bead of sweat above his gray brow.

"He's a bloodthirsty fool. You know that."

"You know he almost shot your son last night, right? So when you scolded me earlier, you—"

"He did what?"

"He had a gun and pointed it at Austin last night." I'd called Fischer by his first name only a handful of times, but this felt like the right time to use it.

This seemed to be news to him.

"Whose idea was it to arrest and drug test Fischer?" I asked, my thoughts forming a completely different situation than the one I had pieced together this morning.

"I'm trying to find the answer to that question. I did what I could, and he'll be free to go in a few, but they're trying to ruin his chances of enlisting."

"Who's they?"

Of course he wasn't going to tell me. The details didn't really matter anyway. What mattered was that Fischer needed to be careful; we all did.

"I've made many, many mistakes in my life, but this time, it's pure spite. The less involved you are the better, but ironically, you're the only one who can help get my kids out of here before anything escalates and my health grows—"

I didn't have to hear the end of his sentence to know something was going on with him—something more than some melodramatic villains from his past trying to sabotage his children's lives. The real reason he was attempting to repent was that he was going to die. I could practically smell it on him, the stench of a rotting man. I should have caught on sooner, but now it was obvious.

"Is it cancer or something else?" I asked.

He ran his hands along the edge of the steering wheel. "Tar pits. Enough about me. Can you make Karina leave with you? I can make sure Austin gets to basic before Thanksgiving, but Karina will never listen to me, as you know." He almost smiled, and for the smallest breath, I felt a little pity for him.

What a miserable existence, what a wasted legacy, and now it was going to be cut short, leaving his relationship with his kids in limbo, even after his last breath.

Karina was not going to be able to handle his death. That was the only thing that made me wish it wasn't coming. I wondered how much time he had and if anyone else knew.

"Why are you telling me all of this?"

"Like I said, you're the only one who can help. Not help me, but help my daughter. She is going to lose her brother to distance and will be left with no one by her side, and you seem determined to stay, so all I'm asking is that you convince her to go to Atlanta with you, and soon."

My head pounded as the rain picked up, mimicking the noise in my mind. I couldn't guarantee that Karina would leave this place, and she 1,000 percent wouldn't move if she knew her dad was dying.

"I can't and won't promise you anything, but I'll do what I can. For her," I finally agreed.

I needed to get out of the damn truck and have space to process this bizarre conversation, the situation with Fischer, the fact that Phillips was roaming around with a gun. As overwhelming as it all was, as I mentally listed it I shifted my process to what Sergeant Martin would do, taking the emotion out of it. I needed to come up with a plan that wouldn't make Karina hate me, and execute it quickly.

CHAPTER SIXTEEN

Karina

"What if they keep him there?" Elodie asked, her hands clasped on her lap, knuckles white.

Her skin was a gray color, under her eyes blue and hollow. It wasn't the time to remind her that stress wasn't good for her baby, but it was so hard not to.

"They won't. Kael will figure it out. He always does."

"This is all my fault. God, how do things keep getting worse, Karina?"

I scooted closer to her and wrapped my arms around her shoulders. Her skin was icy to the touch, increasing my anxiety. There wasn't a single thing I could do or say to make sense of any of this, and she was right—everything kept getting freaking worse. Nearly daily at this point.

"Things always get worse before they get better, Elodie. We will figure it all out, Kael will handle it, and my brother will be fine, and worst-case, you can take my brother and run away to France." I smiled, actually wishing that was in the realm of reality. I would miss them like crazy, but each day felt like another bomb would go off.

She almost smiled. A second later, my front door opened and

Kael, followed by Austin, walked through. Relief washed over me. Elodie jumped up, wrapping her arms around my brother's neck, and finally stopped crying.

"Are you okay?" she asked, placing her palms on either side of his cheeks and moving his head around slowly.

He laughed, as only he would, given the circumstances. "I'm fine. I'm fine."

Kael took his shoes off and hesitated by the door for a moment. He didn't make eye contact with me instantly, which he usually did. He had to be exhausted from being dragged into my brother's shit again, but something felt off. I knew him well enough to know he wouldn't exactly be vocal about anything that was wrong. It wasn't the time to ask him, especially not in front of an audience, so I hugged him instead. He bent his knees a little to meet me at my height and pressed his forehead against mine. I nearly melted at the intimacy of it. Until Kael, I'd never realized how starved for physical touch I was. My mother had been affectionate until she wasn't, and my father . . . I couldn't remember the last time he'd hugged me or so much as touched my arm or brushed my hair away when it covered my eyes.

"What now?" I asked. I didn't breathe as I fired off the questions that had been playing in my head for the last few hours. "Are you in trouble? Did you pass or fail the drug test? Can you still be a soldier? Why did they arrest you in the first place? Where is Phillips? Did Dad—"

"Kare, oh my god." Austin rolled his eyes, drooping his shoulders like he was fifteen and had gotten caught shoplifting, again.

"Don't 'Kare' me, Austin. We have been worried to death and you're acting like nothing happened. We need answers." I looked at Elodie for backup, but with one glance I could tell her alliance was with my brother.

"Let me at least take a shower and eat before you interrogate me," my brother teased. "But seriously, everything is okay. It was a mix-up and I'm not in any trouble," he explained.

I swear the house could be on fire and my brother would sit on the couch and play freaking Xbox. Nothing ever seemed to bother him, and aside from Phillips's behavior toward Elodie last night, Austin floated through life without a care in the world. Must be fucking nice. I stared a hole into his back, cussing him out mentally as he walked down the hallway and went into the bathroom. The sound of rushing water filled the room, and Elodie turned to Kael.

"Is he really okay?" she asked, her brows scrunched together as she leaned toward him as if she was examining him. *"Tu vas bien?"*

"He's all right," Kael said. "Did anyone show up here?" He glanced around the room, doing his usual survey of the place, probably noting that we'd moved the pillows on the couch to the floor and Elodie had brought a glass of water to the coffee table. He noticed everything.

"Non. My husband hasn't, and he didn't call," Elodie told him.

Last night felt like a different lifetime, like it hadn't actually happened to me, to us. It was strange and fascinating, the way my brain was processing the anxiety and intrusive thoughts as they came in. Today, even with the chaos of my brother getting arrested and released, it felt like I was split into two versions of myself. One of them was hiding in a corner with a spinning mind and shaking hands, full-on fight-or-flight mode, and the other was standing in my living room, half smiling, thinking about how Kael's eyes looked like honey under my lights. I kept waiting for a massive, soul-splitting breakdown, but even when I thought about the way the string lights in Mendoza's backyard had reflected off the metal gun in Phillips's hand, the memory was both fuzzy and clear, like a film I had seen but didn't remember clearly.

"Karina?" Kael's voice sounded like it was underwater as I blinked my eyes to focus.

"Huh?"

"Did you hear me?" he asked.

No, I did not. "Um, no. Sorry. What was it?"

"I said I'm going to go to Mendoza's. Do you wanna come with me or stay with Elodie and your brother?"

"I want to go with you." I didn't want to be away from him, not even for a second.

We waited for my brother to come out of the bathroom before we left. Kael gave the two of them a brief lecture on not opening my door and calling him immediately if Phillips showed up. My brother agreed calmly, but I could practically read his mind, and I knew that if Elodie's husband arrived unexpectedly at my house, all rational thought would fly out the window and one of them wouldn't survive. The casual bleakness of my thought surprised me. No, it wasn't the thought exactly. It was that it was true. This was what I had always feared when it came to being too embedded in military life and culture: life and death becoming passive thoughts, a part of the way things were. Would I reach a point where I wouldn't even cry at a funeral, like my father?

"Do you cry at funerals?" I asked Kael as soon as he closed the driver's-side door of his truck.

"No," he said, checking the rearview mirror before pulling out of my driveway.

"Hmph. Did you used to?" I wondered.

He shook his head. "Not since I was a kid and my mom's brother died."

He had mentioned his uncle a few times, in the quiet of the night as I poked and prodded for every detail about his life before I knew him. He had died when Kael was a child, and was the only sibling his mother had.

"Do you cry over other things? Just not death?" I asked.

He glanced over at me before he responded, probably wondering where the hell I was going with this.

His voice was low as he told me, "I cried the first time I killed someone."

My breath caught in my throat at his raw response.

"Oh." I kept my eyes on him. The idea that he might think I couldn't look at him because of what he'd said made me sick. His eyes met mine as he slowed to a stop at the end of my street. In them I saw regret, pain, a man who had lived a hundred lives before his twenty-first birthday.

"And the second, and the third." A lifelong sadness filled his words.

"Did it get easier?"

He shook his head. "I was told that it would, that the first time was the worst. But even though I only eliminated people who were actively trying to kill me or my platoon, it only got harder. Watching my boys—Phillips for one—becoming too comfortable taking lives was something I wasn't trained for. I was trained to survive, to only kill if I absolutely had to, but I had, and still have, a constant fear of slipping, of not valuing human life. It's a thin line when you're told that you're doing the right thing, that you're a hero fighting for the safety of your country. The more I questioned, the more I lost my sanity."

"People who are insane don't think they're insane." I had no clue how to comfort him and knew deep down that I couldn't, but

I needed him to know that he wasn't bad, that he was the most thoughtful, the most levelheaded person I had ever known. He wasn't like Phillips, or my father.

"Right." He smiled a little, raising his brow. "Any other questions about my emotional capabilities, or can I get on the highway?"

I laughed, knowing sarcasm and self-deprecation were how we both handled heavy emotions. Sometimes there was no morally perfect way to navigate things as big and traumatic as war and death and invading countries and taking lives.

"Highway, but I do have more questions." I reached for his hand. It was so warm in mine, and the ointment slathered over his busted knuckles was still wet and shining under the fall sun. "Who was the worst teacher you've ever had?" I asked him as he sped up. The engine roared, and he began to tell me about the awful math teacher he had in the tenth grade.

Gloria greeted us as we pulled up to the house. She was barefoot and wearing a T-shirt that went to her knees. Her hair was down, more wavy than usual, half of it in a bun on top of her head. She looked like an LA girl leaving one of those overpriced organic grocery stores, so effortlessly cool. I realized that Kael never told me why we were going to the Mendozas' house or if it was to hang out with them, but I hoped it was just because. It felt surprisingly nice to have a friend's house to go to.

"Hey, babe." Gloria hugged me with both arms, a *real* hug. A hug that felt like friendship and trust and comfort. I didn't think I would ever get used to that feeling. "How are you?" She gently pushed my shoulders to have direct eye contact with me. "You look like hell." She frowned, brushing my hair away from my face. "Beautiful hell, but hell nonetheless."

"I don't know . . . how I am, I mean." I decided to not edit my response. I almost said, *I'm totally fine! You?* but Gloria had such a comforting vibe that I didn't feel the need to pretend around her, which was also a strange feeling. One I wished I would be used to by now, but which was slightly uncomfortable still.

"Understandable. Last night was fucking wild. I can't believe Phillips had the nerve to pull out a fucking gun."

"Gloria." Kael's voice came out as a warning.

She rolled her eyes at him, clearly not fazed. "What? That's what happened and she was literally there. Stop babying her." She wrapped her arm around my shoulder and led me to the door.

As we were about to step inside she turned around to Kael behind us. "By the way, Manny is on his second bottle and the kids are at the neighbor's house playing, so now that you're here, you can take over babysitting my husband."

Kael groaned but didn't disagree.

Mendoza was sitting on the couch when we walked in. Like Gloria had warned, he had a half-empty bottle of what looked like his usual tequila in his hand.

"Happy fucking Tuesday!" he shouted as we entered the room. "Or is it Wednesday? Anyway, glad to see we're all alive today. Have a seat!" He was cheerful, obviously drunk as hell, but in a funny mood.

A tiny voice in my head reminded me that it shouldn't be funny, but that didn't change the fact that it was.

"Glad to see you're damaging your liver at one in the afternoon," Kael said as he sat down next to him on the couch. I followed Gloria's lead and plopped down on the love seat. She moved closer to me and crossed her legs under her body. The television was on, a football game playing in the background with barely any sound. Kids' toys were scattered randomly around the room, and their house felt like a home full of life. Cup rings stained the wooden part of the coffee table, children's fingerprints dotted the glass center.

"I'm nothing but consistent." Mendoza leaned up to put his elbows on his knees. He was wearing his ACUs.

"Why aren't you at the company?" Kael asked. For a bunch of soldiers, sometimes I wondered when they worked.

"I got the day off. Thanks to your old man." He pointed the bottle at me.

"What?" I couldn't hide my surprise and discomfort at the mention of my father. I wondered how Mendoza could even stand to be around me given how he felt about my dad. I was grateful that Kael had spared me most of the details of what exactly my dad had done; otherwise, my guilt would keep me from being able to have a friendship with Gloria.

"Your old man came and got me off work. Said I can take a mental health day or some shit. I was shocked too. A mental health day?" He laughed, taking a swig of the bottle.

Kael's entire mood changed in a couple of breaths. I watched him try to keep his face still, but I could see the shift in his eyes, his jaw, his hands on his lap, as my father was mentioned. I knew we were seconds away from Kael telling Mendoza to stop talking.

On cue, he did just that.

"You can talk about my dad. It doesn't bother me," I told Mendoza, and looked at both him and Kael. "I hate him, too, so it's fine." I tried to smile, lighten the mood a little, but it came out awkwardly. I really needed to work on my social skills.

Gloria laughed, telling Kael to chill the fuck out, but he didn't. He was only more tense as Mendoza offered me a drink.

"Absolutely not." Kael pushed the bottle away from me before I could decide for myself. I didn't even want to drink, but Kael deciding for me pissed me off, so I stood up and grabbed the bottle with both hands. Drinking in the middle of the day with so much shit going on was a horrible idea and I knew that, but that didn't stop me.

Mendoza was amused; Kael was not. He glared at me and I glared right back, taking a swig of the warm liquor. I tried not to spit it back out as it burned down my chest and settled in the pit of my stomach. I quickly handed the bottle back to Mendoza. Gloria passed me a bottle of blue Gatorade and told me to wash it down.

"Thanks."

The Gatorade definitely helped cool down the fire from the tequila. When I looked at Kael, I could tell he was not impressed with my little tantrum, but now that the liquor had moved to my head, I wanted more. I guessed this was how people became addicted to alcohol. With only one drink everything felt less serious—Kael's annoyance was kind of funny, Mendoza's mood made more sense to me, and Gloria's patience with her husband was even more impressive.

"How's Fischer?" Mendoza asked us. "I tried to call him after his dad said he was a free man, but he didn't pick up."

Mendoza quietly noticed me eyeing the bottle of tequila. He looked at Kael, then back at me, tipping it toward me. He underestimated Kael's awareness of literally everything and I decided to ignore his judgment as I went ahead with another drink straight from the bottle.

"He's fine. At Karina's place with Elodie. Have you heard from Phillips?" Kael kept his composure, seemingly choosing not to try to stop me from drinking with Mendoza.

"Nope. And he's a lucky motherfucker that I haven't. My kids were in the house, and he brought a gun here. I better not see him again."

"Okay." Gloria sounded exasperated as she told me to come to the kitchen with her. "We'll take this," she said, grabbing the tequila and taking it with us.

I didn't look back at Kael as I followed Gloria into the kitchen.

We sat down at their dining table, Gloria on one side and me on the other. Their table was only big enough for four chairs but had five to fit their family.

"Sorry, but I couldn't listen to them talking about Phillips anymore. That's all Manny has been talking about since he woke up." Gloria rubbed her fingers in a circular motion over her temples. "Here." She slid the tequila she'd hijacked from her husband across the table to me. "Don't get too used to that." Her eyes fell on the bottle as I took a drink. "And for god's sake, at least put it on some ice."

She stood up and went to a cabinet. The cups were all mismatched and it reminded me of the way my mom always collected random plastic cups from fast-food chains and kept them. She always said that people who have matching cups and plates lived in a museum, not a home, and sitting in Gloria's kitchen, I agreed with her. I wasn't sure if it was the tequila or the nostalgic feeling of the house, but Gloria sort of reminded me of my mother. A more stable version of her, who would never abandon her children.

"What?" Gloria looked down at me as she poured a hefty amount of liquor into a cup with ice and what I assumed was Gatorade. "Why are you smiling at me like that?" She petted my head, and my smile grew.

"I really like being around you," I admitted. A bubble of panic rose through my buzzed brain as I realized how weird that probably sounded. I tried to cover it up with more words, hoping she wouldn't regret befriending me. "Sorry—that was so weird. I meant like. I—" Gloria's hand gently covered my mouth, ending my fumbling words.

"I really like being around you, too, Karina," she said, a warm, genuine smile spreading across her beautiful face.

CHAPTER SEVENTEEN

Karina

Eventually, we rejoined the boys in the living room. Kael was more relaxed, pulling me onto his lap on the couch. I sank into the warmth of his body; the couch felt like a cloud.

"You guys are coming over for Halloween this year, right?" Mendoza asked Kael and me.

He had finally switched from tequila to water and Gatorade mixed. Gloria explained that Gatorade as a chaser was their secret to never having a hangover.

"Wasn't planning on it," Kael told him in a way that only Kael could without sounding rude.

"Come on! It'll be a good time. No drama," Mendoza promised.

I turned my head slightly to look at Kael's face against my neck.

"We can't guarantee that," Gloria corrected, moving to sit on her husband's lap. "But Phillips is not invited, so we can promise no one will get shot," she said, and smiled as Kael gave her a harsh look. I knew he'd done it for my sake only. This was their usual.

"I want to come," I volunteered. Of course, I'd love if Kael came, but the invite sounded open to both of us, not only him.

He squeezed his arms around my waist a little more tightly. I leaned into him. "Of course you do," he said.

"Sure do. Is it a costume thing? Or a regular party?" I asked, realizing I had never been to a Halloween party in my life.

My mom loved Halloween and, until she left, I had spent it with her at home passing out candy to kids as she scared them. I vaguely remembered trick-or-treating a few times, but I'd had more fun with her, so while Austin ran the streets with his friends, filling his pillowcase full of candy, I spent time with my mother on her favorite day.

"Costumes are optional but encouraged," Gloria replied.

What on earth would I dress up as? I hadn't worn a costume in years. Most women my age dressed as a sexy version of something, a sexy nurse, a sexy witch—even sexy bumblebees were a thing.

"What are you going to dress up as?" I asked them.

"We're going as the Addams family. All of us," she said as the front door opened and noisy children burst through. They climbed onto the couch and life filled the room. Laughter and random noises ensued as they climbed all over us like ants on a tree. "And our adult time is up." Gloria smiled, kissing her husband on the cheek, and embraced her children.

I wasn't sure what to do, so I copied Kael and awkwardly tried to tickle and poke them back. It felt weird at first, but once Julien started laughing and climbed onto my lap, the thought process behind how to play with a child left my brain and some instinct kicked in.

"I want candy now!" Vi told her parents.

"Not yet. You have to save it for Halloween."

"What are you going to be for Halloween?" Julien, the youngest one, asked me.

I don't know where the answer came from, but I responded, "A demon?"

"A demon?" Kael laughed, eyeing me. "Really?"

I nodded. "Yep. I love demons." I squared my shoulders.

"You love demons?" Kael was grinning from ear to ear, noticing how not good at this whole family thing I was.

I nodded again, more confidently this time. "Always have."

"Cooool. I wish I could be a demon, but my mom is making us dress up as a family," Manny complained.

"I'm not *making* you. You said you love the idea." Gloria pouted and her son rolled his eyes.

"Only because I don't want to hurt your feelings," he told her. She reached for him and squeezed his cheeks gently, as if he was a baby and not nearly her size.

"My sweet boy. You can be a demon if you want. Maybe Karina can do your makeup and help you?" she offered.

I hoped he would say no, that he would continue to go along with his mom's plan, but to my literal horror, he grinned at me and nodded profusely. "Can you?" he asked, his hands going to his chest to beg.

Damn it. Damn these cute kids and my tendency to people-please.

"Sure?" I managed.

I could barely manage to do a basic everyday makeup look, let alone a costume, but I couldn't bring myself to tell them all that. YouTube was about to become my new best friend.

When we left their house, Mendoza was asleep on the couch and Gloria hugged me and said she would text me later. We went back to my place to find neither Elodie nor Austin there. I texted them in a group chat, to be sure they were okay, and Elodie responded that they were at the park. The weather was nice, breezy and sunny but not too warm. Fall in Georgia meant unexpected rain, cold fronts, and warmth—sometimes four seasons in one day.

"So, what are you going to dress as for the Halloween party I volunteered us for?" I asked Kael as I plopped onto the couch.

"Us?" He raised a brow and sat on the other side of the small couch.

"Absolutely, *us.*"

His head dropped back and he groaned. "I never go to that shit. Ever."

I climbed toward him, straddling his waist with my thighs. Placing my hands on either side of his face, I met his eyes with mine. His beauty always stunned me. It showed itself constantly to anyone and everyone who laid their eyes on him, but in such a quiet, comforting way. Like a perfectly roasted warm coffee, like a fuzzy blanket on my couch in the fall, like Kael Martin.

He looked away from me and I felt that awkward, subtly uncomfortable feeling creep in again.

"What's wrong?" I had to ask.

He sighed and moved his focus back to my eyes. "Nothing, I'm just distracted."

"By Phillips? Or discharge?" I asked, concern growing inside of me.

Not because he was distracted by something that didn't revolve around me, but because I hated the idea of worry so much as even touching him, no matter what the situation was.

"A little of both." He looked down at my chin, avoiding my eyes.

"It's not something with me, right?"

Kael's already dark eyes turned darker. His expression told me that he was deciding whether to lie to me or not. I knew it could be my own paranoia, but I knew him so well, and my gut was screaming at me.

"Honestly, I—" he began. *Here we go*, I thought to myself. He was going to either tell me he'd been hiding something about

Phillips, or that he was leaving tomorrow for Atlanta, or that he couldn't stand me anymore. My brain was in overdrive, my heart suddenly pounding. I hated the way my thoughts controlled my physical being.

"I really didn't like that you drank so much earlier. I don't care how stressed or anxious or worried you are, downing tequila isn't going to help you, and it pissed me off that you seemed to do it to deal with your emotions, and to piss me off. Both reasons did just that . . . pissed me off."

I pulled back from him and dropped my hands. "That's a lot of pissing you off. Seriously?"

"Yeah, seriously. It's a slippery fucking slope when you start drinking when something goes wrong. I don't want that for you. I've seen it happen again and again. Look at Mendoza, do you want to be like him?"

I shook my head, a little stunned at the shame washing over my body. "Don't judge me. It was one time, Kael."

"One time leads to two, then three, and suddenly you have no control over it."

I felt offended and embarrassed and honestly, it made me want to lash out at him, despite knowing that he was not only right but had my best interest in mind.

"I'm smarter than that. I'm not my mother."

"Becoming an addict has nothing to do with intelligence, Karina." His tone was serious as his hands moved to rest on my hips.

I kept quiet, processing what he'd said. He was right, and it was ignorant of me to assume that addiction had any tie to someone's intelligence. I still felt like it could never happen to me, that I wouldn't allow it to, that I could somehow control it, but I was also aware that that was an arrogant and untrue thought to have, so for once, I kept it inside. Blood ran thicker than water, and her blood ran through my veins. My mom had tried to quiet her ghosts by numbing them, and that certainly hadn't worked. The wreckage she'd left behind should be lesson enough for me.

"You're right," I told him, pressing my chest closer to his. I tucked my chin in and rested my forehead in the space between his jawline and collarbone. His skin was so warm, so full of comfort.

"Don't do it again, okay?" Kael's hands moved to my back and he ran his palms up and down, pushing under the sweatshirt I was wearing and touching my bare skin. I sighed, instantly relaxing, and my brain slowed down with every breath I took.

"Okay," I agreed, hoping that I meant it.

CHAPTER EIGHTEEN

Kael

Karina fell asleep on my lap, likely from indulging in afternoon tequila shots. I had so much on my mind that it was impossible to consider even closing my eyes. I tried it and heard her father's voice, begging me to take her with me to Atlanta. I could still smell the coffee on his breath as I blinked away the thought. How the fuck was I going to bring this up to her? We were in such a good place and the last thing I wanted to do was fuck that up, but her staying here, if it was as bad as her dad made it seem, wasn't safe.

My life had gone from so slow and repetitive, being concerned only for my ma and my sister, to a web of chaos. Even Phillips, the unstable yet stable ticking time bomb, had become a direct threat to the people I loved. It was hard to reconcile that he was now on the other side, the enemies' side, as demonstrated by him pulling a gun out in front of Karina. I had spent years of my life trying to save his, to keep him alive, and now just wanted him to disappear, even if that meant death.

My phone vibrated in my pocket. I dipped my hand in and silenced it, then gently moved Karina's sleeping body to lean against the pillows on her couch. Her eyes moved behind her lids but they didn't open. Her lips parted slightly, and she made a humming noise. I covered her with the blanket from the back of the couch and pulled my phone out of my pocket. It was my ma. I made my way back to Karina's room and closed the door behind me before I called her back.

"Hey, Ma, sorry I missed your call," I said, sitting on Karina's unmade bed.

"You've been missing my calls a hell of a lot lately," she told me. I could practically see her eyes rolling back in her head as she spoke. "How are you? What's been going on?"

"Not much," I lied through my damn teeth. "Getting ready for my discharge and move. Same old, same old. How are you? How's Tay? I haven't talked to her in a while either."

Outside of a few texts here and there, I had barely spoken to my sister. I guess I had been more distracted than I realized.

"She's either at school or studying for school." She paused and I imagined my sister the last time I saw her, around her birthday, and smiled, remembering her kicking my ass in some trivia game she was obsessed with. Fucking genius; thank god one of us was.

"She got herself a tutoring job. Pays well and you know she loves to keep her face in a book." My ma's voice cut off at the end, bursting into a fit of coughing.

"You still have that cough? It's been what? Months?"

"Oh hush. It went away for a while, it just came back," she told me. "When are you coming to visit? It's been over a year and you're only a couple of hours away. I haven't seen my son since you've been home from Afghanistan." I could hear the sadness in my ma's voice, the longing to see me. I didn't have an excuse, except the one I couldn't say to her.

"Uh . . . I'm sorry. I'll—"

"Kael? Are you still here?" Karina's voice filled the hallway and the room.

"Who's that? Is that a woman?" my mom asked. *Fuck me.*

"Yeah, it is . . . I'm in here," I called to Karina.

"Oh, thank goodness. I woke up and thought you left!" Karina's cheeks were red and her eyes were wild with fear.

I dropped my hand with the phone in it and reached for her. "I'm here, I came in here to call my ma back. You were only asleep for a few minutes," I told her.

She looked down at my phone and I picked it back up, realizing my mom was still on the line and that I should have muted the phone or hung up.

"Kael, are you seeing someone? Who is that?" my mom asked three times in a row.

She wasn't the nosy type, but I'm sure my ma, who had never, ever seen me so much as in the same room as a woman, was shocked to say the least.

"No. I mean, yeah. I am. Sorry, I'll call you back. Love you." I hung up and tossed my phone on the bed like it was on fire.

"What on earth was that about?" Karina's brows bunched together. Her expression was a mix of skepticism and curiosity. She seemed slightly amused at my obvious panic.

I felt like a thirteen-year-old boy hiding a girl from his mother.

"I don't know. I never talk to her about girls." The heat was spreading across my face and uncomfortably down my neck.

Karina's smile burst across her face. "Kael Martin, are you nervous right now?" She moved toward me, then sat on my lap, her impossibly large smile growing somehow. "What is this? You're being so cute." She laughed.

I laid down against the bed and covered my face with one of her pillows. Thank god for her messy bed, making the pillows within reach. She grabbed a hold it, trying to pry it away from my face.

"You're embarrassed! I never thought I'd see the day when

you're shaken up like this. How freaking adorable!" she squealed, clearly enjoying herself at my expense.

"Having fun, are you?" I moved the pillow, throwing it to the floor. She nodded, covering her laughter with her hand.

I gripped her hips, yanking her forward. Her hair fell onto my face and her breath caught in her throat in surprise. She audibly gulped as I dug my fingers into the soft flesh of her waist.

"Hmm? Not so funny now?" I whispered into her mouth, our lips almost touching. I lifted my hips, pressing my hardening cock against the apex of her thighs.

Quiet and wide-eyed, she shook her head. I tucked her hair behind one ear and brought my mouth to it.

"Nothing to say?" I licked the base of her ear and she moaned, her body melting against mine.

I fucking loved the noises she made every time I touched her. Sucking on her earlobe, I lifted one hand under the back of her shirt, unclasping her bra as I dipped my tongue down to her neck and bit her hard enough to leave a mark but soft enough to make her soak through her panties.

I pulled her sweatshirt over her head, and she lifted herself up awkwardly to pull her pants off. I gripped her wrists to stop her. I wanted to do it. Undressing her slowly was one of my greatest pleasures. Watching her eyes roll back and hearing her breath hitching and panting in anticipation of my touch filled me with indescribable satisfaction. Staring at her naked body was arguably better than fucking her. She shivered as I lifted her back on top of me, sliding her onto my cock.

Pink-and-orange light from the fall sunset cast across her face as she moved her hips, bringing us both closer to heaven. The light hit her skin so beautifully, making the little marks that she always complained about glow. Her eyelashes brushed against her cheek, golden and angelic, making me lose control. Her hands gripped my shoulders as she came, sounds of pleasure pouring out of her as she ground down on my cock. I pressed my thumb against her clit as it pulsed, throbbing as she came down from the high.

"God, you're so fucking beautiful," I said, tensing and releasing my entire body and soul into her. She collapsed on my chest, and I ran my fingertips up and down her back as it moved rapidly.

The sun had fallen by the time we caught our breath.

"Well, that was—" she finally said when I thought she was asleep.

I smiled even though she couldn't see my face. Her cheek was pressed against my bare chest, her hair a wild nest around us. "I should tease you more often," she told me, lifting her face.

I caressed her cheek slowly with one hand. "No, you should not. I went easy on you, this time," I threatened playfully.

"It really was so cute seeing you all embarrassed."

"Stop saying *cute*," I groaned, and she giggled, making my hand move with her cheek.

She was quiet for a moment, staring into my eyes. I could feel a question growing in hers and wasn't surprised when she asked, "Did you not tell your mom about me?"

I cupped her cheek with my hand. "I don't tell my ma, or anyone, anything about me. Or you."

"Hmph. Sounds about right."

"It's not for any reason other than that's how I am. I've never introduced her to a woman before, even when I was young."

Karina's mouth flew open. "You knew other women before me?" She mocked me in disgust, and my body shook with laughter.

"No, no." I shook my head. "Of course not. You're the first woman I've ever even spoken to." I kissed her soft, wet lips and she smiled, nodding as she kissed me again.

"Good," she said, kissing me a third time, this one lasting a bit longer.

After a few moments I told her that my mom had asked me when I was going to come visit her.

"It's only a little ways away, right? You could go there on a weekend, couldn't you?"

I nodded. "Technically, yes."

"Why don't you?"

Sighing, I attempted to make sense of my reasoning. Karina wouldn't judge me, but would she understand? Maybe not, but she would try.

"It's hard to explain, but I realized I've been avoiding seeing my mom since I enlisted. I haven't seen her since I got back."

"Oh." She stared at me, gathering her thoughts. "I guess I knew that because I've been with you most of the time since you came home. It's not because of me, is it?"

I shook my head. "No. I've been like this since before I met you. I want her to remember the son she was proud to raise. The boy who never got in trouble and wouldn't hurt a fly. Not a man who has taken lives . . . not a man who has blood on his hands and shadows in his mind."

Karina sat up on one elbow and leaned onto my chest, bringing her face to mine. "I know she's so proud of you. Anyone would be. You're still the same boy she knew and loved even if you've been through things that most people can't imagine. And you've handled them better than anyone could have expected. I'm proud of the man you are, and I would be so proud if my son grew up to be the same kind of person."

I could barely stand the overwhelming emotions her words brought on. Shame and relief danced together, both confusing and consoling me.

"I'm not the boy she raised anymore. I've changed, and done so many things she would recoil at the thought of. I can't ignore that, and I'm not sure if I can hide it around her."

"Oh, Kael, that's not true. She's your mom, she will be so happy to see you, I'm sure of it. You should go. It will be good for both of you. Don't you miss her?"

What a complicated question. Of course I missed her, but the son she missed wasn't me, not anymore. He died on the battlefield in Kabul. I didn't want to ruin the idea of the boy she raised, but I knew she missed me like crazy. This was the first time I hadn't seen her the moment I got home. The more time that passed, the easier it was to disassociate from the guilt I felt for being a poor excuse for a son.

"It's more complicated than me missing my mom," I explained.

"There's nothing less complicated than a mother's love," she told me, brushing her fingertips along my jawline. "My family excluded, obviously. Also, helloooo? Look how fucked up everything is around us. Elodie, my brother, literally everything is a mess and, for once, maybe we should run away for a night and leave tomorrow's problems for tomorrow?"

"That's very unlike us," I reminded her.

There was a small twitch in her lips, the dark humor of hers that I loved. "I wish my mom wanted to see me," she added. My chest sank.

Was I being selfish to whine about how my guilt was keeping me from seeing my ma, in front of Karina out of all people? Yeah, yeah, I was being selfish toward her and my ma, my sister, myself.

I wrapped my arms around her back, squeezing her body to mine. I kissed her forehead and hugged her again. I wasn't sure if I would regret it but I asked, "Do you want to go with me? To see my ma?"

Her head popped up, excitement clear in her bright eyes. They were the color of spring grass today.

"Really?"

"Yeah. I'm not sure how good of an idea it is for me to go, but I know I'll feel better if you're with me."

Karina made an exaggerated noise like a squeal and climbed on top of me. She pressed her forehead to mine and wrapped her hands around my biceps.

"Let's go," she said eagerly.

Whether it was from being excited to meet my family or wanting to put together one more piece of the puzzle of my life, her happiness was contagious, and I found myself looking forward to her being in my old town, in my old house. The past and present mixing was not something I usually welcomed, but I would do almost anything for Karina and my ma.

CHAPTER NINETEEN

Karina

The next evening, the sun was low in the sky when we pulled up to Kael's childhood home, and I felt a sense of nostalgia even though I had never been there. It was almost as I had imagined: a quaint ranch-style house with yellow siding, deep-red shutters on the front windows, and a matching door. The porch covered the length of the house and had white railings and balusters, with handrails on both sides of the steps. The driveway was a circle shape with a giant tree in the center, and behind the house was nothing but trees. The front yard was deep, the house pushed far back from the road. It was unique, and I smiled as I tried to collect all the details, imagining a young Kael running around the yard, playing in the woods behind the house.

"What?" His voice interrupted my imagination. He seemed nervous now, compared to the calm guy who drove for almost three hours while I talked so much that I put myself to sleep.

"Nothing. I love it here."

He looked at me, full of skepticism. "But we just got here."

I shrugged, grabbing my purse from the floorboard of his truck. "I don't care. I love it already," I said, as a woman, no taller than five feet, stepped onto the porch and waved.

"That's your mom." I stated the obvious.

His mouth twitched anxiously and he nodded. "Yeah, that's my ma."

"Let's go in?" I suggested, squeezing his hand. It wasn't as warm as usual; the cool temperature of his skin surprised me, but I didn't show it. I squeezed again and he silently agreed, turning off the truck and unbuckling his seatbelt.

"Let's go in," he repeated, his breath falling out as if he had been holding it for the last few hours.

Kael's mom began to cry at the sight of him. She brushed his sweatshirt at the shoulders, her eyes full of tears. "You've grown up in such a short time."

The way she looked at her son made me want to sob. I tried so hard to hold back, to not draw any bit of the attention to myself during their reunion, but damn it, it was so hard. I sniffled, swallowing my emotions the best I could, but I had never in my entire life seen a mother look at her child like that. Like he was the center of her universe, like she would hang the moon and nail the stars to the night sky for him. Without her saying a word, I could feel the immense love she felt for Kael. I tried to imagine how that must feel, to be so loved by a parent, but couldn't.

In a blue-and-white polka-dot cotton dress that nearly swept the ground, she looked tiny as she wrapped her arms around him. He effortlessly lifted her off her feet, squeezing her small frame as she continued to cry.

"Don't cry, don't cry. I'm here," he told her, over and over.

As I stood there watching them, I didn't feel awkward or like an intruder on such a meaningful moment. I was so happy to see Kael this way, loved and admired by someone important to him, someone other than me.

After a few more moments he gently put her down and brushed

her hair back. It was tied back into a low bun but had gotten a little crooked during their embrace. Kael's hands went to work. Turning her around by her shoulders and undoing the hair tie, he meticulously but quickly redid her bun and kissed her forehead, wiping the tears from her cheeks. I could feel the distance he told me he'd put between them evaporating by the second now that they were together.

"Oh, honey, I'm sorry. I'm Dory. You must be . . . well, if my son had any manners, he would have told me your name by now." She turned her attention to me, smiling and trying to put herself together emotionally. Her smile was a carbon copy of Kael's, literally identical.

She was stunning, not an ounce of makeup on her skin, with eyes that were almost too big for her face, which made it even more interesting and captivating. Her eyes were so much softer than Kael's, but I could feel the strength in them. A small woman, but a mighty soul.

"Karina, my name's Karina," I said back, not knowing what would happen next.

She wrapped her arms around me before my worries could take me out of the moment. The smell of honey and fresh-cut flowers filled my senses as she squeezed me like she had known me for years.

I couldn't help but notice the look on Kael's face while I was in his mother's arms. A little uneasy, like he wasn't sure what to do. It wasn't like him to not be able to control his surroundings, so I was sure this entire day would continue to make him anxious. That made two of us.

"Let's get inside. It smells like it's going to rain any minute." She let me go and turned her gaze up to the sky. I sniffed the air, and realized she was right.

As we walked up the porch steps, I thought about how lovely it would be to sit on this porch during a storm. There were two rocking chairs with floral-printed pillows decorating them, and a table full of empty metal coffee cans, stacks of old magazines and newspapers. It felt cozy and antique, but tidy—a kid's bicycle with inches of dust on the metal and a flat tire, another table with a game of checkers that hadn't been touched in a while. It felt like a space full of memories of Kael and his sister's childhood. I hoped I would have more time to look more closely before we left.

The living room was warm; the air was the perfect mixture of breeze and comfortable heat. The smell of food filled the room. I couldn't tell what it was exactly, but it surely came from heaven. My stomach growled audibly, and Kael looked down at me, a slight twitch in his lips. He was still on edge, and I was prepared for him to stay that way for a while. I couldn't measure the time, even guessing, but emotionally this was complicated for him, so my discomfort and anxiety were going to stay hidden to the best of my ability. I needed to be the support for Kael, like he'd been for me since I met him.

"I bet you're both hungry, so I made some of your favorite food, Kael. Have you ever had homemade chicken and dumplings or shrimp and grits, Karina?" she asked me.

"I wish. But no." I shook my head. "Even living in Georgia for a while now, I still haven't. Well, I did have shrimp and grits once, but it wasn't homemade. So, basically, I haven't had them before, so I'm excited to try all the things."

I couldn't stop my mouth from moving even though my mind was screaming at me to shut the hell up and stop being weird.

"Sorry, sometimes I say stuff—but I'd love to try your food," I apologized, almost clasping my palm over my mouth to stop myself from saying another word.

Dory smiled and tilted her head to her son. "No need to be sorry. I'm glad you're a talker, since we know this one isn't." She lovingly glared at Kael, and to his point he shrugged and didn't say anything.

She led us through the living room and into the kitchen so quickly that I didn't have much of a chance to look around. I did clock some picture frames on the wall but couldn't make out the subjects of the photos. It felt like I was in a museum of Kael's life. She waved for us to sit down at the table, and covered her mouth with her arm as she coughed. Kael tensed and patted her back. She told him she was fine and shooed him away. He then pulled out a wooden chair for me. It squeaked against the tile floor, and I sat down with my hands in my lap. He pushed me toward the table and told his mom to sit down, too, pulling a chair out for her as well.

"I want to feed you, it's been so long," she said, refusing to take a seat just yet. "You sit down and let me be your momma." Her voice was soft but fierce, and Kael obliged, sitting down next to me, his leg shaking up and down rapidly, nerves getting the best of him.

Dory filled our plates with a pile of food, and it was delicious. The first bite of a homemade dumpling had me drooling. The texture, something between a biscuit and bread, was insanely perfect, and the broth was flavorful, instantly becoming the best thing I had ever eaten in my life. I devoured my food in silence, as Kael did the same. Dory told us she'd already eaten, and sat down at the table with us, pouring herself some tea from a porcelain pot with little blue flowers on it. She seemed to be used to her son's quiet nature, and the three of us sat in silence, with only the sounds of us enjoying the food and gulps of water to wash it down among us. Kael was on his second plate of food, and I watched him intently, loving the access to him I was being granted by being here in his mother's home while he ate his favorite home-cooked comfort meals. The sudden chirp of a cuckoo clock made me jump and almost choke on my food. Kael laughed, barely making a sound, but the smile on his face was impossible for him to hide.

Dory also found it amusing, laughing and apologizing for scaring me. I could feel the embarrassment burning in my cheeks as I coughed and chugged water. Coughing was one of the most ridiculous things to be embarrassed of, but I always had been. It brought me back to coughing in school; every time was mortifying for no reason. I focused on the beautiful color of the wooden kitchen table. It was a medium shade of oak—the top was made of strips of the same wood but with the grain going in opposite directions in a pattern. It was a long oval shape, and the legs were thick; this table could easily last a hundred years. Memories of time together were stained into the surface, making it even more arresting. The irony wasn't lost on me that my father's table was cold and spotless, never so much as a crumb or a fingerprint on it. Family dinners in this home were obviously the opposite of my Tuesday dinners with my father and Estelle.

"Where's Tay? Didn't you tell her I was coming?" Kael finally asked, wiping his mouth with a napkin.

"She'll be home after her tutoring session. Even seeing you doesn't come before her money." Dory laughed.

I couldn't wait to meet Kael's younger sister. I hoped she liked me, or at least could tolerate me. Even though I was fuller than I had ever been, anxiety found a way to nudge itself into the very pit of my stomach. I wondered what it was like to not worry about every social interaction before they happened, to be able to go with the flow.

"Not surprised." Kael smiled, scooping up the last bit of food from his plate and shoveling it into his mouth.

He stood up to get more but his mom grabbed his plate from his hands and pushed one of his shoulders down, telling him to sit. He looked at me and smiled a little. I could tell he was attempting to quietly check in on me even though he was right next to me. I smiled back and reached for his hand when his mom's back was to us. I kissed it gently and he brushed my cheek, quickly but tenderly.

"Are you still hungry, Karina?" Dory asked me.

Shaking my head, I put my hands on my bloated stomach. "I'm so, so full. It was the best meal I've ever had, and I'm not just saying that."

"Thank you. Let me know if you want any dessert or tea," she offered kindly.

Kael went to town on his third plate of food. It made me so happy but a bit sad, thinking of how much he'd probably missed his mom's cooking. How many sleepless nights full of explosions, gunshots, and screams he must have had while his mom sat in this kitchen worried sick for her son's life. Incredibly selfishly, I thanked whatever or whoever was controlling the universe for me not meeting Kael until after he deployed. I wasn't as strong as Dory or Elodie or Gloria. I wouldn't have been able to handle spending every day wondering if he would survive or not. Even the hypo-thetical thoughts made my stomach and chest ache.

I finally gathered my voice, trying to distract my mind. I didn't want to be awkwardly quiet, but I was terrified of being obnoxious or saying the wrong thing. "Can I ask where this table came from? It's so beautiful."

Dory smiled, running her fingers across the wood. "Kael made it." She beamed, her eyes overflowing with pride and joy.

My mouth fell open. "Really? Wow, it's incredible." I took a closer look at it.

"When he was what, fifteen?" she asked Kael.

"I think so—" He hesitated, uncomfortable with both of us praising him at the same time.

I reached for his arm and put my fingers around it, gently applying pressure. "You made this when you were a teenager?"

"Yeah."

"And the chairs," his mom added. "Except that one," she told me, pointing at the only chair of six that didn't match the rest of the set.

"Wow. Why on earth did you join the Army if you're so good at carpentry? You—" As I realized what I was saying, I pushed my lips shut. "I'm sorry, I didn't mean it the way it came out. I'm . . . This furniture is so beautiful."

My stupid, stupid mouth didn't know when to stay closed. If Kael built a whole kitchen set as a teen, I could only imagine what he was capable of now. His work on my house and his duplex made so much more sense to me now. And building Elodie's baby's crib by hand.

"You're fine," Kael told me. "I know what you meant." His voice was soft, not offended. I was afraid to look at his mom out of fear that I had already ruined any chance of her liking me, so I kept my eyes down.

"I wondered the same thing. I told him to try and sell some of the stuff he made. He was out there sanding down wood from the trees behind the house while most kids were running in the streets. But he insisted on enlisting. He'd talked about it since he was a boy," his mother told me. Her body language was so relaxed, instantly making me relax.

"Okay, you two. Enough about me. I'm going to clean up and leave you two to talk about chairs or politics or literally anything except me. Please," Kael said sarcastically, rising from his chair. He gathered my plate and his, along with the utensils, and went to the sink.

I tried my best to keep eye contact with Dory as she watched me. She lifted the teapot up and filled her glass as she asked, "Where are you from, Karina?"

"All over, really. I've lived in a few different states, but I feel like I'm from Texas because that's where I spent the best years of my life, until this last one. My dad is in the Army, so we went where he was stationed. I've bought a house here, so I guess I like it more than Texas after all." I had so much to say about my dad, but for obvious reasons I kept it simple.

"And your mom? What does she do?"

I tried to keep my back and breathing as strong and straight as possible. I didn't want to come off as unstable, and if I hid my fucked-up childhood maybe she would think I was deserving of her son's time and love.

"She's—" I searched my brain for a lie, an easy one that wasn't technically a lie but wasn't exactly the truth. I made the mistake of looking into Kael's mother's soft eyes, and my defenses melted away as my mouth spoke without my brain's permission.

"I don't know what she's doing. She was an alcoholic, or still is, I guess. I haven't seen her in years, and I don't even know where she's living. Before she left she was a stay-at-home mom and wife, though. But she hated it, so I think maybe she's gotten a job or something by now? I'm not sure."

Until now Kael had been the only person on the planet I openly poured my thoughts out to without editing them. His mom looked at me with the same understanding expression, not overreacting or with false sympathy in her eyes, making me want to keep going.

"My dad remarried, and his wife now is better at being a wife. She hasn't really had the chance to be a mother, but she's sort of trying lately with me. My dad and I have a complicated relationship so it's a little hard to explain the dynamic. He isn't exactly a father, he's so militant and only cares about his wife and the Army." Kael turned off the water faucet and I looked up at him. He leaned his back against the counter, eyes directly on me.

"Sorry. I'm trauma dumping all over you and we've only just met. None of this makes me sound sane . . . or stable."

I knew Kael was seconds away from swooping in and saving me from my own compulsive mouth, but he didn't get the chance because his mom began to speak as he took a step toward us.

"Don't you worry, that's what kitchens are for, isn't it?" She smiled. "The good, the bad, and the ugly. And families are always messy and complicated. I don't know a single person who has a stable or sane family." She laughed a little and continued, "I didn't speak to my dad for nearly twenty years before he died, and my mother developed dementia when I was in high school, so I didn't get much of a chance to know her as I became a woman."

As I processed that that meant Kael's mother and grandfather had had a strained relationship and her mother had developed dementia at such a young age, both situations incomparably hard, she began to speak again.

"I know how hard it is and how fundamental it is for us women to have a relationship with our mothers. It's the most important and the most painful tie we will ever have to another person. I'm sorry about your mother, but I'm more sorry for her that her illness chose for her. I'm sure she regrets it and wishes she could defeat it every day."

Her words didn't slam into me the way I would have expected such an intense statement from someone I'd just met today to; they caressed me, wrapping each letter around my body, filling a little part of me that had been missing since my mother left. Even though it had been six years, I'd never really considered my mom living in regret as a viable option.

"We've just met, but can I tell you the most valuable thing I've learned as a woman, a daughter, and a mother?" she asked me, no hesitation in her voice.

I tried to keep the emotion out of my voice. "Yes, please."

"When you think about your mother, and even your father, try a bit of empathy. It's their first go at this life too."

She reached for my hand, and I couldn't help my shoulders from shaking, my fingers from trembling.

"It's damn hard, and it feels much better to be angry, but we're all trying to figure all this out, mistake by mistake, day by day. When I think about my parents, and myself as a mother, from that perspective, even my children's father, that gives me a little bit of comfort. So I really hope it does for you too."

Her one suggestion, piece of advice, whatever the hell I wanted to call it, changed my entire perception. My mother had been my age when she had me and my brother; my father too. Maybe instead of a villain and a selfish abandoner, my parents had simply been young kids trying to figure out how to navigate the world, like me. My mistakes may not be as harmful or heavy, but who got to decide the weight of our wrongdoings and how long our sentences for them should last?

Dory was right; it felt much better to be angry at both of my parents. I had empathy for everyone else around me, to a fault, so why not them? Maybe my mom was sitting somewhere wondering about me, wishing she could ask me how my day was or if I had eaten dinner yet. Maybe my father wanted to apologize for being so emotionally detached from me and pouring himself into his work my entire life.

Maybe, just maybe, my parents were human too.

CHAPTER **TWENTY**

Karina

I could feel how puffy my eyes were when I opened them. I was curled up on the couch in Kael's mom's living room. I barely remembered moving from the kitchen, but when I woke up, it was dark outside and I could hear Kael and his mom talking in the kitchen. I stretched my arms out and a movement at the corner of my eye scared the crap out of me. I jumped up, thinking it was a dog or maybe even a ghost, but when I looked again, it was a teen-age girl sitting on the other side of the couch, dressed in a white school uniform top and black slacks. Her hair was in double buns on either side of her head and thin metal-framed glasses sat on the bridge of her nose. I couldn't see her clearly in the dim room but I blinked a few times to get the sleep out of my eyes.

"Hi." She smiled, seeming to be entertained by my fear.

"Hi," I responded, clearing my throat. "Sorry, I just woke up and didn't realize anyone was in here."

I could immediately tell that she was Kael's sister, Tay. She was taller than I'd imagined but just as pretty. The genes in this family were insane.

"You're Karina, right?" she asked me, her voice a whisper.

"Yeah, and you must be Tay? Sorry, I was so tired and must have conked out here. How embarrassing," I said, matching the volume of her voice.

"It's okay. It's nice to meet you," she said, still whispering.

"Why are we whispering?" I asked back, checking if there was a reason or if I had just kept it going.

"My ma and brother are going down memory lane like always, and I didn't want to interrupt them yet, so I was waiting for you to wake up or for them to find me in here before I made my presence known." She grinned, like she was breaking the rules.

I matched her expression and kept my voice as quiet as possible. "Makes sense. Family reunions can be so daunting."

She scooted closer to me, to sit on the cushion I was on. "Yeah, for sure. And someone always cries, and it isn't going to be me," she said with certainty, rolling her eyes.

I tried not to laugh as I confessed, "I already did, so you're safe."

Her giggle was playful and louder than our voices had been, so she covered her mouth.

"Oh man, she got you already, huh?"

"She's really good at it."

"Tell me about it." She rolled her head back as the light in the room got much brighter.

"When did you get home?" Dory asked Tay as Kael stepped in behind her, his frame so much bigger than his mother's it was almost shocking.

In less than five steps, Kael was hovering over his sister, and she stood up as he lifted her into his arms and off the ground.

"Kaeellllll." She exaggerated her voice, but I could hear the happiness in it.

"Tayyyyy," he mimicked her, and she tried to wiggle out of his arms.

I thought my heart would burst out of my chest seeing them

together. I couldn't imagine going so long without seeing my brother, especially if he was only a few hours away. Even when Austin had been with our uncle I missed him every day, despite the stress he brought into my life.

I turned my attention to Dory, enjoying the peace and happiness so evident on her face. It must have felt so good to have both of her babies home and on good terms, no matter how long it had been between visits.

"How the hell did you grow a damn foot since I saw you last?" Kael asked her, putting Tay's feet on the floor.

"You haven't been here in so long, so you wouldn't know," she told him. I could see the dent her words made in him, but he took it well, not moving a muscle in his face.

"Yeah, I get it. I get it. I don't come here enough. Anyway, Ma said you got another tutoring job. Shouldn't you be dating or hanging out with people from school at your age?" he asked her.

The look on her face was pure disgust. "Why would I do that? I want to make money. Hanging out doesn't make me smarter, or richer."

"And dating sure as hell won't either," their mother added.

"I'm never going to date," Tay said with certainty. I loved it. "Plus, who are you to talk? You never hung out with friends, you just played football and built stuff." She poked his chest and then turned to look at me. "And you've never even had a girlfriend until now."

Kael's face was priceless. I couldn't have loved this girl more. She was so funny, witty, and bright, and I loved that she was slightly roasting Kael, catching him off guard, which was a nearly impossible thing to do. Also, I obviously loved to find out that Kael had never properly dated anyone before me, and I was the first one to meet his family.

"Okay, enough from you." He shushed her and tried to avoid looking at me. I was so entertained by all of this. I loved being here.

Since Kael had come into my life, I had felt more connected to not only myself, but to other people than I had since the day I was born. Gloria and Mendoza, even Toni and Tharpe, now his mom and sister . . . Kael had given me such a priceless gift without even realizing it. I was never going to be the easiest person to connect with or make friends with, but the people around him were all so warm and welcoming, accepting my awkwardness and even embracing it.

I watched him as he talked with his sister, and Dory disappeared into the kitchen. I didn't feel left out as they caught up and, truly, I loved watching him interact with someone he had known so long, even if he wasn't really telling her anything substantial or detailed about what he had been up to since he saw her last. Neither of them so much as mentioned the Army, and the only person she asked about was Mendoza, briefly, to which Kael told her he was doing well. Was that the truth? I didn't think so, but I guessed it made more sense than the truth.

As I listened to the conversation their voices faded and my eyes grew heavy. When I woke up, Kael was asleep sitting up, on the couch. We hadn't planned to stay the night, but I was glad we had. We wouldn't have gotten home until after midnight if we had driven home. I smelled coffee coming from the kitchen but wasn't sure if I should follow the scent. I checked the time on my phone, and it was four in the morning. I walked into the kitchen and found Dory standing by the back door, gazing into the woods behind the house. I tried to make a little noise so she wasn't startled by me walking up behind her.

"I hope I'm not interrupting you or bothering you. I smelled the coffee and followed it. Habit, I guess," I nervously rambled while fidgeting with my fingers in front of me.

She turned around slowly, a black mug with the United States Army logo on it in her hands.

"I hope I didn't wake you up. I'm not used to having visitors."

I shook my head, ignoring the little pang at the sadness in her voice. I really needed to make sure Kael visited her more. "No, not at all. We're the ones who took over your living room."

"I'm so happy to have you both here. I understand Mikael hates it here, and I don't blame him, but I will say I got the best sleep I've had in years last night knowing he was home. And safe."

After a beat, she added, "As you can see, I don't sleep much. Not since he left for basic training.

"Would you like some?" she asked, without looking up from her own coffee cup.

I glanced toward the living room, where Kael was still asleep on the couch.

"Actually, yes, please." I was absolutely not the "wake up at 4 a.m. and have coffee" kind of girl, but the idea of enjoying a warm cup of caffeine with Kael's mother while the rest of the house, probably even town, slept, was beyond intriguing.

"Hmm, this one is right for you." Dory handed me a heavy ceramic mug with little flowers painted on a white background. At the bottom rim there were thin strokes of green paint like grass. It was handmade, maybe by Kael?

"Mikael made that for me for Mother's Day when he was in grade school." She answered my question without me asking.

"It's so cute." I ran my fingers along the bubbled-up paint and thanked her as she filled up my cup.

I closed my eyes, drinking the coffee slowly. God, it was good.

"I use chicory. It's one of those love-it-or-hate-it flavors, but I've been adding chicory in my coffee for decades."

I had never had chicory, and wasn't even sure what it was, but her coffee was fantastic.

"It's great. Thank you."

Dory kept looking back at the backyard, making my curiosity eat at me until I was suddenly next to her, peering out into the dark yard to see what she was looking at.

"Kael built that shed out there. It's where that yellow light is." She pointed to a small glowing light near the line of massive trees.

"He's so great at stuff like that. Building and renovations and everything in between," I told her, though she knew that even better than I did.

"It's a fully functioning space. It has a bathroom, a kitchenette. I kept thinking he would move back there once the Army got to be too much. Or at least, come to escape here sometimes. But that hasn't been the case." She took a long sip and sighed.

"I'll try to make sure he comes here more. He wants to, he's just—"

I hesitated to speak for Kael, knowing he wouldn't like that, and not wanting to betray his trust by repeating what he'd told me.

"It's complicated." She turned to me. Her eyes were the exact shade of deep brown as Kael's. "And you don't have to promise me anything except that you'll be there for him. Not only with his PTSD, but when my son is the only Black man in the room and someone says something out of pocket, I need you to stand up for him. When he works himself to the bone and forgets to eat, I need you to feed him. When people underestimate his talent because of his background, I need you to remind him he is worthy. As his mother, I'm begging you to be his voice when it's not safe for him to speak up."

I was a little too stunned to speak, absorbing her words as they coated my mind. I wasn't sure if I was going to be able to do those things for her son, not because I didn't want to or because I wasn't capable, but because there was so much uncertainty around our future and, as of now, I wouldn't be close enough in proximity to be there for him in this way. My heart was beginning to feel as if it was staying in a constant state of broken, each day cracking a sliver more.

"I'll do my best. I love him," I admitted. I couldn't bring myself to promise her what she'd asked, but it was true. I loved Kael more than I could explain.

"That's all we can do, is our best."

A cough broke through the air, the sound too big for her small body. I reached over and patted her back softly, handing her a glass of water. She shook me off gently.

"I'm fine. I've had this cough for a while. Damn thing won't go away." She coughed a bit more, covering her mouth as her thin shoulders hunched.

"Tttt—" She struggled to find her words, but I didn't have a clue what she was looking for. "Tay." She finally said her daughter's name, but she looked confused. "Tay keeps harping on me to see a doctor, but I don't have time or energy for that."

"I'm staying out of that, but I will say it's better to deal with crappy doctors than suffer in silence."

She nodded, her eyes focused again. She changed the subject immediately, asking me every question under the moon.

The sun was coming up as I finished telling her more about my job, my house. I realized when she went to her room to get dressed for the day I hadn't thought about the rest of the brewing storm waiting for us back at Benning. For a short while I'd felt like a normal young woman venting to an old friend. It felt so good, but of course my brain reminded me that it would likely be the first and last time.

Kael stirred a little as I sat back down on the couch, and he reached for me, resting his head on my lap. He fell back asleep, his lips parting slightly, and I closed my eyes for a while. When I woke up again I looked up to see his mom standing in the doorway of the kitchen, same coffee mug in hand, watching us with a sweet smile on her face.

CHAPTER TWENTY-ONE

Kael

Waking up to Karina in my ma's living room was more jarring than I'd expected. I was confused as fuck as to where I was and what year it was. I hadn't slept on that couch in years.

"Hi." She smiled down at me, her hair falling over her shoulders.

"Hi," I repeated, stretching my body as much as I could on the small couch. The smell was so familiar, but the circumstances were not.

Karina seemed well rested, a sense of ease over her that typically wasn't there. As we left, my ma hugged me again and again, calling me my uncle's name by accident. She had done that a few times on the phone, but I knew she was usually so exhausted from work that it made sense to mix our names up. That and our names were so similar. My sister had left for a study group earlier, but that was no surprise. Karina and my ma seemed to have a hard time saying goodbye to one another, which I both loved and hated. I knew I was only making things more complicated by intertwining our lives in every possible way.

"Were you nervous about me meeting your family?" she asked me as I pulled onto the highway.

I knew she would eventually ask her questions, but we had a

long drive ahead, so part of me hoped her inquisition could wait until we were a little further into the day. My ma had been a mess when we'd left, but I'd promised her that I could come back more often. Karina made me promise her the same, pouting over not seeing my old bedroom, which I'd built out back. It was about the size of two sheds together and had everything I needed inside. When I was deep in deployment, I had daydreamed about running away and living there, in the back of my ma's house forever.

"A bit, yeah."

I didn't look at her but I heard the subtle inhale she made at my honesty.

"Because of me? Or because you haven't introduced anyone to them?" she asked. I knew she would assume it was because of something wrong with her, even though that couldn't be further from the truth.

"No." I shook my head, putting my blinker on to change lanes even though the road was empty except us. "Because of me. I didn't think I would ever bring my two lives together."

"Two lives?"

"It feels that way. Not as sinister as its sounds, but it does feel like I have two versions of myself," I admitted. "Or more."

She was quiet for a few seconds. When I looked at her, she was staring out the window at the trees as we passed.

"And which version of you do I know?" she finally asked.

"The only one that matters."

"That's not a real answer."

She was too clever to accept my bland response. "You know the me that no one else does, so it is a real answer. The man you know, flaws and all, is someone only you have met. Truly."

Karina looked at me and curled her legs up on the seat, wrapping her forearm around her shins. Her eyes were soft and accepting, deciding to take my response at face value and let it go, for now. She was the one person I'd ever opened up to in this way, one of the only people I'd ever trusted in my life, and that meant a lot. I had fucked up when it came to her, and she had forgiven me, but who knew how long it would be until everything unraveled with her father. I was lying to her, even now, even as she trusted my words, and we drove in near silence with only the sound of her playlist in the car.

Memories flashed through my mind like an open camera roll. Her father the first time I met him, dirt and dust covering every part of his face, his gun against his chest. Her soft, welcoming eyes the first time I saw her at the massage studio. Him again, clean and shaven, threating Mendoza into silence, using his power in the most disgusting way. Her rambling to me on the living room floor as she painted her nails, laughing and unguarded. The silent shock in his eyes when I walked into his home for the first time with his daughter. Her voice when she comforted the darkest parts of me. Him showing up at her house and ruining everything. Him begging me to take his daughter away from here. The devastation in her eyes when she learned the truth. There I was, repeating history, and I couldn't stop it. Technically, I could, but I wasn't. I should have told her everything, but I couldn't bring myself to. I loved her, but I hated him more.

The thought made my stomach turn, and I knew how fucked up it was. But I glanced at her again in the passenger seat and decided to keep the secret a little longer.

Fischer and Elodie were in the living room when we got back to Karina's house. Elodie had just gotten off work and it was Karina's turn to go in. I suspected their boss hated me at this point since both were missing so much work lately and by proxy I was to blame. While Karina showered, I put her laundry in the washer, folding the pile of towels that had been in the dryer. The dryer filter was covered in lint so I cleaned it off, wiped down her counters, and washed the dishes in the sink. When she emerged, her hair wet and in a braid that was falling apart, I was drying a bowl.

"You didn't have to do that," she said, lowering my hand with the bowl and towel.

"I know, but I did anyway." I kissed her forehead and placed the bowl in the drying rack. I put my hands on her shoulders and turned her around gently to fix her braid.

"You're spoiling me and I'm going to get too used to it," she told me, her tone split, half joking, half worried.

It seemed a bit ominous, and paranoia crept in, as if her words were a reminder that I knew deep down that this was all temporary, a fragile hourglass, slowly dropping sand as the time passed.

"You should expect to be treated this way, Karina. Nothing less. Promise me?" I tied the band around the bottom of her hair and turned her around again.

Kissing her forehead, then the bridge of her nose, then her lips, I felt impossibly attached to her with every moment we spent together. But everything was going too well in my life, so I was expecting a tornado to come rip it apart. My fate wasn't to be gifted a happy, comfortable life with Karina—to live in a beautiful home with our children running around. I knew better than that. My sins would catch up to me, and I was practically begging them to by complicating Karina's life day by day and not just going away and leaving her to have a calm, honest life. She trusted me, and that fucking killed me.

There was a war waging inside of me. I wanted the best for her, I really fucking did, and I wished like hell that the best for her could be me at the end. But I wasn't the best for anyone and I seemed to consistently leave a path of destruction in my wake.

"As long as you keep doing it, I'll keep expecting it. Are you hungry? I can reheat some of the food your ma sent home with us before I leave?" she offered.

My ma had sent us off with two stacks of Tupperware full of dumplings, shrimp and grits, bread, steamed purple potatoes . . . I didn't catch all of it. I think some ham or beef too. Food had always been one way for her to show her affection. Even on nights when she worked until dawn stocking shelves at the local grocery store, she would make sure there was always food in the house for me and Tay. I could imagine Karina as that type of mother. Always thinking ahead for her children and doing anything, literally anything, for them. She put me and everyone around her first; I couldn't imagine how extreme her empathy would be for her children. How lucky they would be.

Instead of promising her anything that I wasn't sure I could keep, I lifted her chin with my thumb and had her eyes touch mine. Her cheeks flushed pink, and I kissed her shiny lips, tasting the coconut-flavored lip balm she had been using lately.

"I'll wait for you to get home and then we can eat together. I have a couple of errands to run and I need to put up some drywall, but if your brother helps me I'll be done and here waiting when your shift is over."

"I love the sound of that." She grinned, lifting herself onto her toes to kiss me.

"Can you two get a fucking room?" Fischer groaned, striding into the kitchen.

"This is my house. So if you don't like it, get out," Karina said and kissed me again.

"Come onnnn . . ." he whined.

"You've been having a secret relationship with my *married* best friend, so I don't want to hear a word from you." She pointed her finger at him. She was teasing him, but she was right as hell.

He smiled, the length of it going nearly from ear to ear. "Touché, Kare. Touché."

Fischer grabbed a glass and filled it with water from the sink before leaving us in the kitchen again.

"I'll be back in a few hours," I told her, hugging my arms around her body, inhaling her intoxicating scent.

"Me too," she responded. "I love you, Kael."

I didn't deserve her love, but I needed it to survive for as long as I could take it.

"I love you, Karina."

After she left I got into my truck and brought Elodie and Fischer with me to my duplex. I needed his help today or the drywall would never get finished by the end of the week. He insisted that Elodie come with us, as he didn't want her to be at home alone, and neither did I—not until we knew what mental state Phillips was in. I got a text from Mendoza saying that Phillips was staying with someone from his old platoon, but he didn't know who. That it had been so quiet and no one had heard from him except for hearsay was concerning. I'd been in my Karina bubble the last thirty-six hours. I debated calling him, but I knew Phillips saw me as his enemy now that I had so clearly chosen a side. Now that we were back near post, I hated the idea of not knowing his next move, or if he even had one. In hopes that the other night was a one-off, I put my phone on the counter and got my ass to work.

I was so lost in the manual labor of using my hands and mind to build something that I hadn't realized that Fischer had stopped helping me. I no longer heard him talking to Elodie or any tools being used. I wiped the sweat off my face with the bottom of my debris-covered T-shirt and made my way through the mess to find him. Elodie was in the living room of my side of the duplex, sitting cross-legged on the couch watching a show on my barely used TV, but he wasn't there with her. I passed her and listened closely, following the trail of his voice outside to my front yard. I stood in the doorway but didn't open the door right away.

"I'll send you the money as soon as I can. I'm working more this week," Austin said into the phone.

I shifted my body sideways so he would be less likely to see me listening. This little fucker better not owe people money or be using again. I would kill him.

"Are you really going to come here?" he asked whoever was on the other line.

My blood began to boil, my suspicion growing high. Who the fuck was going to come here? With their father's warnings to me and the situation with Phillips, the last thing any of us needed was someone coming to Fischer to get money he owed them.

"Okay. I'll figure it out. Be safe, okay?" he told them and hung up the phone.

As soon as he stepped inside, I grabbed him by the collar of his T-shirt and slammed him into the wall. "What the fuck are you thinking?"

His entire face went pale and his eyes widened; shock didn't begin to describe the widening of his light eyes.

"What? How long were you standing there?" he asked, trying to push me back by his elbows.

I pushed forward, pinning him against the wall. "Long enough to know that I've worked my ass off to get you into the Army and you're fucking up again." I searched his face, waiting for an explanation. "You better not lie to me. I heard you. You owe someone money and they're going to come after it. As if you don't have enough people trying to come after you."

I could barely contain my anger. I needed him to make it to and through basic, to make a living and have health care, to have stability for once in his life and stop letting his impulses control him. For himself and for Karina. It was the least I could do.

"Are you using again? Empty your pockets." I let go of him with one arm, knowing one was enough to hold him still, and dug my free hand into his pockets, dumping them both onto the floor.

A debit card, a key chain, and his phone fell to the ground. Nothing more.

"What the fuck, man. Get off me!" he shouted, pushing at my unwavering grip on him. "I'm not on anything! I haven't even had a damn drink! Let me go!"

Elodie came rushing to the door. "What's happening?" she shrieked, yanking at my arms to let him go. I dropped my grip, stepped away from him, and her hands flew up in the air. "Why are you guys fighting? Tell me!" she demanded.

Our breath was wild, and my anger began to melt away as I saw how shaken up Elodie was. She had been through enough, and here I was sending her into a panic. Fuck.

"Nothing, just a misunderstanding and him jumping to thinking the worst of me. As usual," Fischer said, his eyes filled with moisture. I could feel the hurt in them as he picked his stuff up from the floor and grabbed the front-door handle.

"I want to get out of here," he told Elodie, not looking at me.

"Fischer, why don't you—" I began. All he needed to do was tell me what the hell was going on with the phone call I'd just heard.

"Martin, why don't you just fuck off with your holier-than-thou shtick. You kept feeding me bullshit, saying how great I was doing, how proud of me you were, how I would make a great soldier."

His voice broke and he began to cry, trying his hardest to stop but failing.

"All that just to accuse me of being high in one flash of a second. Fuck you for making me believe you actually thought I had a chance," he spat, flinging the door open.

Elodie looked confused and afraid but followed him out of the house, and they got into her car. I watched them drive away, hearing his words repeat themselves, echoing through my mind as I slammed the door and slid down the back of it.

About twenty minutes later, a knock at my door made me stand up. Assuming it was Fischer, I opened it, ready to apologize for being so quick to jump to the worst-case scenario when he had been doing so good lately, even passing a drug test two days ago. My worry for him and his future clouded my judgment, and I was about to begin my sincere apology when I realized it wasn't Fischer at my door—it was Phillips.

CHAPTER **TWENTY-TWO**

Kael

"What the hell are you doing here?" I stood up straight, mentally clocking how long it would take me to grab my gun if I needed to.

Phillips seemed to have lost all his rage-induced energy from the other night. His eyes were sunken in, his face more pale than usual, and his cheeks hollow. Purple and blue bruises covered the span of his left cheek all the way down to his jaw, and his neck had a red ring around it . . . all from my hands. To my surprise, he didn't smell like alcohol and seemed alert, for the most part.

"Can I come in? I don't have anything on me." He shook his pockets of his jeans and patted them all.

"Why should I let you in here after what you did?"

His eyes went down to the porch. "I don't have anywhere else to go and I need my battle buddy." He hadn't called me that in so long that it sounded foreign to me.

I looked him up and down, trying to remember the things I used to respect about him, but was at a loss after he'd put Karina in danger.

"You don't have a battle buddy anymore," I told him, point-blank. He visibly shuddered at my words. That was one of the worst things a soldier could hear.

"Martin, I know what I did was beyond fucked up. I came to apologize."

"I thought you came because you don't have anywhere else to go," I reminded him, not buying his apology bullshit yet. He'd pulled out a fucking gun in a yard full of people I care about.

"That, too, but the apology is the first reason. Please, let me in."

Phillips had changed so much since I met him. I had always tried to ignore the subtle shifts in stability, the mood swings, and how easily angered he could become, and put the blame on our circumstance, being at war and trying to stay alive and all.

I stepped aside and let him pass.

In jeans and his gray PT shirt that said *Army* in black font, he stood in the center of the living room, looking like a teenage boy about to get scolded by his parents. Speaking of parents, I wondered if his parents even knew he was home. I should have called them. But then again, he was a loose cannon now and not my problem. Not anymore.

"Did you tell your parents you're back?" I asked him, keeping a few feet between us for both of our safety, especially his.

He nodded, slowly and cowardly.

"Did you tell them that you tried to kill your own pregnant wife?"

His eyes bugged out and he moved his body dramatically, like a fish out of water, swaying and flopping while standing upright. "That's not what that was. I don't know what the hell I was thinking, but I wouldn't hurt her!"

"That's not what it looked like to me. Not only did you almost kill someone, you disrespected her and humiliated her in front of everyone."

"She's been cheating on me, Martin. While pregnant with my baby . . . if it's even mine." As he said the words, I knew he believed them.

"Fischer wasn't even around when you got her pregnant, so use fucking logic."

"Maybe not him, but at this point, who knows what she's been doing since I brought her here." He was evidently distraught. "I'm clearly her meal ticket out of her country, a cash cow."

I couldn't stop the laugh that bellowed out. "A cash cow? You're a private first class and she's from France, one of the most developed countries in the world. You know better than this. She isn't the kind of person to use someone like that, even *you*."

"And you know her so well now? You only hung out with her a handful of times before you left and now that you're fucking that Karina girl—" I held my hand up to save him from what would come if he said another word about her.

"Remember what I said about you disrespecting Karina. This is your last warning. Do not mention her name again in front of me. Do not even think about her name, her face, her existence—unless you want me to rip your tongue out of your mouth."

I was instantly pulled back to the car ride home from my ma's, when Karina asked me how many versions of myself there were. This was one she had not and would never see, but ironically, this was the one that came the most naturally.

"Okay . . . okay. You love her, don't you?" he asked me, looking me dead in the eyes.

I thought about lying, but he needed to know the lengths I would go for her. It could backfire and give him ammunition to try to get back at me through her. If he did, that would be his death sentence.

"I do."

His thin lips turned into a smile. It wasn't the one I was used to; it was like a pencil sketch of the outline of the smile I had known for years.

"Is that the reason you're so nonchalant about my wife cheating on me and leaving me for Karina's brother of all people?" he asked, sinking to the floor as if he couldn't bear the weight of his own frail body.

"I'm not nonchalant about it. I don't think what either of them did is okay. But they did what they did, and I know it must hurt like hell, but risking your life and hers is not going to change what happened and you know it. I won't make excuses for them, it's not my place, but I can tell you that if you try to hurt them to subdue your own pain, you will suffer."

"By my own hands or yours?" he asked, darkness coating his voice like tendrils.

"Both."

He closed his eyes, taking a couple of breaths. "How long have you known? You were my best friend and you didn't say a word to me. After everything we've been through, you didn't love me enough to tell me before I was humiliated."

"I didn't know either. No one did."

"Everyone does now. And someone knew enough to tell me online. Can you imagine how embarrassing it was to find out on fucking Facebook? And to have to find a private who owed me a favor to go around stalking them to get proof?"

I immediately realized that the private was the one who'd sent the photo of Elodie and Fischer to everyone on Phillips's orders. Probably some newly enlisted, easily scared punk.

"You took it too far by having someone follow her around. Why not have a conversation with your wife?"

He scoffed. "They took it too far by fucking behind my back."

"Why would you tell everyone? Isn't that more humiliating?" I circled around him.

His eyes followed me. "Too late for that. I was already humiliated, so they should be too. I had a feeling something was going on with her long before I got the Facebook message, but I needed to see it with my own eyes."

"Unfortunately, Elodie was the only one who was hurt. Fischer couldn't care less, which makes the whole thing pettier. Anyway, your wife cheated on you, so now what? You can't control yourself so you spiral and get yourself in trouble, losing your career and fucking up your whole life?"

I did feel for him, and didn't agree with the choices made by any of them, but honestly, this was the fucking military. Marriages without affairs or scandal were less common than with civilians, and I wasn't going to feed into his pity party, especially when he had been treating Elodie like shit since he left and likely before. People were losing their lives around us; it was hard to find sympathy for him.

"That's up to me." He touched his chest, looking behind me to the wall. "I can't stop being fucking livid about it." He paused. "I don't know what to do with my anger, Martin."

"You transferred your war mentality to home. You're so used to being on edge, checking your back all day, waiting to be attacked. When you found out about this, it gave you a new outlet. I'm sure it hurts like hell, but I'm begging you to try to look at it from above. Are you that desperately in love with her and honestly believe your marriage can be saved or would have been fine if this didn't happen? Or are you used to mental chaos and now you're transferring that emotion? Be honest with me, or at least yourself."

I sat down on the couch, no longer wanting him to feel like a caged animal being taunted. I checked my phone to see if Karina had texted me since she'd gotten to work, but she hadn't yet.

"My marriage was fucked from the beginning."

"Maybe her relationship with Fischer gives you a proper reason to admit that and come to terms with it. You tried, she tried. I might sound like an asshole, but it's better to get a divorce now than waste more time. People get divorced all the time."

Phillips raised a brow at me and came to sit on the other side of the couch. "Is that supposed to be comforting?"

I couldn't help the smile that took over my face. We were eighteen again and back in Afghanistan, sharing the snacks from my ma's care package. He was different then; so was I. The harshness of our reality hadn't developed yet. He was one of the only people I knew who could make me laugh. The memory became fuzzy around the edges, blurring into him holding a gun in Mendoza's yard.

"It's supposed to help you wake the hell up before you really do something you'll regret. Comfort is a luxury that you and I can't afford."

He nodded, closing his eyes slightly. It seemed like he hadn't slept since getting back to the States.

"Are you hungry?" I asked him, noting the shallow dips in his cheekbones.

"Actually, yeah, I'm fucking starving."

I got up and he followed me into the kitchen. Pulling open the cabinets, I grabbed two ramen packs and a small pot.

"At least you still eat like a broke college kid," Phillips said when I pulled a carton of eggs out of the fridge.

"Some things won't ever change," I offered, pointing for him to sit down while I made his food.

He was quiet, complimenting the progress on the place every few minutes. I was feeling extra-hospitable and chopped up some green onion and bacon to add. I grabbed a protein shake and slid it across the counter.

"You're emaciated," I told him.

He looked down at himself, seeming surprised. "I guess I am. I haven't been eating or sleeping."

I poured the noodles into a bowl and handed him a fork and a spoon. "I can tell."

"Thanks for letting me in and listening to me, Martin. I thought you would tell me to fuck off or choke me again." He laughed as he blew on the steam from the bowl.

I didn't respond; there wasn't anything to say outside of warning him that if he didn't get his shit together, I would kill him, but he knew that. After he scarfed down the noodles, I made him a couple of eggs to get his protein up. The color slowly returned to his cheeks as he ate. I didn't fully trust him and never would, but I hoped our heart-to-heart had made him get a grip on what was at stake.

"Go lie down. I'm going to work some but will keep the noise down as much as I can. If you wake up and I'm gone, don't come find me. And remember not to do anything dumb."

He stretched his thin arms into the air and twisted his spine.

"I won't. I won't," he promised, and I hoped for his sake that he would keep it.

CHAPTER **TWENTY-THREE**

Kael

When I walked out of my house to head back to Karina's, my least favorite person was waiting for me. Karina's dad was idling in my driveway in his brand-new, shiny Ford truck. He rolled the window down as I approached the vehicle.

"Are you stalking me now?"

"I can't deny that, sitting here in front of your house." There was a harmless sarcasm in his voice that was completely new to our dynamic.

"What do you want this time? It's barely been forty-eight hours, I haven't managed to convince Karina to leave the county yet." I looked around my quiet street as a semi with a moving company logo drove by us. Military families kept them in business around here.

"Her mom is back," he said blankly. I jerked my head toward him; there was no way I'd heard him correctly.

"What did you say?"

By the unsettled way his face twisted and how much anxiety was in his voice as he repeated himself, I could tell that it was true.

"When did that happen? And why?" I didn't know what questions to ask, or how to process this.

"Seems like she's been here for at least a month, maybe two. I don't know the why yet."

My heart rate spiked. How much more would life throw at Karina? It wasn't fair. Was this a good thing, or another traumatic relationship for her to try to navigate? "How do you know?"

He let out a deep breath. I could instinctually understand that he was unsure if he should share more information with me or not, but he didn't have much of a choice. On the outside he was a high-ranking officer who demanded respect with a single glance, but deep down he was a lonely man with no one on his side when it came to the outside world, and no connection with his daughter. This served as a reminder to him that regardless of his rank and status, things like family and death couldn't be controlled, which I was sure drove him mad.

"I saw her. She was at the PX near my house. I thought I was losing it or the meds my doctor put me on were making me hallucinate. I never thought I would see her again, but after six years she's here, and I don't know what she wants. Or how long she'll be here."

A small part of me was thrilled at the idea of Karina seeing her mother after years had passed. A woman who'd made a mistake now coming to town to atone for abandoning her children and making up for the time lost—but a much bigger, more logical part knew that was naïve and not likely to be the case. If it was, wouldn't she have found Karina by now?

"And what do you want from me?" I asked, genuinely curious what the hell he expected me to do about his ex-wife coming back.

His shoulders slumped a little and his phone rang through the truck speaker. Estelle's name displayed on the screen. He seemed worried, and since he was unable to hide it in front of me of all people, that made me worried too. What kind of woman was

Karina's mother? I'd heard at least a hundred stories about her, and none of them made for a promising reunion.

"I didn't come to ask you to do anything this time. I came to warn you, so when she steps into the light in Karina's and Austin's lives you can be there for them, especially my daughter. She was much more affected by her mom leaving, and I don't want her to get her heart broken again."

"Did you talk to her? Your ex-wife? So I know what kind of headspace this woman is in. Do you have any information that can help me help them?"

He shook his head. "The only information I have is that she won't stay, and she was never ready to be a mother. Her headspace . . . that's going to be interesting to figure out if we can. Her mental health was more than complicated leading up to her departure."

The way he threw out *departure* in such a nonchalant and calm way was ridiculous. He made it sound like she'd simply gotten on a train for a vacation, not left her family in the middle of the night.

"How was she at the PX? Would she still have an ID card?" I asked while trying to dissect the details out of the tiny bit of information I was given.

"No idea. I haven't gotten any notification that she ever applied for anything. She might still be using her old ID, it might not be expired. But she sure as hell was on post."

"Was she alone?"

"I couldn't tell. She was walking out as I drove by, a bottle of Pepsi in her hand," he told me, as if that meant something to me.

"Pepsi. Got it." I tried not to roll my eyes. For such a "great" officer, he sucked at paying attention when it mattered. "Did she look like she was on anything? Drinking or drugs?"

He thought for a moment before he shook his head. "No. Didn't look like it. She looked . . . alive."

He looked at me and I looked at him. He sounded like he was still in shock a bit, or he had believed her to be dead. That may have been better at this point. I got the feeling he wasn't speaking of her literally being alive, but his expression was cloudy and unfocused.

"Call me if you need my assistance," he told me as he revved up his truck to leave.

What an unlikely duo, united against both our wills.

CHAPTER TWENTY-FOUR

Karina

My body wouldn't stay warm for some reason. I kept shoving my hands inside the warm towels and even kept them on my heated bed between clients, but nothing I did would keep the warmth. Mali hissed at me when I tried to turn the heat up for a third time, and Tina, my longtime client, was practically sweating during her session. She didn't complain as she asked about my brother, like usual. She always used her skills as a family therapist during her sessions with me. I told her a little, but left out everything that mattered. I trusted her but I was exhausted as it was, and didn't feel like sharing for once. I checked the clock so many times during my shift, which was unusual since I typically zoned out during my treatments. I really hoped I was just distracted, and not becoming burned-out or bored.

When my shift was over I did my usual closing duties and took the food Mali offered me home—even though I wanted to eat the leftovers from Kael's mom first—because I didn't want the food to go to waste. It was pork and a mix of vegetables and a sauce that smelled spicy and sweet. Tons of rice on the side, which usually lasted Elodie and me for days. I walked across the dark alley and pulled my phone out to tell Kael I was on my way back. I thought

I heard footsteps and turned toward the sound, but no one was there. Less than thirty seconds later, I heard the steps again. I shot around faster this time, and my phone fell out of my hand as I looked at a woman who looked so much like my mother that it made me freeze in place. Before I could blink, she was gone. Or was she even there to begin with? I looked around, kneeling down to grab my phone and wipe it off, but there wasn't a trace of anyone. No sound, no motion lights from the other businesses turning on. Nothing.

Okay, Karina, you need to freaking sleep.

I picked up the pace and got out of the alley before my mind played any more tricks on me. Relief filled me as I saw Kael's truck parked on the street. I practically skipped home and rushed up my stairs. I couldn't shake the feeling and the memory of the mirage of my mother, so I chose to compartmentalize it and pretend it hadn't happened.

"Honey! I'm home!" I announced, smiling at myself because, corny or not, I always loved when husbands and wives would say that to one another on sitcoms.

Kael came into the living room from the kitchen and smiled, setting down a plate on the chair and scooping me into his arms. He was so warm that I shivered, some of the cold leaving my body instantly.

"You okay?" he asked, putting my feet down on the floor. He dipped his eyes down to look at me.

"I'm tired, I think? I've been cold all shift, nothing could make me warm. Even now, isn't it freezing in here?" I looked at the thermostat on the wall. It said seventy-four but it felt like fifty-something.

"I'm the wrong person to ask that," he told me, touching his warm hand to my forehead to gauge my temperature. "You don't have a fever, but you should eat, take a hot shower, and sleep. Do you work again tomorrow?" he asked.

I nodded and bent down to pull my shoes off. I dropped my purse by the door and followed Kael into the kitchen with the bag of Mali's homemade food in hand. My house smelled almost as good as Dory's, and I was surprised by how much I missed her already. I had only spent one day with her, but it felt like many more. I wondered when we would see her again, and hoped it would be soon. What she'd said about accepting my parents for who they were had such an impact on me. It was the first time someone gave me decent advice about how to deal with the loss I felt from both of my parents.

"It'll be done heating up in about two minutes, have a seat," Kael told me.

I looked at the stove and there were two pots on it, and the oven was on. "You could have used the microwave," I reminded him, feeling a bit bad about the pile of dishes that I knew he wouldn't let me wash.

"It wouldn't taste the same." Kael shook his head, stirring one of the pots with a wooden spoon.

"I know this sounds crazy, but I thought I saw my mom," I told him, full of embarrassment. I knew he wouldn't judge me, but he was right. I was so on edge lately and really needed freaking sleep.

He turned to face me, resting the spoon on the edge of the pot. "Your mom?"

I nodded. "It obviously wasn't her. I don't think anyone was even there, but that's a little more worrisome for my sanity, you know? But I felt like I was being followed and looked up and imagined my mom there. It felt so real. I really wish she would quit haunting me. Literally." I tried to laugh it off, but the image of the woman was so fresh that it was nearly impossible to shake.

"Baby," Kael said, his eyes full of sympathy.

Crossing the tile, he came over and stood behind me. I tilted my head back to look up at him. He didn't have a bad angle, and the more I looked at him the more devastatingly beautiful he was. His lips were wet and warm as he bent down and kissed me. He cupped his hand around my chin, keeping my head tilted toward him. His tongue slid into my mouth and the groan that escaped was impossible to keep in. The relaxation he brought should be bottled up and sold.

My body began to finally warm up as he pulled away, kissing my forehead. He kept his eyes on me as he used both hands to rub the tops of my shoulders.

"I'm not a professional," he warned me as his fingers worked against my tired and stiff trapezius.

"You're doing great." I rolled my neck, and the relief was instant. "I don't know the last time I've gotten treated, professionally or not," I told him. He pressed his fingers into the muscle, keeping pressure there for a few seconds. It hurt but I knew it would feel better after.

"Let's eat and I'll give you a full-body treatment, for free." He playfully winked at me; it was very out of character, adorable and corny at the same time.

"That sounds . . . suggestive," I teased him, raising my brow as he walked backward to the stove. He turned the fire off and laughed.

"It might be."

I pressed my thighs together, trying to hide how easily my body reacted to him. I could tell by the look in his eyes that it was obvious, that I wasn't hiding anything. He plated the food and put the pots in the sink. My mind was much quieter than it had been all day—what a relief. Instead of thinking about every single thought I've ever had, I only thought about Kael, the food, and how glad I was that he was here and in my life in general. I finally felt tethered to the earth, not in a suffocating way, but in a safe way. I was so tired of always floating around, solving everyone else's problems, and never taking a breath for myself. With Kael I felt agency; I felt heard and protected. As my mind wandered to what would become of us in the future, he set a plate of steaming food in front of me. I hadn't eaten at all, and my stomach growled angrily at me for starving it all day.

"If you're still hungry after this, I'll heat up Mali's food," he offered, sliding a fork between my fingers.

"Thank you." I dug in, taking a huge bite of the dumplings. They were even better today; how was that possible? I needed to get the recipe from his mom immediately.

We ate in comfortable silence. I started to get sleepy as my plate neared being empty. I couldn't stop yawning. Kael stopped me when I tried to put my plate in the sink.

"Go take a shower. I'll take care of this." He kissed my cheek, smiling as I yawned again.

The shower was warm and even though I was exhausted, I went through a whole everything shower. I shaved, double shampooed, and exfoliated my entire body. I felt so much better by the time I got out. Self-care really was so healing. I went to my room and put on a pair of shorts and a sweatshirt. I heard the water running in the kitchen—the great thing about my tiny house and its shoddy pipes. I tried to keep my eyes open, listening to the water run.

I thought I was dreaming when I woke up to warm hands moving up and down my calves. I opened my eyes just enough to see Kael kneeling on my bed behind me.

"Thank you," I managed to say.

"Do you want to sleep instead? My offer will still stand tomorrow," he told me.

"Both. You rub and I'll sleep?" I closed my eyes again as he moved his hands down to my feet.

I hadn't realized how much my body had needed a massage. I spent my time treating others but hadn't been treated in so long. It felt like a metaphor for how I lived my life, but I was so tired that I didn't want to spend my last bit of energy dissecting it.

CHAPTER **TWENTY-FIVE**

Karina

It was pouring outside when I woke up, and so my room was filled with humidity. Freaking Georgia and its unpredictable weather. Kael's body was practically a heater, and the more it rained, the warmer he grew. I mentally scanned my body, which felt so much better than it had when I went to sleep. I was still a little tired, but my mind felt so much clearer than it had been in so long. Maybe all I'd needed was a good night's sleep?

Kael's arm was tight around my waist, his breath warm against the back of my ear. I wondered how I'd ever slept a night without him and what would happen if I ever had to again. I hated the way my mind always went to the worst-case scenario instead of to the next step and the immediate future. I couldn't seem to enjoy a moment for too long without thinking of its expiration. My eyes shut, I counted backward slowly from one hundred to calm my thoughts and slow my breath before Kael woke up midpanic. I wanted him to sleep soundly, not be disrupted by my mental gymnastics.

I kept having to restart the countdown, but I finally began to zone out around fifty-four and dozed back off to sleep. This time when I woke up, Kael was no longer wrapped around me. I sat up to look for him, but he wasn't in my room. I made sure I had enough clothes on to leave the room if Elodie and my brother were here, which was growing a bit tiresome. Not them being here, I was happy to help them, but that I never knew when I would have the house to myself again, and I felt selfish even entertaining the idea, but sometimes I did miss my alone time.

I made my way into the living room and checked the clock on the wall. It said midnight, which couldn't be true given the sun was out. When I looked out the window, there was a break in the rain and the sun was shining. But that only meant the rain would show up again soon. Kael wasn't there either. I instantly panicked, struggling with the way I was depending on him so much lately. My attachment to him was alarming, and according to the internet, I had an anxious-avoidant attachment style. On the one hand, I was clingy and insecure, not fully trusting but desperate for attachment and on the other, I was hyperindependent and not willing to fully merge my life with another person's.

I grabbed my phone from the couch and called him. His voice was close by when he picked up. His silhouette appeared in front of my screen door, and he walked through.

"You okay?" He assessed me, a touch of worry lifting his scarred brow.

"I didn't know where you were."

"Working on your birthday gift during the break in the rain." He craned his neck toward the door and porch.

Ah, my most favorite and the most thoughtful gift I'd ever received: a deck and a porch swing, built by Kael Martin.

"I didn't want you to think I'd forgotten about it, but between the rain and all the drama, it's taking longer than expected. The rain's supposed to stay at bay for another three hours or so, so if you don't mind, I'm going to keep working. I can finish the base of the deck at least, since all the wood is cut and measured." He sounded excited, and I sure as hell couldn't wait to see it finished. On top of that, I had to go into Mali's soon.

"I have to work at some point anyway, so you can take all the time you need. My shift is about five hours long—I have two regulars, one new client, and space for a walk-in. If there isn't one, I can leave after three treatments."

"Great. I'll get back to work then, and you get yourself ready. There's food in the oven if you have time to take a few bites at least. And coffee in the pot."

"But you don't drink coffee," I noted.

He smiled, dazzling as ever. "You do."

I moved to wrap my arms around his waist, and he made a dramatic sound like I was squeezing all the air out of his lungs.

"I'll miss you," I told him, leaning on my toes to kiss him.

He bent his head down to give me an achingly slow, luxurious, and tempting kiss. I slid my tongue between his parted lips and he gently gripped my hair behind my neck, tugging. My body prickled with desire.

"If you want to make it on time to work, I wouldn't do that," he warned, pulling away from the kiss.

I blinked, mesmerized by the seductive tone of his threat. I couldn't afford to be late today—Stewart was coming in for her last treatment before her big move to Hawaii with her wife.

"Rain check?" I asked, sucking at the inside corner of his full lips.

"Always." He pulled away, kissing my cheek, my chin, my forehead, then lifted my hand and kissed each finger.

"I'll be here when you get back. Now go eat and down some caffeine, baby." He swatted my ass as I skipped away, high off the adrenaline rush he gave me and from hearing him call me baby.

I went into the kitchen and got the food out of the oven. Grabbing a spoon, I dug into the dish. It smelled familiar, but I hadn't had it at Dory's. From the pan it was in, though, I could tell it'd come from her. It tasted like the best version of a cinnamon roll mixed with bread pudding, and had big salty chunks of pecans throughout. It was so, so good. I grabbed a cup of coffee and felt creative when I dunked the bread into the coffee. Oh my god, was it delicious.

An eye on the clock told me I had about three minutes until I needed to splash water on my face and brush my teeth. My hair was in a braid that was coming loose, but it would make it through my shift. Kael making it possible for me to have my own porch swing made me so energized, so excited for the day. I wished all days started off so well.

I brushed my teeth and rinsed my face, putting a thin layer of moisturizer then sunscreen on, and was done with my routine for the morning and went to my room to put on my work clothes. I opted for a pale-purple work set, even though I usually wore black. Saying goodbye to Kael on the porch felt like we were playing house again. He was here more than he wasn't lately, and I kept coming back to the fact that I found myself depending on him more with each thoughtful gesture, each action that made my day a bit better, a bit easier.

When I got to work, my mood was much better than the day before. I had a smile on my face and a little pep in my step. I was a bit worried yesterday that I was getting sick or something, but I'd just needed a break, mentally and physically. And sleep and warm food.

"You're better today." Mali echoed my thoughts as she pulled one side of the curtain to my workroom open.

I nodded, lighting my candles. Since it was fall, I was using both vanilla pumpkin and cozy fireside scents. The sweetness of the one and the earthiness of the other blended together perfectly.

"Good. I don't want to worry about you too. You're the stable one here." She smiled at me while running her index finger over my counter to make sure it was clean. Of course, it was.

I laughed, knowing that there weren't any clients there yet. "I'm the stable one? We're all screwed then."

"We're all screwed anyway. Taxes are up, wages are down, the economy is shit. People can barely feed a family of four anymore." She used my small mirror on the counter to mess with her eyelashes. "Enough small talk, are you two going to keep calling out of work? My husband is taking me on a cruise in two weeks and I need someone to stand in as the manager while I'm gone."

Ah, so the vacation fever has set in, that was why she was more dressed up and cheery than usual. A vacation . . . I couldn't wait for the day when I could take a vacation that I paid for myself. Maybe Mexico or Barcelona? That day was a long way away, but a girl could dream.

"Are you asking me?" I brought myself out of the daydream of a beach chair, a book, and no responsibilities for a solid week.

"Yes. And if you don't burn down or remodel the place while I'm gone, maybe you can take over some of my workload. As a manager."

I couldn't hide my surprise. "Really?" I nearly shrieked. I went to hug her but she backed away, swatting at me in true Mali fashion.

"Don't get too excited. Nothing is happening until I see what you do while I'm gone, but I can't work forever."

I poked a finger toward her cheek but knew better than to touch it. "And you trust me," I teased her in a singsong voice.

She shook her head. "I knew I shouldn't have said anything!" She wagged her hand in annoyance as she left my workroom.

I was smiling ear to ear. A manager? That would mean more hours, a raise, even if it wasn't much, and more control over the spa and the chance to make it better and busier than it was now. I didn't want to get ahead of myself, but who was I kidding? Of course, I grabbed my phone and texted Kael, telling him that I might be getting a promotion. My heart was beating fast as I moved around my room, waiting for my client to come. Stewart was right on time, and she hugged me as soon as she saw me.

"I can't believe this is my last time seeing you," I told her as we pulled away from the embrace.

"I'm going to miss you and our chats here. You know more about me than my therapist does." She smiled, her unique green eyes shining with kindness.

I led her back to my space and gave her time to get situated on the table. I thought back to the first time I ever had her as a client and how we'd immediately clicked even though I'd been having the worst day ever. I had just started working here and I'd been late—my brother had gotten in trouble at our uncle's and my dad wouldn't stop calling me to complain. I'd been worried sick for Austin and of course, he hadn't answered my calls. Stewart had been so empathetic; she could immediately tell that I was off, but that I wouldn't want to say so or let it affect my job.

So I'd held my own problems in, suffering in silence, as usual. She'd confided in me about her life, not all at once, but in a slow and intimate conversation that had distracted me from my crappy day. She'd been so generous emotionally and we'd had a great session. Stewart had booked her next appointment on the spot, given me a huge tip, and made me feel so much less anxiety over whether I would make a good therapist or not. Over the last year we'd bonded, and though I'd kept it as professional as I could, I considered her to be someone I truly cared about. I was so happy for her and her wife and their new life in Hawaii, but I would miss her.

After her treatment, she gave me another hug and another too-high tip, but refused to take it back when I refused it. I wished her well and off she went. The provisional lifespan of military friendships and relationships was not something I would ever get used to. I never planned on entangling myself with the enlisted or their families, but plans were just that, and I'd clearly failed. I could not be more entangled than I was.

My shift continued to go well and by the time I finally looked at the clock, it was time for me to go. I tidied up my space and put a load of towels in the washer to make Elodie's shift a bit easier for her. I wrote a little note for her and left it on her cabinet with a small candle from my room that she had complimented a few days ago. She walked in the back door as I was leaving, but she either didn't see me or was ignoring me. Since she had no reason to ignore me, I brushed it off and went on my way, eager to get home, hoping Kael was there waiting for me.

He was still outside working on the deck. A tremendous amount of work had been done in a short time. I looked for Austin, assuming he had been helping, but only Kael was there, on his knees, hammering one piece of wood to another to cover my concrete steps.

"Did you see Elodie?" I asked as I approached him.

He turned to me, wiping his brow with the bottom of his T-shirt. It wasn't remotely hot outside to me, but I hadn't been working on a deck for hours.

"Yeah, but she's upset with me, so she didn't talk to me."

"Why would Elodie be upset with you?" I asked. Elodie had a soft spot for Kael, taking his side even over mine sometimes.

Kael looked away from me and stood. "Are you sure you want to know?"

"Do you know me?" I asked, wondering what on earth they could be fighting about.

"I gave your brother a hard time over something, and was wrong about it."

"Don't be cryptic. What did you give him a hard time over?"

Kael sighed and sat down at the beginning of my sidewalk. The grass was still wet from the on-and-off rain, but the sun had dried the concrete. "I heard him talking on the phone with someone about money and I accused him of using."

My scalp prickled. "Why did you assume he's using just because he was talking about money?"

I knew why, and couldn't say I wouldn't think the same, but Kael had always been so hard on my brother and quick to accuse him of being on drugs. Whether he was right sometimes or not, it pissed me off. My dad once told me that if my brother murdered someone, I would make the best defense for him even if I caught him with the gun in his hand. I liked to think he was wrong, but I couldn't be sure.

"Because of his history, I guess. I feel like shit over it and am going to apologize. I haven't seen him, though."

"Where is he? It's not like he has many places to go these days," I said, pulling my phone out to text Austin.

"Not sure. Maybe he's at mine." As he finished the sentence, his eyes went wide and his nostrils flared.

He reached for his phone as it vibrated in his pocket. Gloria's name and photo popped up on the screen. He answered instantaneously. Less than thirty seconds later, we were in his truck, driving way over the speed limit to get to Kael's place. I kept asking Kael what was going on but he was dead silent, intent on getting there as fast as possible. I was panicking. Was my brother really on drugs? Did he overdose with Mendoza there? Was Mendoza drunk and out of control and had Austin called Gloria? None of the scenarios made much sense, and each one made me more nauseated than the last.

"I know you won't, but I really wish you would stay in the truck," Kael told me as we pulled up, his voice tight.

Like always, I climbed out of the truck, and noted Mendoza's van parked on the street. Was Gloria here? I was about to text her when I heard shouting coming from inside. Kael moved faster than my eyes or feet could follow. When I got to the front door, it was locked.

That bastard.

My brother's voice mixed with another man's, which I didn't recognize. I made my way to the back of the duplex, hoping to god that the back door was unlocked. It wasn't. I began to feel helpless, which sent me into rage. I hated feeling helpless more than any other emotion. Kael was doing what he thought was right, but so was I. I pounded on the door as the not-familiar voice clicked in my brain. Phillips. A line of ice water trickled through my veins. I pounded harder.

"Let me in!" I screamed.

Somewhere in the back of my mind, I knew that me being there wasn't going to help a single bit, that it would distract Kael and my brother from whatever the hell was happening inside the house, but I couldn't help it. I was that idiot in films who never listened and kept adding fuel to the fire. Before I could change my mind and go back to Kael's truck and hope for the best, the door flew open and Phillips met me eye to eye. He looked like a madman, his front teeth covered in blood. I looked past him to see my brother, panting and holding his waist. Mendoza was propping him up and Kael was standing in the middle of the room with his hands spread out like wings, keeping distance between them.

"Oh, look who joined us. Now the party can really begin," Phillips said, bloody smile gazing down at me.

A sharp pain ran through my body and I yelped, not realizing that he had grabbed a fistful of my hair and was yanking me farther into the room. Kael's expression turned murderous, and he flew toward Phillips. I was tossed to the ground, and staggered backward on my hands to get out of the eye of the storm.

"Karina, leave!" my brother spat.

I could barely register what I was seeing—a piece of blue plastic was dangling from his side, and his T-shirt was lifted and covered in blood. A screwdriver. There was a screwdriver hanging out of his side. I could taste bile in my throat as I tried to move closer to him without Kael stopping me or Phillip noticing.

"What the fuck happened? You said you were going to stop this!" Kael shouted, grabbing Phillips by the shirt and lifting his body like he was a rag doll.

"You should have kept him away from me! I was going to leave today to go to my parents', but he fucking came here to taunt me!"

"I didn't come to taunt you. I didn't know you were fucking here!" my brother coughed out.

As I pulled my phone out to call the MPs, Mendoza noticed and silently shook his head at me. So I put my phone away. I crawled closer to where my brother was and stood up. His skin was turning slightly yellow and the area around the puncture was already purple. Dark-red blood seeped down his torso onto the top of his jeans. I swallowed, trying not to vomit.

"You all think you're so much better than me. You think you can get away with fucking my life up. And you—" Phillips turned his chin toward my brother as Kael slammed him against the wall. "I'm going to fucking kill you. I don't have anything to lose now," he threatened.

My brother lunged at him before Mendoza or I could stop him. The room was spinning. I felt like I was having an out of body experience. Things like this didn't happen in reality; blood and death threats were only on the screen.

Mendoza grabbed me by the shoulders, holding me back from trying to get my brother. "Go. Fucking go," he said in my ear. "Martin or your brother will get killed if you don't go."

I froze at his warning, knowing he wouldn't say that if he didn't believe it. But as my feet carried me toward the door, I heard Kael groan in pain. Whipping my head around, I tried to keep up with what was playing out in front of me, and was suddenly back in Mendoza's backyard, Phillips standing there with a gun in his shaking hands.

"Put it down," Kael warned him, a trinkle of blood running down the side of his mouth. Phillips must have hit him with the weapon. "Put my gun down," he said again, this time slowly.

"Fuck all of you. You've all been planning this. You wanted me to fuck up and get locked away so you can steal my wife and my baby. My whole life." He began to sob.

I could see his mind splitting in front of my eyes. Paranoia and pain were driving this man into madness, and with each second that passed I could see the humanity leaving him. It was terrifying, and I couldn't move.

Were we all going to die?

Just like that? I had never feared for my life until now, and it was shockingly not as terrifying as I always thought it would be. The last time Phillips did this, I was so shocked that I couldn't even consider it. But now, as Phillips turned his gun on me and Kael shoved my brother away from him, I wondered what the news would say.

What my dad would feel.

If my mother would see our faces on the news and wish she would have come back.

I thought of Kael's mother and sister. The two of them never seeing him again.

That drove me up, toward Phillips.

Kael screamed my name, and everything shifted. Phillips turned the gun on my brother, and I moved toward him. The bullet was fast but so was Mendoza, who dropped to the floor as my brother screamed.

CHAPTER TWENTY-SIX

Karina

The room was completely red. Blood everywhere, coming from the corners of the hospital wall, dripping down the wall art and all over the beeping machines. I startled awake, cupping my mouth to keep from screaming. My brother wasn't asleep but he didn't move, just stared blankly at the wall behind me.

So much had changed in one day. Austin would be fine; the doctors stitched him up like a doll and the psychiatrists kept giving him something in his IV bag every few hours to calm him down. Elodie nearly went into labor from the stress of what had happened and was now waiting on her parents to arrive from France. And worst of all, Mendoza was in his third surgery within twenty-four hours. He was breathing, that much I knew, but we'd had no other news. I tried to call Gloria but her phone kept going to voicemail without ringing.

I looked at my brother, propped up and beyond distraught. If Mendoza died, my brother would not survive it.

"Do you need anything?" I asked him, my voice cracking. My throat burned. I couldn't remember the last time I'd had a drink of water.

Austin shook his head but didn't look at me. His eyes were bloodshot, and his entire face and all his visible skin was a blueish tone.

"Are you hungry?"

He ignored me.

"Austin—" I began, but his eyes snapped to mine, startling me.

"Stop, Kare. Please, for the love of god, just stop."

His words hit me right in the stomach. I could feel how much he meant them, how he was refraining from saying something harsher.

"I'm sorry, I'm just trying to help," I explained, my eyes prickling with tears.

He let out a sigh and looked back at the wall. "Can you go, please?"

I grabbed my purse and keys. My need to be there for him was so strong it was making me sick, but this wasn't about me. He had been through hell and didn't know what was going to happen to the person he loved the most. I left the room quietly and didn't turn around as I heard my brother begin to sob loudly. The sound haunted me as I walked down the hall, hoping to see Kael, or Elodie, or anyone. I felt lost and useless, like somehow all of this was my fault. My brain was so scrambled that I couldn't decipher if that was a rational thought or not, but as soon as I saw Gloria I realized I was right.

She rushed toward me, an unreadable look on her face. When she raised her hand I thought she was going to hug me, but her palm slapped my cheek, knocking me to the floor. I managed to get to my feet, holding my face in shock as she screamed at me. Black mascara lined her cheeks and her eyes were swollen nearly shut from crying.

"This is your fault! If you hadn't shown up there and if your brother could have kept his dick in his pants, none of this would have happened! My husband, the father of my children's life is ruined, all because of your family, again!" she shouted, her mouth twisting. "He's never going to walk again and it's all your family's fault!" she screamed, her hand again flying toward me.

I couldn't move. But before she hit me, someone grabbed her arm from behind. Kael. He gripped her arm and pulled her to turn her away from me. She kept cursing at me, each sentence worse than the last.

"Get her out of here! How dare you fucking be here!" she yelled, twisting in Kael's arms.

"It's okay, it's okay," he said calmly. Kael squeezed her into a hug, and she thrashed harder.

"If I get my hands on her, it's fucking over!" Gloria screamed.

The look in her eyes as Kael dragged her away from me and down the hall was heartbreaking. She hated me, and I couldn't blame her.

I made my way out of the hospital. No one came after me—why would they? Step after step, I felt like a robot, unable to coordinate my moves, tripping over my feet but somehow able to keep going. I made it to the parking lot and realized I didn't know how I had even gotten here, not just to the lot, but the hospital. I grabbed my keys and pressed the unlock button to find my car. Not a sound. I tried my damnedest to remember how I'd gotten here. Kael's truck was there, and I moved toward it. I didn't have a key, but even sitting by it would give me some sort of grounding. As soon as I made it there, I heard my father's familiar voice calling my name. I was so lightheaded that I couldn't tell if it was him. I ran my hands over my chest and torso to make sure I was awake.

His arms wrapped around me, and I closed my eyes, a dizzying feeling rushing over me like waves. I could hear myself vomiting but didn't feel anything as my body lurched and lurched.

When I woke up, I was in my old room. There was a candle burning and a space heater next to the bed. A tray of food was on the dresser next to my bed, untouched. My eyes felt heavy, and it took me a few seconds to remember why I was so out of it. I sat up too quickly, heaving as my head spun. Estelle was there suddenly, holding a small trash can. She put it under me as I attempted to vomit. My body was empty so nothing came out, but I couldn't stop gagging. She gently rubbed my back, making comforting noises as she caressed me.

Eventually I stopped, and she brought a glass of water to my mouth. My lips cracked as I tried to refuse, and I tasted the blood as it entered my mouth. The smell shot me straight back to Kael's living room, back to Austin's screams and Kael's calls for help. My mind playing through what happened was like treading through a pool of thick mud.

"Sorry." I coughed as the water came back up as soon as I tried to swallow it.

She smiled, soft and sad. "Try to drink a little more if you can."

Her dark hair was pulled into a low ponytail away from her face. Her face was bare and shiny, and she wasn't wearing any jewelry, not even earrings. I wasn't used to seeing her so naturally. She was wearing sweats, which I was surprised she even owned a pair of. I looked around, piecing together that she was in my room taking care of me.

I didn't know how to react to that. I took a few sips of the water she was offering and managed not to cough. The bedspread was different from my old one, and a dark heavy blanket covered my body. I touched it with my fingertips; it was heated.

"You've been so cold since you got here, so I plugged in the heated blanket. If it's too hot, let me know," she offered softly. The subtle dimple in her cheek was made more prevalent by her nervous expression.

"Thank you. Where is my brother?" I asked, closing my eyes and putting my head back on the pillow.

"He's still at the hospital. They'll keep him one more night, to be sure."

"And Mendoza? Do you know anything about his condition?" I didn't think she would, but I had to ask.

"He's—" Estelle's voice sounded like the words were being squeezed out one by one. "He's alive, but as of now, he's paralyzed."

I shot up, ignoring the screaming pain in my head. "What?"

What Gloria had screamed at me made sense now. He would never walk again. Oh my god.

"It might change, it's too soon to call it."

"Oh my god," was all I managed to cry out.

Estelle brought her hand to my forehead, then to my cheeks, wiping away my tears. It shook me to the core that in one split second, with one decision made by one person, everything had changed. Mendoza had saved my brother's life, but the idea of him never being able to play with his children, never being able to pick Gloria up and hug her . . . I got sick again.

I watched Estelle crush a pill and put it into my water, but I didn't decline it. I would drink or take whatever she was offering if it made all of this hurt less. I needed to feel less.

"And Kael? Has he called or anything?" I was full of shame as I asked.

He had way more important stuff to worry about than me right now. His best friend had been shot by someone they'd both trusted and now one of them was paralyzed. The weight of it all was too

188

much to bear. I couldn't begin to imagine how Kael felt. I moved to take the blanket from my body, to look for and grab my phone, but whatever magical potion Estelle had given me was already kicking in. I felt woozy, then tired, then darkness covered my eyes and my mind as I fell into sleep.

CHAPTER TWENTY-SEVEN

Kael

"You need to eat." I slid a bag of take-out burgers and fries toward Gloria. She glared at me and pushed them back.

"What good is it for your kids if you starve to death and both of their parents are fucked up?"

"Fuck you," she growled.

The kids were at Gloria's parents in Arizona for now, but they wouldn't be there forever, and it was partly my responsibility to make sure their mother took care of herself while their father held on to his life.

"Please, eat something, and I'll leave you alone," I told her, pushing the brown bag across the small plastic hospital table again.

"I doubt that." But she opened the top of the bag, pulled out a burger, and unwrapped it. The smell made my stomach growl. "Eat some. You ordered enough for the whole platoon. Eat." She handed me a paper-wrapped burger and I didn't argue.

I'd had a few protein shakes in the last few days but hadn't had a solid meal.

"Did you see Karina yet?" Gloria asked, taking a big bite.

I shook my head. "I went to her dad's place but she was passed out."

"I can't believe what I said to her." Gloria hung her head. "I wasn't in my right mind."

Gloria hadn't meant what she'd said to Karina, and she was going through hell. But Karina was so sensitive, and she valued Gloria's friendship so much. There had been nothing but heartbreak on Karina's already devastated face as Gloria had slapped her.

"You can apologize when you see her," I reminded her.

She pushed her long dark hair behind her shoulders with her fingers. "That won't undo what I said and did. It's not her fault, or Fischer's. It's not one's fault except Phillips's and my dumbass wannabe-hero husband. You know?"

She slid her elbows across the small table and laid her head down. I hoped Karina wouldn't take it personally, but it would have been impossible not to. Karina was probably still in shock. I would never forgive myself for failing to keep her out of that situation, and it was my fault for allowing Phillips into my place at all that day. I shouldn't have trusted that he would have changed his perspective so quickly. Then again, I hadn't realized Fischer would go walking into the lion's den so soon. If it was anyone's fault, it was mine. My head was throbbing and my eyes burned like they hadn't been closed in days, which was true, and my chest felt like it had a hole in it as if I were the one who'd been shot.

"We can't undo anything that happened. We have to live with it, all of it. What we did, what we didn't do, it's ours to bear. All we can do is try to do better from now on."

"How philosophical." She rolled her eyes, a fry hanging out of the corner of her mouth. "I don't know what the future looks like anymore," she quietly admitted. "If he will never be able to walk again, what does that even mean? For him, for our babies?"

I wish I knew the answer. Deep down I was terrified of what it meant. Mendoza was so lively, so young and full of passion. All of that being contained, him unable to move for the rest of his life, was absolutely fucking terrifying. I would carry the guilt of not being able to stop Phillips for the rest of my life. Every time I looked at Mendoza, Gloria, or their children, the weight of what had happened would push against my chest, twist my insides, and make me wish it had been me who'd been injured.

"It means life fucking sucks sometimes. It means everything is going to be even harder from now on. It means the life you knew is gone." I couldn't keep my honesty at bay, even if it was too harsh for the moment. Gloria wouldn't want someone to bullshit her and tell her that everything would be fine, because it wouldn't be.

We didn't talk much as we both inhaled enough food for four people. I could taste the blood from my busted lip every time I took a bite. I was sure it was bruised but didn't have the capacity to care enough to look in a mirror. A little bit of color came back to her cheeks as she finished eating. The beeping monitor made her twitch every time it went off. The physical and mental exhaustion was all-encompassing on her small frame.

"Why don't you go home and sleep a bit? I'll stay here in case he wakes up," I offered, half expecting her to cuss me out.

She looked at her husband lying in the bed and then back at me. "I think I will. He's still out, and now that I'm full, I don't know how much longer I can keep my eyes open."

She leaned over Mendoza's still body and kissed his forehead, running her long fingernails over his slightly grown-out hair. He didn't move a muscle as she left the room, whispering a thank-you to me on her way out.

When the room was silent, with only Mendoza and me and our mistakes, I began to speak to him.

"Manny, we've really done it now. I can't believe you took a bullet for Fischer, you fucking idiot." I was conflicted on whether that had been a noble or a dumbass thing to do. If Karina's brother had been shot and paralyzed or dead, her entire world would have changed. She would have never been the same again. But Mendoza had a wife and children, a career in the Army. Just because I loved Karina didn't mean her brother's life held more value than those of my closest friends.

"I wish I would have stopped it, I never meant for it to get this bad. Phillips came to me saying he was going to leave them alone and not do anything stupid. But, fuck, now you're lying in the hospital. Goddamn it, none of this is fair."

His voice scared the shit out of me as he replied, "Life isn't fair."

His eyes were barely open but his mouth twitched into a small smile. I wanted to punch him for smiling at a time like this, though I wasn't surprised. He always had a way of making a joke out of the worst possible situations.

"Do you want me to call the nurse?" I asked, not sure if that was what I was supposed to do now that he'd woken up.

"No. I don't want to be poked and prodded right now. Where's Gloria?"

I nodded, knowing I would want some peace, too, if I were him. "She went home to sleep. She hasn't slept since you got here."

He closed his eyes softly, like it took a lot of effort to keep them open. "How long has it been? Feels like a goddamn month."

"Only two months." I fucked with him. He cocked one eye open and shook his head back and forth.

"If I could move my arm, I would be giving you the finger. But they've got me so doped up right now, I can't move shit."

"Glad to see your personality isn't gone."

"Just my nerves from the waist down." He was joking, but the reality hit me hard. I found myself blinking away tears but did my best to keep it light for his sake.

193

"How's Fischer?" he asked, his voice dry and raspy.

"Better shape than you. But he's here too. The screwdriver really did a number on him."

"Where's Phillips? That motherfucker." Mendoza began to cough, and I jumped up to his side.

"I should call the nurse. At least drink some water." I held the carafe to his chapped lips. He downed more than I'd expected him to.

"Where is Phillips? Did they lock him up?"

I didn't know how to respond to that.

"No. They can't find him."

Mendoza tried to sit up but failed. The movement killed me. I had never believed in miracles or praying, but I found myself talking to the unknown, begging for all of this to be undone, for Mendoza's life to not be this way forever.

"They can't find him?" he repeated, refusing to accept that.

"They will. They just haven't yet."

I should have been surprised that the justice system and the MPs had failed us, but sure as hell wasn't. I would chase that man to the end of the earth if they didn't find him within the week. He could come back at any time to finish what he'd started.

"And Karina? How is she?" Mendoza inquired.

"Not sure. She's in better shape than you, physically at least. I'm going back to her dad's after I leave here. She's been staying there the last two days."

Both of us turned our attention to the door as Fischer limped in, holding his side with both of his hands.

"What the hell are you doing up?" I scolded him, moving to help him walk.

"I could hear you two from next door and wanted in on the fun." He half smiled, and if he didn't have a literal hole in his body, I would have elbowed him.

"You crazy fucker! Why did you do that?" Fischer sat down on the edge of Mendoza's bed. "You could have died!"

"You almost died," Mendoza responded simply, like they were talking about picking bread up from the fucking commissary.

"I can't believe you," Fischer groaned. "You crazy bastard, stepping in front of a bullet for me. An actual bullet!"

"I'd do it again." Mendoza's voice was clear, dead serious.

"You bastard." Fischer leaned a little to try to hug Mendoza but winced in pain when he bent his torso. "Thank you, but you should not have done that. You have a family."

Fischer began to cry, and Mendoza's fingers twitched, trying to reach for him, but he couldn't.

"I told you I had your back. I'd take a bullet for both of you, any day. My life has been over for a while now, yours are just beginning," he whispered, growing tired from talking as soon as he woke up.

The idea that Mendoza believed his life was over already was devastating enough, and amplified the fact that so much had been taken from him, again and again. I could see the dark edges of my mind creeping in, remembering cold sleepless nights in the desert, recalling the faces of the innocent people Mendoza would never forget killing. He wasn't to blame for what had happened in Afghanistan, it had been an accident, but that didn't make it any better. His alcoholism spoke for itself. I pushed the shadows back, unsure how much longer I would be able to do so.

"No more bullets," Fischer begged, wiping his wet cheeks.

In another reality, this scene would have been funny, the irony of this entire situation being so damn heavy but all of us trying to find the humor in the darkness.

"Are you still going to be able to enlist?" Mendoza asked.

"No clue." Fischer rubbed his chin, his blue eyes full of worry.

"Let's worry about that later. You both need to rest and recover so you can go home," I told them.

"I don't have a home, and no offense, I never want to go to your place again," Fischer confessed, rightfully so.

"How's El?" Mendoza asked Fischer.

"I don't know, she hasn't been here." Fischer's eyes met the floor.

"I'm sure it's because she doesn't want Phillips to come here, since he's still running loose for now," I reminded him.

"My sister is in bad shape too," he added, looking back up at me.

"I'll worry about your sister, you worry about yourself and Elodie. And you"—I gestured at Mendoza—"you worry about yourself only. Your good deeds are done for the year. Got it?"

"Got it." He saluted me and the three of us laughed. Even in this completely fucked-up situation, wounded and unsure of what was coming next, we managed to laugh.

"You're not supposed to be in here." A nurse walked into the room, a look of disapproval on her round face.

Fischer turned on his charm and flashed a big flirty smile at her, and of course it worked. "I had to check on my friend. He almost died for me, the least I could do was crawl over here."

"That's sweet and all, but you need to get back to your bed before I get in trouble for losing my patient. And there's someone here to see you." The nurse checked the watch on her wrist and scanned the three of us with her gaze. "You have two minutes. I'll tell your visitor you'll be back then."

"Is it a young woman with light-brown hair?" I asked the nurse, wondering if it was Karina, but hoping to god she was still in bed at their father's house.

The nurse shook her head. "No. She says she's his mother."

CHAPTER TWENTY-EIGHT

Karina

The bedroom was dark except for the little blue light on the humidifier perched on the nightstand. Estelle had really gone all out in her role as my nurse and caretaker. A humidifier, candles, a heated blanket, a fresh tray of food. My mind was still a bit foggy as I pushed myself up to sitting. I rolled my neck in circles, trying to relieve a bit of the ache from lying down for so long. I couldn't find my phone without any light, and panic settled in, growing by the second as I moved the heavy blankets around.

"Are you okay?" Estelle entered the room, flicking on the light.

She turned the dimmer down as I covered my face from the shocking light. Her outfit was different from the last time I saw her, but still extremely casual compared to what I was used to seeing her wear.

"Do you know where my phone is?" I asked as she got closer.

"In the drawer." She pulled the top drawer of the nightstand closest to me open and handed me my phone.

The power was off, which gave me even more anxiety. As the phone turned on, notifications came through. A few texts from Elodie asking how and where I was. Gloria's name popped up, and I held my breath. I would never forget the way she'd looked at me, full of hatred. My heart was broken, but I couldn't feel sorry for myself because she was right. If I hadn't gone to Kael's, none of this would have happened. Pushing through my fear and pain, I clicked on her name and read the message.

I'm so sorry for what I said. We should talk in person, be safe and please try not to take what I said to heart. I didn't mean it. I took my anger out on you and I'm so sorry.

Reading her message filled me with two types of emotions. On the one hand, I was relieved, and felt like I could breathe again, but on the other, I felt undeserving of her forgiveness. When tragedy happened, it was much easier for everyone involved to have a clear villain, and I was more than willing to take on that role for the sake of those around me. Especially Gloria, who had been so welcoming and kind to me from the beginning. Her life would never be the same now.

I stared at my phone, unsure how to respond, and decided to wait until my thoughts were clearer and I could give her a better reply. I looked up at Estelle, who was standing over me, her brows pushed together in worry.

"I know you probably don't feel like it, but can you please try and eat some crackers? Or the broth? You'll get sick again if you don't." Her request came softly, borderline maternal.

Instead of being snotty to her, I agreed, and reached for the tray of food. She beat me to it, grabbing it and setting it on my lap.

"Kael came by," she told me as I took a sip of broth. I almost spit it out.

"When?"

"A few hours ago. You were asleep, so he said he would come back."

I wanted to vent to her about how selfish I felt, how I knew that I was suffering the least out of everyone, and that I felt like a freaking idiot for feeling so defeated, so exhausted, so afraid. I wasn't the one whose husband wasn't going to walk again, I wasn't the one who had an actual screwdriver sticking out of them, I wasn't the one whose husband had caused all of this and was now nowhere to be found. I was just a stupid girl who'd thrown herself into the middle of the fire and was now being babied by her stepmom.

"I need to get up," I told Estelle after finishing the broth. "I can't just lie here anymore. I need to shower and . . . I don't know, but I need to do something."

She didn't try to persuade me; she grabbed the tray and moved it, then pulled the covers off me and turned the light all the way up. My bones ached as I stood up, and my head was tender from Phillips's grip on my hair. I patted the spot to see if he had ripped any out, but it didn't feel like he had.

When I got out of the shower, there were brand-new clothes waiting on the bed for me: cotton pants and a thick sweater, both pale green and as soft as fur. Estelle ignored no detail, so there were also panties and a bralette tucked under the outfit, even a pair of new socks to match. I brushed my hair into a tight bun at the nape of my neck and pinched some temporary color back into my cheeks before I made my way downstairs.

My father was sitting at the table, his phone to his ear.

"You have two hours to find him. Whoever finds him first will be heavily rewarded and whoever doesn't will be equally punished," he threatened.

I knew who he was talking about, so there was no need to ask.

"You're up," he stated, looking me up and down from head to toe.

"I'm up," I repeated.

"We're going to find him. I have my best scouts looking for him. He won't touch you, any of you, again," he promised.

"Thanks." I didn't have the energy to grill my dad over his involvement or why he would bother helping any of us.

"I never meant for this to happen, Kare. If I'd known how unstable he was, I would have never requested orders to bring him back."

I didn't think my heart could sink any lower, but it did. I should have expected my father to somehow be tied to this tragedy.

I gripped the back of the dining room chair to keep me upright.

"What do you mean? You brought him back?"

"I did not know about your brother and Elodie's involvement. I thought I was doing the right thing, but evidently, I couldn't have been more wrong. I never imagined this would be the outcome."

Something in my father's tone made me believe him, for once.

"I'm going to do everything in my power to see to it that Mendoza gets the top care this post can offer, and if that's not enough, I'll send him up to Walter Reed in Maryland," my dad promised.

Maybe it was the concoction that Estelle had given me or my desperation for something good to happen, but I chose to believe him and find comfort in the fact that he was finally going to use his power for good.

"Your brother will also be fine, and Elodie can file for an emergency divorce, given the circumstances. Her parents are arriving any minute, I sent a driver to pick them up from the airport."

"Why are you doing all this?" I asked. I didn't want to get involved in a trade-off with my father, him doing something good and expecting something from me or Kael, or any of us.

My father pressed his palms gently on the table. "I never wanted to be the villain in your story, Karina. I know I have done many, many wrongs in my life, to you and to my soldiers, but while I have time, I want to spend it doing the best I can. I always put my job before you, before myself, and I can see that has had the worst impact on our family."

"I'm sorry, but this is very sudden. Are you dying or something?" I meant it as a joke, but as the words fell between us, my dad's face changed—his eyes dropped and his jaw ticked.

Oh my god.

What the fuck.

"Dad." I could barely speak. "You're—"

"I figured he would tell you. I thought it would be better coming from Martin than me."

The room began to spin. I sat down in the chair in front of me, farthest from my dad's seat at the head of the table.

"Martin—I mean Kael—knows?"

My father's cold military expression was nowhere to be found. "Only recently. He likely hasn't had the chance to tell you what with everything that's happened. I'm sure I was at the bottom of the priority list."

I didn't have a damn clue what to say or how to process what I was being told. I focused my attention on the centerpiece on the table. Fall-colored ornaments surrounded a woven cornucopia with little pumpkins.

"What is it exactly?" I asked him as the silence got to be too much.

"My liver is failing."

"How? You're not even fifty."

My dad had gone to PT every morning for the last twenty years, so how could his health be failing? It didn't make sense.

"Well, illness doesn't seem to have any age limits, Karina. It sounds worse than it is, I'm not going to die right now. I don't know when, but there's still some time for me to get things right."

I almost laughed at how outrageous this was. He refused to call it what it was, and was keeping the details to a minimum, but his eyes were full of vulnerability, the only time I had witnessed such an emotion from him. My father was sick and now wanted to make amends with everyone around him, Mendoza was wounded and couldn't use his body from the waist down, my brother may or may not be fine, Elodie's baby was coming in a few weeks . . . I was so overwhelmed I wanted to scream. It felt like every time I turned around, something bad was happening to someone I cared about. My father and I had our issues, but I would never wish death on him.

"Does Estelle know?" I thought about how much she had been taking care of me the last few days and how overwhelmed she must be. My dad was essentially all she had.

"Yes. Your brother doesn't, and I don't think it would do any good to tell him right now," he confessed.

I hated the idea of lying and deciding when the right time to share devastating news was, but my father was right in this case.

"Why did you tell Kael before me?" I asked him, genuinely unsure how and when the two of them had even been around one another.

"I trust him with your life, Karina."

Trust . . . what an interesting choice of words for a man who proved again and again to be the opposite of trustworthy. It seemed everyone around him trusted him, except me. Did he blatantly lie to everyone else, too, or was I the special one?

"Well, that's a mistake," I warned him, standing up to leave. I couldn't stay cooped up here any longer, moping around while the world continued to go on.

CHAPTER **TWENTY-NINE**

Kael

I followed Fischer back to his room. As he shut the door behind us, he turned on his heel and faced me, shame clear on his exhausted face.

"It's a long story, but my mom has been around for a little bit now. She hasn't seen my sister yet," he explained quietly, his words coming out in a rush.

I immediately thought of how Karina thought she'd imagined her mom in the alley; had it really been her after all?

"You've seen her?" I tried to make sense of the situation as a knock tapped at his door.

He nodded and pulled the door to his assigned room open. A woman, appearing no older than thirty but who had to be, sat on the bed with her hands in her lap. Her dark-blond hair was the color of sunflower petals covered by a shadow. She stood up and her long dress swept the floor as she greeted Fischer with open arms.

"My god. Are you okay?" Her face was shockingly similar to both of her children's but especially Karina's.

The shape of her eyes, the slightly wide bridge of her nose, her square chin, they were nearly identical to Karina's. I could see now how much Fischer looked like his father compared to how much Karina looked like her mother. From all the stories I had heard about her, I felt like I had met this woman at least a dozen times.

The beaded bracelets on her wrists clinked together as she cupped his face. Nothing about the way she had decorated herself or her embrace with her son made any sense to me.

"I'm okay." Fischer began to explain the short version of what had happened. I could barely follow his words because I was too busy staring at the ghost in the room.

Even her reactions were exactly like Karina's, from the way she nodded slowly as she followed along with the story to the way her eyes went wide at the violent parts.

"This is Martin, by the way. He's the main reason I'm alive today. He's saved my ass more than a few times, and he's the one I told you about, who helped me enlist."

Her attention turned to me. "So you're the famous Martin?"

From what Karina had told me about her mother's emotional relationship with the Army, I expected her to get angry with me, or at least be cross. Instead she smiled at me, the same smile I'd seen on her daughter's face a million times. The same heart-shaped face, the same thick dark eyelashes. It made me uneasy as hell. According to Karina, her father was the only one who had a photo of her mom, so I'd never seen one and now wished I had, so I wouldn't have been so caught off guard. Genetics were strong, but this was uncanny. No wonder Karina's father couldn't help but compare the two of them.

I realized I hadn't responded to her question. Fischer was watching me with an anxious smile.

"Yeah. That's me," I managed to say.

"My boyfriend is in the Army too. Newly stationed here." She perked up.

I always considered myself to be an extremely grounded person, someone who could make anything make sense, but I was dumbfounded. Not only by the realization that Fischer had been in contact with this woman and his sister didn't have a clue, but that she had a boyfriend in the Army and was acting like she hadn't left her family in the middle of the night. It was obvious that she didn't have a clue who I was or that I had a connection to Karina. It took every bit of my self-control not to be rude to her. In my head, I was screaming at her, telling her that she had some fucking nerve to just show up here like nothing had happened. I could feel my jaw ticking, it was so fucking hard to bite my tongue.

"Mom, Martin is also Karina's boyfriend," Fischer told her when my silence became awkward.

He knew me well enough to know that it would be impossible for me to smile and simply ask her about her boyfriend or pretend that I didn't know how big of a deal this would be for Karina and should be for him. Her entire demeanor changed as she took in this information. She went from breezy and smiley to nervous and mildly defensive. She reminded me of a prisoner I had to babysit once in Afghanistan. The sudden change in behavior when held in captivity was a very specific human behavior. It said a lot about her that the mere mention of her daughter made her react this way.

"Oh. Karina's dating a soldier?"

Her words weren't what I had expected. I assumed she would ask where Karina was, what she was up to, how she was.

"I'm discharging, medical retirement, so technically only a soldier for another week or so," I explained.

Fischer looked like he was going to vomit.

"I'm surprised, honestly." She stared at me, taking in the details of my face. She had a curious, attention-to-detail gaze, just like her daughter.

"I was too. She always said she would never date a soldier, but these two are pretty serious. Like, marriage serious," Fischer claimed.

Were we? I guess we were, but I had a feeling Karina would not like her brother talking about our relationship without her being present.

"Marriage? Really? I can't imagine Karina married. Wow, she must be really infatuated with you."

My fist tightened at my waist, and I tried to ignore the burning feeling of wanting to speak for Karina and wipe that look off her mother's face. What did she know about her daughter? She had left when Karina was in high school and didn't have a clue who Karina was as a woman, and her blasé tone made it evident that she didn't feel nearly as guilty as she should.

I couldn't help it, I had to react. "And what do you imagine Karina to be, exactly?"

The playfulness disappeared from her face. Her brows turned down and she glared at me. I hadn't expected her to be so hostile. From the image Karina had painted of her, she was fragile, lost, and dreamy, desperate to be loved and have a purpose in the world. And maybe she *was*, but the woman in front of me was not.

"I imagine her to be like you. Harsh and cold. Like her father."

"Mom." Fischer tried to interject but both of us ignored him.

"She couldn't be further from that." I defended Karina, entirely sure that she was wrong. Karina was nothing like her father; she didn't have a ruthless bone in her body.

Their mother studied me further, looking for a hole to probe. I could practically read her mind now that the idea of who she was had evaporated.

She shrugged, and the butterflies on her chaotic dress looked like they were dancing. "I guess people change."

"Are you planning on telling her you're back?" I asked her. All pretenses were gone now. I may as well ask the most important question.

She turned to Fischer, as if looking to him for guidance. He was lost, unable to help her, but I could tell he would have done anything to make the room less tense. The machine in the corner beeped steadily as the seconds passed. It suddenly dawned on me that the person Fischer had been on the phone with was his mother, not a drug dealer. I didn't need to know how long the two of them had been in contact—it would only make it worse that he'd hidden it from Karina. She overlooked all his bad behavior, his addictions, his selfishness, but could she overlook this?

"I do. I just need to get my grounding here first. I just moved back. Everything is going so well with my boyfriend, and I don't want to rock the boat by throwing in any variables."

Variables? What the fuck was this, a science lab? She was not equipped to be a mother and certainly didn't deserve Karina's empathy or sympathy. And her boyfriend? What kind of person puts something as trivial as a boyfriend before the child they'd abandoned?

Nothing I could say would change her mind, and I didn't want to. If she didn't want to see her daughter, I wasn't going to force her. Karina deserved better than that. She was already a mess from Phillips's breakdown, and with her not being aware of her father's illness, it was too much.

"I'm going to go." I didn't want to spend another moment breathing the same air as this woman, and I wasn't in the business of cussing women out.

Fischer nodded. His face told me that he had a lot to say but couldn't. I wanted to flip him off. That casual little fucker always stirred up a storm and walked away unscathed. He had somehow become the favorite, easier child, and it didn't make any damn sense to me. Given his current state, you know, being in the damn hospital because of a screwdriver being stabbed into his torso by his girlfriend's husband said it all. What a headline.

I didn't turn back around as I left, disappointment and worry filling every crack in my armor.

I couldn't shake the memory of Karina's mother's face as I drove to Karina's. She texted me that she was leaving her dad's and going home, so I wanted to meet her there. I called my ma, hoping to get some advice. She was enraged and confused by Karina's mother's return and behavior. She immediately advised me to tell Karina, that I couldn't hide something like this from her. While I knew she was right, she always was, I couldn't imagine breaking Karina's heart while it was already in recovery. By the time I pulled up to her house, I felt sick. I could have just walked in and told Karina that her mother was at the hospital, and she could go see her right now. As many times as I'd played the scenario in my head, I couldn't bring myself to do it. I went back and forth as I walked up the nearly finished deck and heard Elodie's voice coming from inside.

Okay, so it wasn't the time. I would have taken any excuse, and was grateful for Elodie's presence. I knocked lightly on the door before stepping inside. Elodie had a small suitcase in one hand and a duffel bag over her other shoulder.

"Going somewhere?" I asked her as she greeted me.

She nodded. "I'm going to meet my parents at their hotel. They're staying for a little while."

"That's good," I told her, realizing how uninterested I sounded. "Not good, given the circumstances, but I'm glad you get to see them and be with them right now."

She smiled, waving her hand. "I knew what you meant."

"Sorry." I nervously brushed my hand over my chin. "I'm a little out of it."

"I think we all are." She kissed my cheeks and yelled bye to Karina, who I assumed was in her bedroom.

I moved with caution, as if I was approaching a war zone. Little did I know, I was. Her room was a disaster, clothes thrown everywhere in little piles that looked like visible land mines. She was standing by her dresser, tossing clothes over her head.

"Karina?" I said her name slowly as I approached her.

She didn't turn around. Had she found out about her mom's return on my way here? Her brother must have called her.

I moved closer to her and put my hand on her shoulder.

"Are you okay? Why did you leave your dad's?"

Her eyes were bloodshot with lilac circles under them. Her lips were a deep pink, and I could see the blue veins in her forehead. She looked exhausted, mentally and physically. She looked away, avoiding eye contact with me. I began to feel more than a little on edge.

"I couldn't sit there anymore. I have to work tomorrow since Mali is leaving, and my house is a mess."

It wasn't the time to point out that she was in the middle of covering her bedroom floor with clothing. On cue, she tossed a purple sweater over both of our heads.

"Do you need help cleaning?"

Both of us were on edge. I tightened my light grip on her shoulder and turned her around to face me. She opened her mouth, then closed it. I was about to blurt out that I just met her mother, but she lifted her hand up to cover my mouth.

"I don't want to talk about it. Or anything. I want to clean my house and have a normal day. I feel like I'm losing my mind, Kael, and I can't talk about anything that has happened in the last seventy-two hours. So, please, I know you want to talk it out and have a therapy session, but can we just pretend like everything is fine and have a normal night as twenty-one-year-olds? Please?"

That was the last thing I wanted to do, but I couldn't imagine how overwhelmed she felt. I didn't blame her for wanting to ignore everything and pretend, but I knew that disassociating usually caused more pain in the long run, so it was difficult for me to agree to her plan. I did anyway, nodding in silence while my mind screamed at me to fix this for her, to take her pain away. It wasn't possible, and I knew that but hated it all the same.

"Thank you. I don't want to fight with you or talk about how I feel or what the future means. I want to be a twenty-one-year-old girl manically going through my clothes and ignoring reality for a bit."

I sighed. "Okay. Let's ignore reality for a bit. What exactly are you doing with these clothes?" I looked around the room. How could one person have this many clothes?

"Not sure. Donating them? I need a fresh start. A new style. I wear the same clothes all the time and I can't afford to buy new ones, so I want to get rid of at least half and restyle the rest. Oh, and I bought hair dye. Want to help me dye it?" She was speaking a mile a minute.

My eyes found the box of hair dye on her dresser and the pit in my stomach grew. I wished I had her ability to be so spontaneous, changing parts of my identity every time something was out of my control, but I wasn't programmed that way. I was a dweller, a hyperfixator.

"Sure?" I agreed to her plan, and we spent the day organizing every inch of her house, dyeing her hair dark brown, and ordering Chinese takeout.

As the hours passed I began to settle, coming to the realization that maybe sometimes the answer to handling trauma was to temporarily shut it off. Processing it immediately didn't have to be the only response. Karina's sporadic yet meticulous way of thinking was contagious, but I knew deep down that the clock was ticking and Karina's bottled-up emotions were going to explode without a warning.

CHAPTER **THIRTY**

Karina

I found myself at my father's house by choice. What a complicated emotion regret is. I had gone from declaring that I was never going to see my father again to driving to his house after work. I hadn't called ahead, so I was relieved that his truck was parked in the driveway and the interior lights of the house were on. It was so hard to make sense of what I was feeling when it came to every aspect of my life. Everything had changed so rapidly, and I couldn't get a grip on it. Before I could mentally spiral any longer, I got out of my car and walked up the sidewalk and onto the porch.

Estelle was the one who answered the door. She was dressed casually, in dark jeans and a white scoop-neck top. Her hair was down, like she had let the air dry it, which surprised me, but it looked effortless and pretty on her. I wanted to tell her that, but my father's voice sounded out between us.

"Who is it?" he asked, clearly in a bad mood. The tone of his voice sent me straight back to my childhood. It had been an awful idea to come here. What the hell was I thinking?

"Karina," Estelle and I responded in unison.

"Oh." He stood next to Estelle and looked me up and down, taking in my work clothes. I felt underdressed and suddenly insecure.

I hated that one look from him could do that to me, no matter how old I was.

"What's wrong?" he asked me, softening the smallest of bits.

Shaking my head, I held my hand up. "Nothing. Nothing's wrong, I just . . . I don't know. I wanted to come over. I should have called or something before but—"

"You can always come here, no need to call ahead," Estelle said. The look she gave my father felt like she was coaching him or reminding him, like she was forcing him to agree with her.

"I didn't say you couldn't come here. I assumed something was wrong because you never just come here out of the blue," he said.

What the heck was my plan now? To sit in the living room and watch TV with him and Estelle? To ask about the weather? His health? My head ached at my own stupid, spontaneous choice to come here.

"Have you eaten dinner?" Estelle asked as she closed the front door behind me.

"No, actually." I hadn't eaten since the morning when Kael handed me a piece of toast as I left for work. I'd overslept, my body tired from organizing and rearranging every inch of my house all night.

"Why don't we order some pizza?" she suggested, looking at my dad, who would never in a million years turn down pizza.

"Not Domino's," he said, as always.

It had been years since I'd thought about his boycott of Domino's, and it made me laugh a little that he was still holding strong to such a petty thing. When I was in middle school I won a certificate for a free pizza for reading the most in my class over winter break, and when my parents took me to get my prize, they wouldn't accept the coupon. My father argued with the manager for nearly an hour while my mother doodled all over their wooden table with a hairpin, carving thin swirls into the wood. I sat quietly, no longer wanting the pizza at all, but wasn't used to my father fighting for me over anything, so gladly sat there waiting for a resolution. We left with no pizza and went straight to Pizza Hut, and my dad vowed to never eat Domino's again in his life, which he'd apparently kept up with.

"I know, honey." Estelle smiled, making me wonder if he had told her the story. If we'd had a normal relationship, I would ask her or tell her about it, but we didn't, so I relived the memory myself as we moved to sit down in the living room.

Estelle called Pizza Hut herself, which felt nostalgic. No one called places to order food anymore; apps and laptops and iPads were the way now, but I kind of liked that she called even though it took forever for such a simple order. While we waited, I could tell my dad was uneasy, not sure what to do with me. This was different than the forced family dinners; I'd come here of my own free will. He kept glancing at me, then at the football game on the TV, then back to me.

Once the pizza arrived, I stood up from the couch to go to the dining room.

"Let's eat in here. I'll grab some plates," my father suggested.

I'm sure to most people it wouldn't be out of the ordinary, but I had never seen my dad or Estelle eat in any room of the house other than their dining room. The casual pizza, to eating in the living room, to my dad being the one to offer to get the plates? Was he worse off healthwise than he was acting? It sure as hell seemed like it.

"I heard Mendoza's been healing better than expected," my dad said when we were done eating.

"Yeah, thank god," I agreed, wondering if my father even cared about Mendoza or any of the soldiers under him or if he was just making conversation with me.

"Karina . . ." The tone of his voice sounded a bit like he was choking. "When I got that call, hearing that you and your brother were in danger—" He paused. "I understand that you don't see me as a protector and barely as a father, but it was the scariest moment of my life. I never wanted you to be affected by this part of military life, and I always expected you to stay away from it the best you could, like your mother."

"Dad . . ." I was just as fumbly and speechless as he was. We had never had a conversation like this before, and I thought I even saw a gloss of tears in his eyes as he found his next words.

"I will do everything in my power to make sure Phillips is off the streets and locked away somewhere. He won't be coming near you or Elodie again. And if he would have succeeded in killing my son or my daughter, I would have ended his life myself."

The intensity of my father's words and the way his mouth twisted was overwhelming but felt good, a relief that he actually gave a shit about us. Or maybe I was being naïve, I didn't know, but it felt better than nothing, which was what I'd expected.

"How are you feeling, Karina? You must have been so scared," Estelle asked me, holding a paper towel in her hands, tearing at the edges with her eggplant-hued painted nails.

"Thanks again for taking care of me after it happened," I told Estelle. "I'm okay. I think? Yeah, I'm okay." My response was jumbled, but it was how I felt.

Her eyes widened in concern. "If you need to talk to anyone, I have some friends who work in mental health, all across the spectrum, so don't hesitate to ask."

"Friends?" I blurted. It was absolutely meant to be an inside thought.

Her laughter surprised me. "Yes, I know it's hard to imagine, but I do have friends. Not many, but I do have some."

Her lighthearted response to my insult made me feel a little better. I was genuinely surprised at the idea of her with friends, or with anyone who wasn't my father. From my perspective, it seemed like her life began and ended at the front door of this house, but I was glad to know that wasn't true.

"Thank you for the offer. I'm still processing what happened, but thank you."

"I'll make sure Mendoza and his family are taken care of," my dad added. "He saved your brother's life."

I felt a little sick, the memory still fresh in my mind. It played through like a film on an IMAX screen. Gloria's screams and the blood soaking the floor, everyone scattering, Kael . . .

"I'm going to get some air," I said as my chest heaved. Without looking at my dad and Estelle, I stood up, the room slightly blurry, like the lines of everything were fuzzy around the edges. When I stepped outside, the air was chilly, bringing a little more awareness to my mind. I sat on the swing, lifting my feet, waiting for my body to come down from fight-or-flight. I pulled my phone out to call Kael. His voice would calm me. The swing moved slowly as his soothing voice came through the line. I hadn't forgotten about him knowing about my father's situation, but right now none of that mattered.

"Hey, you okay?" he immediately asked.

"Yeah. I think so? I'm at my dad's and he started talking like an actual dad, Estelle was offering me her therapist friends, it was a lot. I needed some air. I came out to the porch swing and just wanted to hear your voice."

"I agree with Estelle," he told me.

"Are you being sarcastic?" I kicked my feet up. I had left my shoes inside by the door and my socks had little penguins on them. I wiggled my toes, pretending to be a girl on the phone with her boyfriend, no life-changing events happening around her, no near-death experiences.

"A little, but I do think she's right that you should talk to someone. What happened isn't something you should brush off or ignore. I know you want to show yourself that you're strong, but sometimes strength lies in admitting when you need a little more than yourself to lean on."

"Hmm. I've been to therapists many, many times about my childhood and my mom and honestly, I'm not sure that it—" I blinked at a movement in the yard.

I was positive I was losing my mind. That Estelle and Kael were both right. Or had I fallen asleep at some point and was dreaming? The woman walked toward me, her eyes set straight on me. I wiped my eyes with my hands, sure as hell that it wasn't possible that I was seeing what I thought I was. Or whom I thought I was.

My mom.

She was here?

In person?

At my father's house?

"Karina?"

The way she said my name made it sound like she was the one who should be surprised to see me.

I pushed my socked feet into the concrete porch to stop the swing from moving. My phone slid off the edge and hit the porch, face down. I couldn't move to pick it up. My mom hadn't changed physically since I last saw her. Her already long hair was a few inches longer, now passing her waist. She was dressed in a long, colorful patchwork tunic and leggings with large wildflowers printed on them. The tunic had long patterned sleeves that flared out at the ends. She looked like she'd walked out of a photo from Woodstock, a bohemian flower child of a woman who was floating toward me. I wasn't sure her sandaled feet were even touching the ground.

"What are you . . . why are . . ." My heart pounded so hard that it felt like I was shaking the ground beneath us. She'd finally, finally come back to find me. I couldn't believe it, even though she was right there. I didn't know why she'd chosen now, but I was so elated to see her that tears involuntarily poured out of my eyes like they were water sprinklers.

I jumped to my feet and confusion washed over me as her face shifted into a frown. Was something wrong with her? Did she come back to tell me that she was sick? Oh god, I thought, both of my parents were sick? My mind couldn't keep up with the theories flying around.

"Is your dad home?" Her voice carried through the light wind. Her eyes went to the window behind me, the yellow glow of the light through the window casting a shadow onto her face.

"Yeah. And Estelle." I realized my mom probably had no idea that my dad was remarried. "Estelle is—"

"I know who she is." My mom's lips turned into a smile but the shape of it made me take a step back, my knees knocking into the front edge of the wooden swing. There was something off about the way she was behaving. It didn't seem like she was drunk or anything, just off. Or maybe I had created a version of her that wasn't reality, but when I imagined our reunion, she was always running toward me with open arms and teary eyes, telling me how sorry she was while she stroked my hair and hugged me tight.

Instead, she stood at the bottom of the porch like she was a vampire who hadn't been invited in. I was at a loss for words and waited for her to say or do something.

The door creaked open behind me and Estelle stepped onto the porch. I felt like the porch was spinning—it had to be a dream.

"Karina, who are you . . . Michelle, what are you doing here?" Estelle's tone was one I had never heard from her.

"I'm here to see Dennis. To finish our conversation from the other day," my mom replied, equally as hostile.

"The other day?" I interrupted. "You were here the other day?" None of this made any sense.

"Karina, could you please give us a moment?" Estelle asked me. I jerked my neck, snapping at her.

"Give you a moment? She's my mother and I haven't seen her in—" I trailed off, digesting the disinterested look on my mother's face.

"Where is he?" my mom asked, not acknowledging my outrage and confusion. Was this the same woman who'd told me tales and hummed me to sleep? Maybe she was on drugs? Or suffered from memory loss? Nothing made any damn sense.

"He's inside, but he will not be talking to you." Estelle was firm, to which my mother laughed, covering her mouth.

"Is that his choice or yours? Dennis!" My mom shouted for my father.

He stepped onto the porch with lighting speed, rushing down the stairs, his finger pointing directly in my mother's face.

"What are you doing at my house, yelling at my wife?" He was only inches away from her. Given the past, my instinct was to protect my fragile mother, but in the moment, she didn't seem fragile at all.

I stood still, my world becoming more and more confusing by the second.

"We never finished chatting the other day. You said you would call me, but you didn't," my mother said to him.

A look of disbelief flashed across his face. "So you thought the appropriate response would be to show up at my home, again? I was very clear last time, and I'll say it again. I don't have anything for you."

"Dennis, if we can just talk alone." My mother was practically begging. What on earth could she possibly want from him? She hated him, or at least I thought she did. Was it money? A place to stay?

"I don't have anything to say to you that I haven't already said. You should explain yourself to your daughter, who looks as if she's seen a ghost. She should be your priority right now." Disgust echoed in his voice.

She looked at me, her expression unreadable. She seemed to be looking for some sort of escape, but I wouldn't allow that. If she tried to leave, I would chase her, like I hadn't been able to the first time.

"Mom . . ."

"We will be inside," my dad said before my mom could respond. Estelle crossed her arms at her chest.

"I don't think we should—" she began, but was interrupted by my mom.

"She's my daughter. Give us privacy," my mom snapped.

Clearly she had a major issue with my father's new wife, even though my mom was the one who'd left him in the first place. I didn't even know when she and Estelle had met, but it was clear they had.

Estelle's worried expression stayed in my head as she went inside the house, leaving me on the porch with my mother. My heart was racing; I had so much to say to her. I had so many questions.

"This is probably a shock to you, seeing me like this. I had no idea you would be here, or that you're even on speaking terms with your father. And I didn't realize you were so close with Estelle."

"I'm not close with her."

Anger bloomed inside of my chest as I realized that her focus was on Estelle and me having a relationship with my dad, not that she missed me or was happy to see me. She hadn't even hugged me yet.

"That's what you have to say to me after all this time?" I crossed my arms in front of my chest.

She shook her head and took a step closer. I inched back without intending to, but I was shifting into fight-or-flight mode, completely on edge.

"I have so much to say to you, Kare. I have been so busy, on a journey to find myself and who I am. Without being your father's wife or a mother." She smiled as if what she was saying was the best news on earth and not devastating for me to hear. I was too stunned to speak. "After I left, I spent a lot of time alone with my thoughts. And you know what I realized? I was never meant to be a mother. Being a military wife, an officer's at that, was not for me. I spent my entire life living for you guys and not for myself. I was a shell of a woman, miserable, and had no sense of self. But now, Kare, I know exactly who I am, and it's wonderful." She was beaming, a bigger smile than I could ever recall seeing on her face.

"Wonderful?" I choked out.

She nodded as the air left my lungs. Was I supposed to be proud of her and her fucking self-discovery, which made her feel like what she'd done was right? Was it right? It seemed like it'd been the best for her, but what about me and Austin?

"Yes. I hope you have this feeling someday, Kare. Of just complete peace." She spun around at the bottom of the porch, her tunic rising up and dancing around her.

"Mom," I began.

"Please, call me Michelle," she corrected me. If heartbreak had a sound, the entire neighborhood would have heard mine.

There were no words for the pain searing through me. Shock,

ANNA TODD

torment, rejection, envy of her carelessness—it was too much. I could taste the vinegar-like bile in the back of my throat. I swallowed it down, squared my shoulders, and tried my damnedest not to collapse in front of her.

"You're totally fine with the fact that you abandoned your family without so much as a phone call or even a letter, only to come back here now and have the audacity to tell me how great your life is now that I'm not in it?"

She scoffed. Literally fucking scoffed at me, like I was the one in the wrong here.

"You sound like your father." She half laughed.

Maybe she was on drugs? Or had she really convinced herself that her perspective was okay? She seemed genuinely happy and at peace; maybe her perspective was just that, hers. Did that make it okay? I wasn't sure anymore.

"I've been traveling around the South for a while, deciding where to settle, and ironically, I started dating a soldier! Who would have thought? He's younger than me, embarrassingly so, but he's a good guy. And he's stationed here for now, but got orders for Hawaii." She tried to cover her smile with her hands, looking like a smitten schoolgirl. "I get to live in Hawaii, Kare. You know I've always loved Hawaii."

"You've never so much as mentioned Hawaii in my life, but good for you?" I pushed my hands through my hair, tugging at the roots in an attempt to ground myself.

"You're being a little judgmental."

If I was a violent person, I would have slapped her across the face right then and there.

"I am judging you. Not because you're dating someone or moving to Hawaii. I'm judging you because you basically told me that you've decided being a mother wasn't for you, like it wouldn't hurt

222

or impact me to hear that. Like I'm supposed to just smile and be happy for you? As if I hadn't spent the last six years wondering where you were, worrying about you, thinking you missed me. You haven't asked me a single question, like if I'm okay or what I've been doing since you left. You haven't even given me a hug." My emotions took over and I couldn't control my voice as it cracked, but I refused to cry even though it felt nearly impossible not to.

"I was just filling you in on my life, I thought you would be happy for me. I haven't gotten the chance to ask you anything yet," she said, manipulation covering her words.

"You've had years."

"I told you I was finding my way. You really are like your father, always focusing on the negative, always demanding."

"Stop saying that!" I screamed. "You don't even know me! You chose not to, and you show up here for what? What do you need from Dad anyway? Money? Are you on drugs?"

My mother lunged toward me but I dodged her before she could touch me. "Drugs? Don't you dare accuse me of being on drugs because you can't accept that I'm happy."

"All I've ever hoped for is that you're happy, but this entire time I had this idea in my head that you were pining for me, missing me every day, hoping that I was taken care of, but in reality you've completely erased me from your life, memory, and future. I thought you were here to, I don't know, apologize, or at least feel a little bit bad for all the pain you've caused."

"I was also in pain," she had the audacity to say.

"I was a child!"

"But you're not anymore. You should be able to understand what I went through and why I had to leave and stay gone. I did what was best for all of us."

The words clicked and I realized she was right. Her leaving was probably the best thing that had happened to me and my brother, even if it had hurt like hell and given us both different forms of trauma. I couldn't imagine how much worse it would have gotten, and she had already left us in a house that was burning. As I was about to remind her of that, an orange hatchback car pulled up in front of the house. I couldn't make out the face but there was a man behind the wheel. He called her name and she waved, smiling like we had been simply talking about the weather.

"You're right. You are not meant to be a mother and should have never been one," I told her.

"Karina, that's harsh. I don't want to leave on this note, but I have to go. Your brother has my number if you want to call me, but I assume you won't."

As pathetic as it was, I was still hoping for her to hug me, one last embrace before disappearing from my life again. But there was no embrace, no affection, no comfort. Just a narcissistic woman I had longed for when I shouldn't have.

As she got into the car she waved at me, and I tried to memorize her face one last time before I broke down, crumbling onto the hard surface of the porch, crying not for me, but for the little girl who'd created her own fantasy of a mother she never had.

I didn't hear the door open, but before I knew it Estelle was next to me, her arms wrapping around my shoulders as she hugged my shaking body. Flashes of my childhood ran through my mind; both versions of my mother were there as we danced around the living room, made beaded bracelets, braided my hair, then as she sat lifeless on the couch for days, screamed at my dad for working too much, told me stories of escaping and never coming back.

"Karina, I'm so sorry," Estelle cried, stroking my hair.

I untucked my chin and looked at her. Her eyes were blood-shot, her face blotchy and full of anguish. She felt more for me than my mother did, and that revelation made me even more emotional. I hugged her back and the porch swing rocked in the wind, bumping into my arm and scratching it. I pushed it away, suddenly disgusted by it, but it swung back and almost hit me again.

"This swing! Fuck! I never want to sit on this again," I told Estelle.

She looked at it, and back to me. "Let's take it down?"

"Really? Don't you like it?"

"I like you more. And I've always hated that fucking thing, if I'm being honest."

Estelle being the person to comfort me was not what I'd expected, but I welcomed it. I stood up, brushing my work pants off.

"How exactly do we take it down?" I wanted to smash the thing into a million pieces, but logically, I didn't know what to do unless she handed me a hammer.

We looked at one another and shared a laugh. Both of us were still wet from crying, but we stood there laughing as my father joined us. He was beyond confused as he took in the sight of two half-mad women on his porch laughing and crying at the same time.

"Honey, can you take this dreadful swing down for us?"

"Are you sure?" He looked at me, knowing how much I had always loved that thing. I nodded, never wanting to see it again.

A part of me healed as my dad got his toolbox and began to take the swing down. Estelle kept rubbing her hand along my back, a movement that I think would normally have made me uncomfortable, but it didn't. It felt nice, calming. I couldn't wrap my head around what had just happened or process the years of abandonment I had felt, only to have that feeling multiply by a thousand within the last ten minutes. My conversation with my mother had lasted less than five minutes; she couldn't even be bothered to stay longer than that. The sound of the wooden swing falling onto the porch was music to my ears.

I felt so stupid for putting so much emotional value on an object, somehow tying my mother's memory to the stupid thing. Now that it was on the ground, it looked so worn and useless. It felt like a metaphor for my life, or what I thought my life was.

CHAPTER **THIRTY-ONE**

Karina

The day after the confrontation with my mother, I walked into the hotel lobby to find Elodie already waiting for me. I was so damn tired and my entire face was swollen from not sleeping and being hysterical for hours. When I saw Elodie, I instantly felt a little better. She was dressed in a beige floor-length linen dress with a thick brown cardigan on top and white sneakers. Her hair was pulled back, and she was wearing tiny star-shaped stud earrings.

She grabbed me into a hug and squeezed me as if we hadn't seen each other in months, not days.

"Are you all right?" she asked, pulling back to look at me, then hugging me again.

"I'm fine. Are you? I should be asking you that first."

She nodded and took my hands, leading me to sit on a couch toward the back of the lobby. I had never been to this hotel before even though it was one of only a handful of decent ones around post. Elodie's family was staying here for now, and they'd gotten her a room next to theirs for as long as she needed. I hadn't met them yet, but the timing couldn't be more awful. I would have loved to meet them under different circumstances, as in, literally any other circumstance.

"It's nice staying here. Not that your house isn't my favorite, but I feel more independent, even with my parents right next door. Does that make sense?" She smiled, tucking a piece of her hair back into her ponytail.

"It makes perfect sense. How are your parents handling everything?"

"Actually, not so bad. They don't understand how no one has caught him, and they're worried he'll come find me, but they haven't forced me on an Air France flight back home. *Pas encore*, not yet."

"That's good." I offered a small smile. "Do you think they will? Want you to come back with them?"

If I were them, I would likely drag her onto the plane for her own safety. She was only a few weeks from delivering the baby, and her environment was incredibly important, now more than ever. Some parents actually gave a shit what happened to their children, what a thought.

"I'm not leaving. *Non*. I have many reasons," Elodie responded, straightening her back and looking into my eyes. "*Mon amour*, Austin, my job, and you, I don't want to leave you." She added, "Any of you.

"I don't know what the future holds for me, but I know it's not back home," she continued. "It sounds *fou*, no, crazy, Austin almost lost his life because of me, but I can't imagine mine without him now. The right thing to do would be pack up and run away, but I'm done running. We all deserve a happy ending and I want to at least try for one. So much has been taken from all of us, it's not fair."

"Fair left the conversation a long time ago," I told her, speaking to myself as well.

"I'm sorry about your mom, Karina. The reason I didn't tell you wasn't to hurt you. I hoped she would change her mind or realize that she was wrong. It doesn't make sense, she's not a good person."

There it was. I knew my mom would be brought up, but as much as I thought I was ready for it, I wasn't. It had been less than twenty-four hours since my "encounter" with her, and it still hurt so damn bad. One minute I was fine, reminding myself that nothing had changed, she'd left me once and hadn't cared, why would I expect her to now? But the next I found myself wondering what I had done so wrong at sixteen that would make her hate me enough to abandon me twice.

You remind me so much of your father. Her words played in my head, again and again. Both of my parents had unfairly punished me over their hate for one another. I had spent my entire life trying to not be like my father, only to have the one person who knew him best throw that in my face.

What made me romanticize the memories of her and who she was? Was it loneliness, or my own way of rationalizing her choice to leave us? I didn't want to consider the idea that I wasn't enough for her to want to be a part of our family. She'd made it clear that she had no remorse and felt like she'd done the right thing. I desperately wanted to find compassion for her instead of anger, but after yesterday, all I felt was disgust and shame. Some people weren't meant to be parents. Some people shouldn't have kids.

"I'm not upset with you for not telling me. It's not your responsibility, and it's no one's fault but hers." *And mine.*

"I wish we knew the reason. My *bébé* isn't here yet, and I can't imagine doing that. She's not a mother," Elodie hissed. "Not a mother at all."

"I'm sort of learning that there's not always a reason for everything. People are who they are and we can't love them out of it. Why didn't my mom want to have a relationship with me? What about me wasn't as good as my brother? I'll never know, but at least now I know that I don't need to waste any more time guessing what kind of person she is or making excuses for her."

Elodie rubbed my hair and I leaned against her, not able to put my head on her lap anymore because of how big the baby had gotten.

"*Je promets*, I promise, your life is better without having to guess about her," she told me, doing her best to comfort me. "You're too good for all of us. Too understanding, but that's why I love you. I'm so sorry that it ended up this way, Karina. I really am."

"Thank you, Elodie. Can we change the subject?" I asked her, not sure I could handle talking about my mom anymore. I was grateful to have at least one person I could depend on, but if I kept talking about my mom, my brain would explode. I had gone round and round in my own head since it happened and was near my breaking point. I stared at the painted ceiling.

"Sure." Elodie smiled. "I took my parents to Waffle House, and they loved it." She grinned. "My mom was scared at first, but they went back twice already."

This made us both laugh. Nothing like a good Waffle House meal to welcome them to the States.

"Are they staying long?" I asked.

"Not sure. I think they're scared to leave because Phillip is out there somewhere. But according to Toni, he's been put into a treatment facility. Even though we're technically married, they won't tell me anything, so I don't know if it's true."

"Are you afraid?" I asked, my voice barely above the sound of the lobby music.

"A little bit. But there is not anything I can do, so I will just live my life and hope things turn out well for me, for all of us."

"I wish I could think like that. Every time I hear a noise when

I'm home alone I think it's him looking for you. I tried to work yesterday and couldn't catch my breath every time the bell on the door went off. I always thought I was equipped to handle trauma, but I'm not. I gave myself too much credit without the experience, and it shows."

"You can't measure how strong you are based on how you handle trauma, that's not fair or reasonable."

"I would tell you the same thing, but unfortunately, that's how my brain works. This week has been such a tale of how well I can handle things and it's made me realize how weak I am, even though I've spent my entire life thinking I'm not."

Elodie looked at me, sighing but not trying to talk me out of my idea. She knew it was no use. Instead she changed the subject again and we both pretended like life hadn't drastically changed for both of us.

CHAPTER **THIRTY-TWO**

Karina

Kael was waiting for me in the lobby at work when I got there. I had been ignoring his calls, so I couldn't say I was surprised. I wasn't sure what to say to him now that he had lied to me again. Hiding things from me was lying any way I looked at it, and I was so fucking tired of everyone around me acting like I couldn't handle the truth. Even if I couldn't, it wasn't their choice to make for me. Kael had known my mom was back, had known she had no interest in seeing me, had known about my father's health failing, and he'd kept it all from me. If this was the first time he had done something like that, I may have forgiven him, but not again.

No matter how much I loved him, I was too tired to continue on this hamster wheel chasing something that I would never be able to be sure was real. Not only could I not trust him, he had done it all under the guise of knowing what was best for me, and if he'd truly known what was best for me, he would have understood that I'd needed some kind of warning and time to process. I was so damn tired of being surprised and having one thing after another pop up and turn my already barely manageable life upside down.

"How can I help you?" I asked him, plugging in the vacuum.

We were opening in less than five minutes, and I still needed to vacuum and wipe down the counters in the lobby. I was working even harder to show Mali that I deserved the promotion she was offering. There were no clients scheduled for the first thirty minutes, so I had time to clean up a bit.

"You haven't taken any of my calls. I was worried last night but knew you were with your dad and Estelle . . . and your mom," he said as I turned the vacuum on.

It was much easier to act like I couldn't care less what he had to say. I would deal with my emotions later, but being cold was the only way to keep myself somewhat sane. The rejection from my mom for the second time and the fact that everyone knew except me, it was a pattern in my life that I was not willing to keep.

"I've been trying to decide what to say," I admitted, putting all my willpower into keeping a neutral face and tone.

I ran the vacuum over the small space and of course, he waited until I was done to speak.

"Karina, I'm sorry. I know you're probably tired of hearing me say that, but I am truly sorry."

I didn't look at him as I wrapped the cord around the holder. "You're right, I am tired of hearing you say that."

He stepped toward me, his feet directly in line with the spot on the floor I was staring at to keep myself from looking at him.

"I thought I was doing the right thing. I didn't want you to get hurt."

I made a dramatic noise, anger growing in my veins. "Yeah? And how did that work out? How does it always work out when you hide shit from me?"

He dropped his head. "Not well."

"You keep lying to me, since I met you, and I keep taking it. Every single time. I'm tired of expecting the best from you only to be let down. You're supposed to be the one person I can trust in this world, yet you have lied to me more than anyone, my dad included."

"I know it sounds like an excuse, but every choice I made was to protect you. I always had your best interest at heart, Karina. I would do anything for you. You have to know that. I was just waiting for the right time."

"You—or anyone else for that matter—don't get to decide what's right for me, Kael. It always ends up hurting more in the end anyway. Didn't you learn that the first time? Or the second? How many times has it been now? My father, my mother, is there anything that you've actually been honest about since we met?"

"That I love you."

My heart pounded, my pulse screaming behind my ears.

"You have a funny way of showing your love for me. You always tell me how strong and capable I am but you keep taking the power of choice from me. That's not love, that's manipulation."

He stepped closer to me, desperation on his gorgeous, traitorous face.

"I'm sorry. It's in my nature to take on everything, and with you it's nearly impossible to just allow things to hurt you. I can't bear it. I will try if you forgive me, but please try to understand my perspective and how difficult it is to untrain my brain of my way of thinking."

I let out a dramatic scoff. "Your perspective? You can't expect me to put your perspective before my own, Kael. I get that you're brainwashed by the Army to just take tragedy and silence your own trauma, to not have an emotional tie, analyze it, and come up with a solution, but out here in the real world, it's not like that."

I didn't mean to hurt him with my words, but I couldn't sugarcoat my feelings anymore. The fact that I knew he was a good person made this harder, and it was easier if I tried to be like him, emotionless and analytical. I had been rejected by my mother and that absolutely killed me, neglected by my dying father, and lied to by the man I loved. Again. When I listed it out, it was nearly unbearable, and there was no solution. I couldn't force my mother to want anything to do with me, I couldn't wish my father's body back to health, and I couldn't pray for Kael to stop being Kael. Knowing that his intention was to protect me made it worse because it made me feel helpless, spineless, and codependent, the three worst things to me. I held my independence to a high, high stature and losing it, even to love, was not something I was willing to do.

"I can't live with you handling all of this on your own. Let me be here for you." Kael interrupted my internal battle.

"And I can't live depending on anyone else being here for me. I need to deal with all of this on my own. There is way too much going on in my life to have to worry about my heart and not my head. It's easier to be alone. I want to be alone. I *have* to be alone, Kael."

"I'll give up Atlanta for you, Karina. I'll sell the house and stay here. I've already contacted a Realtor. I'll give up whatever I need to, I'll do whatever you need me to. Please—"

"Kael." I swallowed the pain as I spoke. "That's the thing, I don't want you to give up anything. I can't live with myself if I hold you back either. We shouldn't have to sacrifice our entire lives and identities to be together. No one should."

"Love is sacrifice, Karina."

I shook my head, refusing to allow my fate, or Kael's, to be like everyone's around us. "No. Not to me."

The front door opened, and the bell dinged. I was surprised to see Toni standing there. She looked tired but smiled at us, clearly not able to read the room. Kael stood as still as a statue; I wasn't sure he was even breathing as Toni spoke. What awful timing.

"I tried to call but got voicemail. Any chance you have time for a thirty-minute walk-in? My back is killing me from yard work and cleaning up the house for the move," she explained, her hands at her chest in a prayer gesture.

"Move?" I repeated.

"We got orders for Texas, didn't Martin or Elodie tell you?"

I glared at Kael. "No, Martin didn't tell me."

Add it to the fucking list.

"When do you go?" I asked her.

"In about two and a half weeks. Right before Fischer ships off. I guess all of us are leaving," she said, a hint of sadness in her voice.

"Wow." I wouldn't say I was Toni's biggest fan by any means, but I was a little sad that everyone around us seemed to be getting shipped somewhere else.

One day soon it would be just me here. The thought was chilling, but I had made my mind up.

"I've got time. Can you just write your name on the sign-in sheet while I put this away?" I gestured to the vacuum and looked at Kael. "I have to work now, so you should go," I told him, low enough that Toni wouldn't hear me. The last thing I needed was to be the topic of gossip at her last few FRG meetings.

He looked between Toni and me, clearly deciding whether to go or not. But in the end, he gave up, throwing his arms in the air in defeat and frustration. I knew the conversation wasn't over, but at least it would be stalled so I could gain some strength before we continued.

"Are you two okay? He seemed a little tense," Toni told me as we walked back to my therapy room. "Well, he's always tense, but it felt like even more than usual."

I almost laughed at her instinct to pick up on anyone and everyone's business, but kept my mouth shut and just told her that we were fine. During her treatment she did not stop talking, not even for a second. She told me how stressed she was, how she didn't know a soul in Texas, and that all her friends were here. She was worried about fitting in with the new group of wives in Tharpe's new platoon. That was particularly ironic given the fact that she had been so hard on Elodie at first.

She also told me that she had heard about my dad being the one responsible for catching Phillips and how grateful she was that he was off the street and no longer a threat to any of us. She told me that Lawson would be taking Kael's place in the platoon now that his discharge was final. She talked and talked and talked, but I found it soothing since I didn't have to think or speak about anything going on in my life. It was a nice distraction provided by an unlikely person.

Her session went quickly, as most half hours do. She paid and tipped me. I didn't know whether the tip or the random hug she gave me surprised me more. After she left, my day was fully booked, and I stayed late to clean the old poster glue off the wall in the lobby. I had already had new signage printed, and even though Mali had told me not to remodel, I knew once she saw it she would be happy I had. It was nearly ten at night when I finally ran out of stuff to do at the spa. I couldn't think of another reason to keep me from going home, so I took a deep breath, locked the door, and walked home as slowly as I possibly could. Bradley was sitting on his couch with his blinds and curtains wide-open. He was watching some action movie that I didn't know the name of, but I recognized Tom Cruise flying around the screen on a motorcycle, which did not help narrow down the possibilities since there were at least ten of those films.

Kael's truck was parked in front of my house, no surprise to me. I braced myself again, repeating all the reasons I had to be livid with him, to finally distance myself from him. It was easier when he wasn't in front of me, and I knew that. I wished I could go back in time to that first time he came into my work to meet Elodie and just tell him she wasn't around instead of taking him as a client. If I would have turned him away, none of this would have happened and I could have gone on with my already miserable life without adding having my heart shattered on top of it. I'd thought I'd known what heartbreak was, but looking back on my life, I had never been in real love until Kael. The first time he broke my trust was painful, but having opened up to him again only to be betrayed again was something else, something I had never felt before and never wanted to feel again. I had to protect myself above all.

Even if I didn't mean it, I wished to myself that I would have this same revelation someday when I met someone else. I couldn't stomach the idea of even speaking to another man, but there would have to be a time in my future when I wouldn't be in so much pain, wouldn't there? But was being alone so bad? I'd done it before, I could do it again.

I took one last deep breath and opened the front door. Kael was standing in the center of my living room, his hands behind his back. He was wearing the same outfit, matching navy sweatpants and sweatshirt, as earlier, likely meaning that he had spent the entire day in my house waiting for me. I wanted to slap myself when the thought made me feel mushy and cared for. How quickly my mind took his side pissed me off.

"You didn't have to wait here all day," I told him, hanging my keys up on the holder as I slid my shoes off.

"I wanted to."

"What do you want to say, Kael? You're sorry? I've heard it before, and I really don't want to hear it again. I don't want to argue with you, and I think both of us could use some space." The reserve was clear in my voice, and his eyes told me that he could feel it too.

"I don't want space. Not from you."

"Then what is it you want exactly?"

He reached for one of my hands and caught me off guard. I didn't have time to pull away.

"I want to be by your side until your hair is silver, until our backs hurt and our joints ache. I want to stay next to you as we make something of our names, struggling then succeeding, and until our memories fade. That's what I want. And I know you do too. I don't understand why you're fighting against yourself so hard."

Using every single tiny ounce of energy I had, I blocked his words from entering my chest. Once they settled in there, I would be a goner. I would forgive him and wrap my arms around him and lose my sense of self in him, again, and I couldn't allow that to happen. Everything from my mother's hatred for me to my brother's aloofness and my father's coldness reminded me that I could only depend on myself. Maybe Kael was used to having a platoon, an incredible mother, and a group of friends by his side, but I wasn't. I had never known what it felt like to know that if I fell someone would be there to catch me, or at minimum help me up.

"There's nothing left here for you, Karina. Your father might not be around long, your mother left again, your brother is leaving in a few weeks. Come with me and let's start over, please."

"I have memories here, Kael. I have a life here. I have a job and my house and Elodie."

"Elodie is going to move to wherever your brother gets stationed," he harshly reminded me. I knew that, but there was a small chance he would be stationed here.

"Estelle will be here, and eventually she will be alone."

"And? You can barely stand her." He was onto my excuses, but I kept them straight.

"We've been getting along." I defended myself by a thread. "For better or worse, she's my family."

I had grown closer to Estelle in the last two weeks than I ever imagined possible. She wasn't my only reason for wanting to stay here, but she honestly was one of them. At the bottom of the list, sure, but still on it. I wasn't even sure what the hell else was on my list, but I was so damn afraid of feeling trapped, giving up the only things that make me *me*, like my house, my job, all for a man who continued to hide things, very fucking important things, from me, and an uncertain life.

"I can't pack up and follow you to Atlanta. And a few hours ago you said you were ready to give up that dream."

"And the offer still stands, but what the hell can you do here that you can't do there?"

"A lot . . . nothing? I don't know!"

"Can you please think of yourself for once? Every choice you make is based on someone else's feelings or well-being and never your own! It's always about your brother, Elodie, your father, even the damn neighbor. Everyone except you and your happiness." He raised his voice, clearly exasperated.

I took a step toward him; my living room felt like it was shrinking.

"That's exactly what I'm doing, Kael. Thinking of myself. I told you from the moment I met you that I was never going to be a woman who follows a man to another city, abandoning her life and her goals for his. I can't do it."

"And what exactly are your goals?" His voice turned dark, defensive.

"Don't you dare act like I don't have any goals. Just because my dreams are smaller and less lucrative than yours doesn't make them irrelevant. I want a quiet life, Kael. One where I don't have to worry whether I can believe the person I'm sharing it with. I want to be alone. That's all I want."

He scoffed. I knew his emotions were getting the best of him, and it wasn't like him to be ruled by his anger more than logic, but that made two of us.

"A quiet life? Like being in constant danger and constant hustle? Always chasing something that you don't even know you truly want? Is that the kind of life you want, falling apart? Like your house for example?" He pointed to the crack in my ceiling that had been growing as the weeks passed.

I threw my hands in the air. How fucking dare he. If he wanted to be harsh, I could be fucking harsh. My sadness was drowned by my anger.

"And what? You're going to keep me safe, Kael? Before I met you I was never in any danger, I had never had my trust betrayed in the worst way, and I had never, ever questioned my own sanity while being gaslit by a liar who claimed to hide shit from me to 'protect' me!" I used air quotes for the word *protect* to emphasize my point.

He stared at me, eyes full of fire.

"Go ahead, what's your next excuse? If you were serious about having a future with me from the beginning, you would have consulted with me about Atlanta in the first place instead of buying a place there and hiding it. Now you think because you waited until the last minute that I'm going to jump when you say jump? And don't talk about my house like that. I work my ass off to have this house, and you know what it means to me. And my father is slowly decaying? So what, I should just leave before he dies and pretend he doesn't exist, like you do yours?"

I knew I had gone too far, but so had he. We were both taking our anger out on one another and neither of us seemed to be able to stop. This was for the best anyway; he should hate me and leave me too. If he longed for me after we split he would be even more miserable, and even if it didn't seem like it at the moment, I didn't want that for him.

He looked at me like I was a stranger he had never met, never touched, never claimed to love.

"Wow. My father? You're bringing up my fucking father right now?"

I'd been shocked into silence by my own words. I waited for him to say something else as both of us paced around my living room, but he didn't. He grabbed his key chain from the table and slammed the front door on his way out. I was still catching my breath as his truck roared to life and he drove off.

An hour later my temper had calmed, and I already missed him. I didn't feel the closure or the ultimate ending that I'd expected to feel. I felt like complete shit for bringing up his father to purposely hurt him. I stared at my ceiling fan and felt my body sink lower and lower into my mattress, digging my fingernails into my palms until the tears stopped coming.

I texted him an apology but never heard back. I had finally managed to push away the only man in my life who had ever loved me. The real me. I felt accomplished and defeated at the same time. A devastating and shameful mosaic of my parents.

CHAPTER **THIRTY-THREE**

Karina

When I arrived at the Mendozas', I was stuffed full of nerves.

How would things go?

It felt so ridiculous to celebrate Halloween with everything that had happened just a couple of weeks ago. I had practically gone into hiding the last few weeks, only working, sleeping, working, sleeping. I missed the feeling of being surrounded by this group, the first time I had ever found my people. In reality they were Kael's people, but I was grateful they'd still invited me.

The yard was decorated with fake skulls and headstones and cotton spiderwebs. I briefly thought of my mom, but fuck her. She didn't get to represent Halloween anymore. She was probably having the time of her life—childless, no responsibilities, living her life with her new boyfriend, pretending I didn't exist—so I should try my best to do the same. My Uber driver wished me a good night as I adjusted my dress and glanced at my reflection in the window one more time before I climbed out of the car. My face was painted red with black circles around my eyes and thin gray lines across my face from my forehead to my chin. I was a demon, but not a cute one—an angry one. The face paint had definitely looked better in my head, and Pinterest hadn't been as much help as I'd hoped, but there I was, red face and all, walking up their sidewalk.

The music wasn't as loud as I thought it would be. Drake played through the windows, and I tried my best to stand up straight as I knocked on the door. I could have rung the bell, but that kind of attention seemed overstimulating to say the least.

"Who's knocking? Come the hell in!" Mendoza's voice sounded through the door.

I turned the knob, wondering if they actually wanted me there or if I was making a fool of myself by showing up, but it was too late. I was already in the living room. I spotted Gloria first, dressed as a witch, the sexiest one I had ever seen. The slit on her black dress went all the way up her thigh to show her exposed hip. Her mesh stockings left little to the imagination and she was wearing at least five-inch heels. Black-and-silver eyeliner feathered out like wings traced around her oval eyes.

"Karina, baby!" she cooed, rushing toward me with a clear cup full of red liquid.

The interior of the house was decorated too; red, orange, and black balloons touched the ceiling and there were carved pump-kins everywhere. Some of them were colorful and some plain.

"Wow, you look awesome!" I told her. The tension I thought would exist between us was nowhere to be found as she wrapped her arms around me.

"Thank you. I was supposed to be Morticia but the kids fought me too much to match, and with everything going on, I said fuck it and morphed into a sexy witch instead." She rolled her eyes. "You look scary as hell by the way." She laughed, her high ponytail whip-ping around us.

"I think I went a little too far," I admitted, a little embarrassed as I looked around the room to see that every woman there was dressed in some version of sexy.

She touched the fabric of my black floor-length gown and shook her head.

"You look great. Plus, if I see one more fucking sexy nurse, I'm going to gouge my eyeballs out."

"You made it. Happy Halloween, almost Thanksgiving." Mendoza rolled near me in his wheelchair.

I would never get used to the guilt I felt knowing he would likely be confined to that chair for the rest of his life, but there was nothing I could do to change that. *Confined* wasn't the right word, and I had no way of knowing how Mendoza felt, but I knew how privileged I was even to have the thought. I would make sure I found the right way to discuss this so I was as educated as I could be and not hurt anyone unintentionally with my words.

He looked lively, from the flush in his cheeks to his wide smile. He was wearing a white T-shirt with big green eyeballs on it. It took me a second to realize what his costume was. A brown fabric square was draped over his chair. White teeth were glued to the front. A plastic hook was attached to the back.

"I'm Mater," he said in a fake Southern accent. "From *Cars*, you know?"

"Oh my god." I didn't know how to react.

I wanted to laugh but felt horrible doing so. It was so creative, and the more I looked at it, I could tell that Gloria had spent a lot of time making it. I was sure the kids loved it.

"What? It's fucking perfect." He honked the makeshift horn on his costume, and I covered my mouth.

"It really is," I agreed, letting myself laugh with him.

"I made it myself. It ruined our family costume, but this is pretty good, right?" Gloria asked, hooking her arm around her husband.

She kissed his cheek, and he stuck his tongue out to lick her lips as she pulled away.

She playfully swatted at him and he grabbed her wrist, bringing it to his mouth, gently biting her skin. I looked away, my cheeks warm. Despite how lonely I was and would continue to be, I didn't feel even a ping of jealousy around them. Over time I would come to terms with the fact that I wasn't as lovable as I desperately wanted to be. What a monumental realization to have at such a young age. I knew if I said it aloud whoever was listening would roll their eyes, tell me I had my whole life ahead of me, and promise that someday I would find my true love. What if that wasn't what I wanted? Was the taste of being loved addictive? Sure, but the pain that came with it didn't feel worth it to me anymore, and I couldn't imagine spending my entire life trying to prove to myself and someone else that I was capable of being loved and hoping that they didn't betray me. Not every story is a fairy tale, not every person has their person. Speaking of pain, there he was.

Kael was sitting on the edge of the couch, staring straight ahead. He wasn't in a costume, which didn't surprise me in the least. Dressed in a beige Henley, light-wash jeans, and his usual stark-white sneakers, he hadn't seemed to notice me arrive, not that he should, but of course I wished he would have. Together or not, we were supposed to be soul mates. His body was supposed to know when I was around, his skin was supposed to crackle, missing my touch, and his heart was supposed to ache knowing that he would never touch me again.

All that being said, he stared at the wall like he couldn't have cared less who came and went, even me. It was childish and narcissistic to care or expect anything from him, but I couldn't help it. Even in death, I would wish for him to notice me.

It had been a little over two weeks since I saw him last. Halloween had come and gone, too, but since Mendoza was still recovering, we'd all agreed to wait and celebrate the holiday together. No one had been expecting Kael and me to break up, again, but neither of us would ever cause a scene, not under these circumstances. I couldn't stop staring at him, waiting for him to look up at me. What did I want him to do when he looked at me? I didn't have a clue, but I needed him to. Momentarily I forgot that I was painted red and couldn't find anyone else in the room dressed in a scary costume. I felt like Lindsay Lohan's character in *Mean Girls* when she shows up at the costume party and everyone is dressed as Playboy Bunnies and sexy versions of everything under the sun.

Kael took a drink of his beer and finally lifted his eyes. Confusion flashed across his face as he took me in, then a bit of humor lifted the corner of his mouth. He nodded to me like we were old pals, not lovers, and I couldn't decide if that was what I wanted or not. I'd been the one to initiate the breakup, and I knew I'd done the right thing, but it hadn't been long enough for me to be capable of pretending I was over it. I would love him for the rest of my life, that was evident. Our book was nearly closed, and as a romance lover, I hated third-act breakups, but unfortunately for me, I was living one.

I nodded back, lifting my drink cup to him. He did the same with his beer bottle and went back to staring ahead. Even though that was what I'd asked for, it felt fucking awful. My brother's voice interrupted my pity party as he and Elodie came through the front door and into the living room. Elodie was dressed as a mouse, wearing a light-blue onesie and big floppy mouse ears. Her face was painted, the tip of her nose pink, and white whiskers splayed across her cheeks. She looked freaking adorable, all belly and costume. My brother was dressed as a chef, and it clicked. They were dressed as Remy and Alfredo from *Ratatouille*.

Elodie rushed to me to hug and double-kiss me. "What a cute idea. And what a hard launch as a couple! Couple costumes and all?" I smiled at her. It felt good to see her smiling.

"We thought we may as well, everyone on this whole post has heard about us anyway." She winced but seemed to be handling it pretty well, considering.

Austin hugged me, lifting me off my feet. I swatted at his arms, embarrassed and feeling Kael's eyes on me again.

"You look fucked up." My brother laughed. "In a scary way." He bent down to assess my face paint, smiling from ear to ear.

"Oh, fuck off. It's a Halloween party, not Disneyland," I teased him back.

Something about his energy had changed. I had no idea what it was, but something was different. More mature, calmer? He and Elodie had been staying in the free side of Kael's place for the last week, so my house felt extra-empty. My brother was leaving in a few days and as much as I still didn't love the idea, it had grown on me now that he would need to have a steady income, health insurance, all the adult things he had never cared about having before Elodie. I hated to admit it, but I was grateful that Kael had pushed him to join the Army. Even the silent confession pissed me off. I stared daggers at Kael, and of course he looked over at me at that exact moment. I looked away quickly, and excused myself from my brother and Elodie, telling them I had to pee.

I found my way to the bathroom and locked the door behind me. The breath of relief that fell out of me felt like a lifetime of anxiety being released from my body. I leaned against the sturdy doorframe, reminding myself of a breathing technique I'd seen on Instagram. I closed my eyes and thought, *I breathe in, I breathe out,* until my breath steadied and I could feel my feet grounding into the tile floor.

The sound of the party outside quieted and my heart rate slowed. If I hadn't met Kael and he was simply another stranger here, everything would be fine. Still, if I hadn't met him, I wouldn't know anyone here, and I wouldn't have a friendship with Gloria. I also wouldn't know what it felt like to feel so deeply understood by another person. There was a silver lining after all, even though it fucking hurt to see him acting so casually. Seeing him at all would hurt anyway, but him acting like a stranger was too much. What if someone hit on him? What if one of the sexy nurses or the blond dressed as a hot version of Alice in Wonderland approached him? The thought made me sick.

I gathered myself enough to move away from the door and look in the mirror. My own reflection scared the crap out of me, black and red and utterly freaking ridiculous. I laughed, full-on Joker style. I washed my hands and opened the bathroom door, jumping out of my skin at the sight of Kael towering over me.

"Oh my god!" My hand flew toward him but I stopped before it hit his chest. "You scared the shit out of me."

"Sorry." He lazily moved his shoulders up and down.

"What are you doing here?"

"Here as in the party, or the bathroom?"

Of course he would play semantics with me. "Bathroom."

"I was planning on using it for its intended purposes." He glanced behind me, nodding to the toilet.

How embarrassing. My ego deflated immediately, and my eyes went down to the floor.

"Oh, sorry, I—"

His fingers were warm as he gently held my chin, tilting my face up to look at him. The touch nearly set my body on fire. It was devastating and soothing. *Kill me.*

"I wanted to make sure you're okay. I saw you come in here, and you were in there a while. I was worried about you."

249

I sighed, shaking my head a little to release his grip. "I'm fine. Overwhelmed by the party and people." *And you.*

"I like your costume," he said calmly.

I was about to thank him when I caught myself smiling like an idiot. "What are we doing? Acting like we're friends or like we don't know each other? I can't do both."

He looked around us, confused for half a second before he went back to neutral.

"I don't know. I have to leave that up to you. I told you what I want but I assume you haven't changed your mind?"

"No. I haven't."

"My ma said you called her."

I snapped my head up. "Yeah, she told me I could call her whenever, so I did."

"I wasn't telling you not to. If anything, I'm glad you did."

"Did she tell you what we talked about?" I asked, my gut telling me she would never, but my mind needed the verbal confirmation.

"No. And even if I asked, she would never tell me, so please don't worry about that."

I didn't know what to make of the way I felt. Being there, standing in the hallway of a party with Kael, was way more calming than roaming around, being forced to be social, but it was incredibly selfish of me to use his presence while keeping him at a distance emotionally.

I wanted so desperately to hug him, to take his hand and run away from our past, the pain we'd caused each other, the lies, but I couldn't. I had to absorb the deep sting of longing inside of me and swallow it down. I wasn't meant to be with anyone, and that felt abundantly clear.

"I'm leaving in a few days. I wanted to make sure I was the one who told you." He caught me by surprise.

I'd known this time was coming but hearing it out loud still wrecked me. I nodded, internally screaming but managing to keep my face straight. "Thanks for telling me. I'm relieved I don't have to find out another way." I stared past him when I said it.

I wasn't trying to rehash anything, but it was true. I would have been much more devastated if I would have heard it through the grapevine, or if he would have just disappeared without a warning.

"I'll come back to see your brother off, if you're okay with that. I don't want to cross your boundaries, but I would love to be there when he leaves for San Antonio for basic."

Kael was leaving, my brother was leaving, my mother had reappeared and left again. I tried to come to terms with the fact that I was going to be alone again, without Elodie, maybe soon without even my dad.

"Of course you can be there. I'm not going to keep you away from him. I wouldn't do that."

Kael nodded and took a small sip of his beer. The music got louder, and the group was obviously getting more intoxicated as the minutes passed. I spotted Elodie and my brother out of the corner of my eye and Kael followed my attention to them.

"I'll let you get back to the party," I said to Kael, not knowing what else to say to him. I hated how awkward it felt, but also hated the idea of never seeing him again.

"I don't want to get back to the party."

"Me neither, but I don't know what to say to you. It's like I'm walking on pins and needles and you must feel the same way. I know you're sorry, and I accept that, but I don't want to tempt myself or confuse you, so I need to go. This isn't fair to you, either, that I'm clinging to you here when you should be enjoying your limited time with your friends," I rambled away to him like I always did. I didn't know if I could turn it off once I began, but I was relieved to find that I could still be honest with him.

"There's no one else I would rather spend time with than you, Karina. Not here in this house, not in this state, not on this fucking planet."

His words whittled away at the tiny bit of composure I had left. I forced myself to go through the list of reasons why we couldn't be together, why I couldn't let his words change my mind, then walked away from him, without a word, without a glance, and kept walking until I found myself at the end of the block, calling an Uber to take me home.

CHAPTER **THIRTY-FOUR**

Kael

The day had come for Fischer to leave, and to say I was proud would be an understatement.

Was I also worried? Hell, yes.

Was I anxious? Absolutely.

But most of all, I was relieved that he would have a steady paycheck and a source of stability. When I pulled up to Karina's, Elodie, Fischer, and Karina were in the front yard. The sight of Karina standing there nearly broke the composure I'd convinced myself I could maintain throughout the day, and I hadn't even gotten out of my truck yet. It hadn't been long since I last saw her at Mendoza's, but each day felt like a year.

I tried my best to understand where she was coming from, and recognized that I sure as hell didn't handle things the way I should have with her, but I hated that she was so cut-and-dried about it. It was my fault for underestimating her ability to handle the chaos unfolding among her family, but I loved her and wished she wouldn't have completely ended things. I respected her enough to follow her rules but that didn't mean it didn't drive me fucking crazy every time I thought about her. Settling into my life in Atlanta had technically gone smoothly, but there was something missing. Karina. I tried to keep myself as busy as possible by start-ing the demo on my house the second I moved in, but nothing quite worked to keep her off my mind.

"Martin!" Fischer's voice broke my train of thought.

I turned my ignition off and climbed out of my truck. Karina's stare burned into me as I approached, and I tried not to focus on the tight black jeans and turtleneck that were practically poured over her body, clinging to the curve of her waist and accentuating her breasts and thick thighs. God help me, she looked stunning. She always did, but I could tell she'd spent extra time blow-dry-ing her hair, lining her eyes, and blushing her cheeks. She had to be as on edge as I was—probably more so, considering it was her brother leaving, after all.

The day she found out he'd enlisted felt like a lifetime ago. That had been the first crack in the trust I had tried to build with her, but looking back, I can honestly say I would do it again without a second thought.

"Can you believe I'm going? I'll be Private Fischer as of tonight. It's wild, right?" Fischer said to me in a tone that reminded me of a child seeking praise from their parent. I patted his shoulder, pulling him toward me.

"You've come a long way, Private Fischer," I told him, struggling to not look at Karina.

It was impossible, though, and when I did, I found her already looking at me. She looked happy, as happy as she could be given the fact that she was so against her brother enlisting. I gave her a weak smile and she looked away, turning to Elodie, whose face was soaked with tears.

"I'm happy. It's . . . I'll miss him, you know?" Elodie said, break-ing into a full-on sob.

She had been through hell filing for divorce from Phillips,

and she was only a few weeks away from reaching the mandatory thirty-day waiting period that Georgia law enforced. Phillips had gotten some fucking sense and wasn't contesting the divorce filing. Elodie's visa status was up in the air, but I wasn't worried about it, considering I knew her and Fischer were going to get married the moment they were legally allowed to. They hadn't said it, but it was beyond obvious that they couldn't be apart. We were all hoping that Elodie wouldn't have the baby until he was out of basic training, but the timeline was tight.

"You're on Karina duty until I'm back, remember?" Fischer wrapped his arms around Elodie from behind, kissing her cheek. "Making sure she's eating and leaving the house, not just crying on the—" He shut up when Karina's elbow landed in his ribs.

"Sorry." He winced, realizing that I was the cause of her misery.

"Anyway, Dad has been texting me all day. I know it's annoying to do the rounds, but you should see him before you go," Karina told him.

"Can't he come here?" Fischer whined, and Karina rolled her eyes.

"You better come back more mature. You'll have a baby to raise," she scolded him.

Her hair was blond again, a warm tone at the top fading into a lighter blond near her ends.

"Let's take some pictures to remember today," Elodie said through her tears, pulling her phone from her pocket and holding it up. "Come here, Martin."

I stood next to Fischer and he draped his arm over my shoulder, smiling as Elodie took photo after photo. She gave us a few different commands of different poses before she had Karina join in. Fischer clearly didn't get the memo because he stood on the side of his sister, forcing her to be between us.

"Closer, please." Elodie shooed me with her hand in the air. I stepped closer to Karina, so close that I could smell her shampoo.

God, I missed her so much. Now that I was physically near her, I longed for her so much more. It was excruciating.

After we posed and posed, Elodie stepped in, and I stepped out. I took as many photos as I could before Fischer had to leave. I reached into my pocket and pulled out a note I'd written him and shoved it into his hand, warning him not to read it until he was on the plane.

"What is this? Martin, you romantic, you didn't have to write me a love letter," he teased, batting his lashes at me.

"Shut the hell up." I laughed with him. "It's not much, so don't get your hopes up," I told him as he hugged me.

I didn't want to make a sappy speech in front of Karina or an already distraught Elodie, so I'd written down my thoughts for him, to express how proud I was of him and how much his life was going to change.

Karina was staring at me, expecting more information, I assumed, or maybe she was surprised by the gesture, but she didn't say anything as she hugged her brother goodbye. A few tears escaped her eyes as he got into Elodie's car and they drove away. We stood in silence for a few minutes, her sniffles coming less and less frequently. I didn't want to leave, and I knew she would tell me to, so I stood as quietly as I could. Eventually she turned to me, and I held my breath, having no fucking clue what she was going to say.

"Thank you," she breathed out, her eyes soft and wet.

The words confused me, but right as I began to ask her what she meant, she continued, "Thank you for helping my brother. I hated you at the time, but enlisting really was what's best for him and I see that now. So thank you, Kael. I know you love and care about him like family."

I broke eye contact with her; the intensity of it was too much for me. "I did what I could, he's the one you should thank for having the strength to save himself."

I thought back to the boy I'd met, the one with bloodshot eyes and slurred words. The one who continuously got himself into shitty situations and made really dumb choices again and again but who had a heart of gold. That heart was what had gotten him where he was now and would continue to lead him through his life. With the war calming, he likely wouldn't be deployed, until the next one at least, which gave me some peace.

"Still, you helped him, even though you knew the consequences. Just take the compliment, will you?"

The corners of her mouth turned up into a half smile and I couldn't stop myself from wiping my thumb under her eyes. She sighed but didn't stop me.

"You know I hate compliments," I said, brushing away the little flakes of black mascara that had landed on the tops of her cheeks.

A small laugh fell from her lips. "Yeah, I know."

"I miss you," I told her, not caring if she told me to go to hell.

Her eyes opened and she narrowed them at me. "Don't," she protested.

"I can't help it. I'm not going to say anything else, but I miss you and my life is miserable without you," I confessed, knowing it wouldn't change anything but needing her to hear it anyway.

"Kael," she groaned, exhaustion and pain filling her beautiful face. "I'm trying so hard to focus on myself, my new promotion, and keeping a tiny bit of sanity. I got a new therapist, I've even been hanging out with Estelle of all people, so please, don't make me waver. Not yet."

The end of her sentence gave me the tiniest bit of hope. I would wait however long she needed me to. I would wait until my last day on this earth if it meant she would have me again.

"Are you saying you're capable of wavering?" I asked her. Before she could cuss me out, I added, "Not now, but someday?"

Quietly, she stared into the cloudy sky above us. "Maybe," she told me, breaking into a smile.

TWO YEARS LATER

Karina

The wind whips around the coffee shop each time the old wooden door creaks open. It's unusually cold for September and I'm pretty sure it's some kind of punishment from the universe for agreeing to meet up with him today of all days. What was I thinking?

I'd barely had time to put makeup on the swollen pockets under my eyes. I'd held two freezing ice cubes to my face and moved around my kitchen while they dripped down my cheeks, melting quickly. It was humid in my house and the smell of cool Georgia rain filled the place, not that it took much. And this outfit I'm wearing? A simple fall ensemble that took me an hour of digging around my drawers and my closet—with a mini fashion show in front of my bedroom mirror—to decide on the same thing I usually wore to anything formal: an all-black outfit, pants with a crease that looked very grown-up and like I'd tried, even though I felt like wearing sweatpants. To go with them I put on a thick black turtleneck and only discovered an annoying drop of toothpaste on it as I was driving, which I turned into a big spot by rubbing it with water and a paper towel. After so much effort, I look like shit. Complete shit.

Sitting here, my head aches, but I'm not sure I have any ibuprofen in my purse. I'm thinking that it was smart of me to choose the table closest to the door in case I need to get away quickly. Or if he needs to. This little place in the middle of Edgewood? Another good choice—it's neutral and not the least bit intimate. I've been here only a few times but it's my favorite coffeehouse in Atlanta. The seating is limited—about ten tables; they want to encourage a quick turnaround. There are a couple of Instagram-worthy features, like the succulent wall and that clean black-and-white tile behind the baristas, but overall, it's quite austere. Harsh gray and concrete everywhere. The whistle of an espresso machine. Loud blenders mixing kale and whatever fruit is trendy.

There is a single door: one way in, one way out. I look down at my phone and wipe my palms on my black pants. Another stain. I need to get my shit together.

Will he hug me? Shake my hand? Was he preparing for our reunion obsessively, the way that I have been? Did he toss and turn like I did, thinking about what to say and how to present himself? The new awkward. Mature and like I've gotten my shit together, that's who I want him to think I am: a better version of the girl he knew so well.

I can't imagine him shaking my hand and using such a formal gesture. Not with me. But maybe he's just as anxious as I am; maybe his head is spinning with memories and regrets like mine? He isn't even here yet and my heart is pounding. For about the fourth time today I can feel the panic bubbling just below my rib cage, and it pisses me off that I can't control the physical effect he has on me. It pisses me off even more that he will probably walk in completely calm and steady, his own version of masking. I have no idea which mood of his I'll get today, controlled or turbulent? Will he bring up the one thing I don't want him to? I haven't seen him since last winter and I don't even know who he is now. And really, did I ever?

There were little things I should have let go of, but there is one big thing that I still can't accept. Even now the thought twists my insides and makes me want to change my mind about this whole Atlanta ordeal. I could go check out of my hotel, pack up my carry-on suitcase, and drive two hours back to my house, a place now off-limits to him. Did he remember that? I'll be able to tell if he often thinks of me by the way he looks at me. He isn't a mystery anymore. He is now a memory. Maybe I only ever knew a version of him—a bright and hollow form of the man I'm waiting on now. I must keep reminding myself that this trip isn't about him; it's bigger than him, bigger than both of us. Kael will be hurting. He'll hide it like a professional soldier but I know he'll be hurting. I don't know how much contact he's had with our friend over the last year, but I know Kael can't afford to lose anyone else around him.

I suppose I could have avoided him for the rest of my life, but the thought of never seeing Kael again seemed impossible and worse than sitting here now, driving myself insane with anxiety. At least I can admit that. Here I am warming my hands on a coffee cup, waiting for him to come through that raspy door after swearing to him, to myself, to anyone who would listen for the last few months, that I would never . . .

He's not due for another five minutes. It feels like the longest five minutes of my existence, but if he's anything like the man I knew, he'll strut in exactly on time with a straight face, not showing one hint of emotion.

When the door opens, it's a woman who walks in. Her blond hair is a nest stuck to the top of her tiny head and she's holding a cell phone against her red cheek.

"I don't give a shit, Howie. Get it done," she snaps, pulling the phone away with a string of curse words.

God, I hate this about Atlanta. Too many people here are like her, tetchy and forever in a hurry. Zero patience and not seeming to care that other people have shit to do too. The city wasn't always like this. Well, maybe it was? I wasn't always like this, though. Or maybe I was? But things and people change. I have. He probably has. I look around the shop again and watch the door for a few seconds. If he doesn't arrive soon I'm going to end up talking myself out of this whole meetup. I used to love this city, especially downtown. The dining scene is full of small, privately owned restaurants, not just chains, with actual chefs who create dishes that I've never even heard of but love. There's always something to do in Atlanta and everything is open later than it is around Fort Benning. The exception, of course, is the strip club—there's always at least one outside every military base. But the biggest draw to Atlanta for me back then was that I wasn't constantly reminded of military life. No camo everywhere you look. No ACUs on the men and women waiting in line for the movies, at the gas station, at Dunkin' Donuts. People speak real words, not just acronyms. And there are plenty of nonmilitary haircuts to admire.

I wanted to love Atlanta, but he ruined that.

We ruined that.

We.

That's the closest I'd get to admitting any fault in what went down. His lies, my stubbornness.

"What are you staring at?"

A few words, but they pour into and over me, shocking every one of my senses and all of my sense. And yet there's that calm, too, that seems to be hardwired into me whenever he's around. I look up to make sure it's him, though I know it is. Sure enough, he's standing over me with his hickory-colored eyes on my face, searching . . . reminiscing? I wish he wouldn't look at me like that. The small café is actually pretty packed, but I hardly notice. I'd had this meeting all scripted, and now, with five words, he's disrupted everything and I'm unnerved.

"How do you do that?" I ask him. "I didn't see you come in."

I worry that my voice sounds like I'm accusing him of something or I'm nervous, and that's the last thing I want. I need to be cool and make it clear that he doesn't have the power to get to me, not anymore. But still, I wonder—how does he do that, really? He was always so good at silence, at moving around undetected. Another skill honed in the Army, I guess.

I gesture for him to sit down. He slides into the chair, and that's when I realize he has a full beard. Sharp, precise lines graze his cheekbones, and his jawline is covered in dark hair. This is new. Of course it is: he always had to keep up with Army regulations. Hair must be short and well groomed. Moustaches are allowed, but only if they're neatly trimmed and don't grow over the upper lip. He told me once that he was thinking of growing a moustache, but I talked him out of it. He has never looked better. I hated and loved that at the same time.

He grabs the coffee menu from the table. Cappuccino. Macchiato. Latte. Flat white. Long black. When did everything get so complicated?

"You like coffee now?" I don't try to hide my surprise.

He shakes his head. "No. You like hot coffee now?" he asks me.

I look down at the mug between my hands and shake my head. "No."

I hate that he remembers small things about me. I wish I could erase them all from his memory. And from mine. I'm lying to myself, and I know that, but I try to keep a straight face.

A half smile crosses his stoic face, reminding me of one of the million reasons I fell in love with him. A moment ago, it was easy to look away. Now it's impossible.

"Not coffee," he assures me. "Tea."

He isn't wearing a jacket, of course, and the sleeves of his denim shirt are rolled up above his elbows. The tattoo on his forearm is fully visible and I know if I touch his skin right now it will be burning up. I'm sure as hell not going to do that, so I look up and over his shoulder. Away from the tattoo. Away from the thought. It's safer that way. For both of us. I try to focus on the noises in the coffee shop so I can settle into his silence. I forgot how unnerving his presence can be.

That's a lie. I didn't forget. I wanted to but couldn't. Just like sometimes I wanted to forgive him, but I never could.

I can hear the server approaching, her sneakers squeaking on the concrete floor. She has a mousy little voice and when she tells him that he should "so totally" try the new peppermint mocha, I laugh to myself, knowing that he hates all minty things, even toothpaste. I think about the way he'd leave those red globs of cinnamon gunk in the sink at my house and how many times we bickered over it. If only I had ignored those petty grievances. If only I had paid more attention to what was really happening, everything might have been different.

Maybe. Maybe not.

I don't want to know.

Another lie.

Kael tells the girl he would like a plain black tea, and this time I try not to laugh. He's so predictable.

"What's so funny?" he asks when the waitress leaves.

"Nothing." I change the subject. "So, how are you?"

"Don't do that. Don't act like we're strangers."

I tuck my lips together and look away before I reply, "Aren't we, though?"

He sighs and his eyes roam around the room before they land back on me. "Should I go?"

"I don't know, should you?"

He moves his chair out slightly and I reconsider. I don't really want him to go, but there are so many reasons to be mad at him and I'm afraid that being around him will soften me. I can't have that happen.

"Okay. Okay. Please, sit. I'll be nice," I promise him, with a small smile that's about as convincing as my attitude.

I don't know what bullshit we're going to fill this coffee date with, but since we're going to see each other tomorrow, it seemed like a good idea to get the first awkward encounter out of the way without an audience. A funeral is no place for that. And I had to be in the city today anyway.

"Kael, how are you?" I retry this whole being-nice thing.

"Good. Given the circumstances." He clears his throat.

"Yeah." I sigh, trying not to think too much about tomorrow. I've always been good at pretending the world isn't burning around me. Okay, I've been slipping these past few months, but for years denial was second nature, a permanent habit I mastered between my parents' divorce and my high school graduation. Sometimes it feels like my family is disappearing. We keep getting smaller and smaller. Sometimes I feel like I'm disappearing too.

"Are you all right?" he asks, his voice even lower than it was before.

It sounds the same as it did those damp nights when we fell asleep with the windows open—the whole room would be dewy the next morning, our bodies wet and sticky. I used to love the way his hot skin felt when my fingertips danced across the smooth contours of his jaw. Even his lips were warm, feverish at times. The southern Georgia air was so thick you could taste it, and Kael's temperature always ran so hot. Another thing I pretend to forget. We aren't here for a romantic reunion.

He clears his throat and asks again if I'm okay. I snap out of it.

I know what he's thinking. He can tell that I've left earth with my thoughts and he's trying to bring me back. I can read his face as clearly as the neon *But First, Coffee* sign hanging on the wall behind him. I hate that those memories are the ones my brain associates with him. It doesn't make this any easier.

"Kare." His voice is soft as he reaches across the table to touch my hand. I jerk it away so fast you'd think it was on fire. It's strange to remember the way we were, the way I never knew where he ended and I began. We were so in tune, so different from the way things are now. There was a time when he'd say my name and just like that, I'd give him anything he wanted. I consider this for a moment. How I'd give that man anything he wanted.

I thought I was further along in my recovery from us, that whole *getting over him* thing. At least far enough along that I wouldn't be thinking about the way his voice sounded when I had to wake him up early for physical training or the way he used to scream in the night. My head is spinning, and if I don't shut my mind off now the memories will split me apart, on this chair, in this little coffee shop, right in front of him.

I force myself to nod and pick up my latte to buy some time, just a moment so I can find my voice. "Yeah. I'm all right. I mean, funerals are kind of my thing."

"Tell me about it."

I don't dare look at his face. I don't want to see his grief or share my own, so I try to diffuse the intensity of what we're both feeling with some dark humor.

"We're running out of fingers to count the funerals we've been to in the last two years alone and—"

"There's nothing you could have done, regardless. Don't tell me you're thinking you could've—"

He pauses and I stare harder at the small chip in my mug. I run my finger over the cracked ceramic.

"Karina. Look at me."

I shake my head, not even close to jumping down this rabbit hole with him. I don't have it in me. "I'm fine. Seriously." I pause and take in the expression on his face. "Don't look at me like that. I'm okay."

"You're always fine." He runs his hand over the hair on his face and sighs, his shoulders leaning into the back of the plastic chair.

He's not buying it. He can feel my anxiety.

He's right. That whole fake-it-till-you-make-it thing? I own it.

What other choice do I have?

"How long are you in town?" he asks, scooting his chair a little bit closer.

Should I lie to him? Why don't I want to?

"For two days. Maybe less. I booked a room at the W."

"Oh, fancy." He smiles.

"It's so loud . . ."

He nods and thanks the server as she sets his tea in front of him. Her eyes take him in and she tucks her hair behind her ear with a big, beautiful smile that makes my stomach burn. I want to disappear.

He doesn't look away from my eyes.

"And so unlike you," he says.

"Huh?" I've already forgotten what we were even talking about.

"The hotel." He takes a drink of his tea and I try to catch my breath.

Being around him is still so dangerous for me. Sometimes warning signs and butterflies are one and the same.

Kael

The sea of black clothing makes my eyes hurt. It's been a while since I've been around such a uniformed crowd. I was so used to the camouflage I wore daily for years that even though I'm out of the Army, I still look for the camo out in the civilian world. Sometimes I miss not having to think about my choice of clothes every day. When I take one of my freshly dry-cleaned jackets off the hanger, I remember my ACU jacket, which had fabric so stiff from caked-in sand and dirt that it crinkled as we marched for hours in the Georgia heat. My hand reaches under my shirt to touch the dog tags hanging around my neck. For comfort? For punishment?

I'm not one of *those* soldiers who wears them as a prideful decoration or to get free drinks at local bars; I wear them because the weight of the metal on my chest keeps my feet on the ground. I'll probably never take them off. Yesterday morning at the coffee shop I noticed Karina's eyes scanning my neckline and I knew she was looking to see if I had taken them off yet. The answer will always be no.

"It's a little cold in here," my mom says, and I drop the dog tags and bring my hands to my lap.

"Do you want my jacket?" I ask her. She shakes her head.

"They have to keep the body cool or it will start to smell," a familiar voice says.

"Still a sick fuck, I see." I stand up and hug Silvin. He's a lot thinner than the last time I saw him. His jawline sticks out like that of a villain in an action film.

"Never gonna change either." He hits my arm.

My mom looks at him with disapproval. "You better quit that." She hits him a little harder than he hit me.

"How many times have I heard that?" Silvin hugs my mom and she breaks into a smile.

She always liked him the few times they met, despite the fact that he could be an offensive prick with a crass sense of humor. His beyond dark sense of humor kept us all laughing through the lowest times in our lives, though, so I always liked him too.

"How are you, man?" I ask casually, even though I know he's probably hurting more than most of the people in the church right now. Like I had been at the last one.

He clears his throat and blinks his red eyes. A puff of air blows from his cheeks before he answers, "I'm good. I, uhm—I'm good. I'd rather be in Vegas playing slots with a porn star and *her* money." He laughs awkwardly.

"Wouldn't we all," I joke back with him, careful not to add weight to his mind. Sometimes it's better to stay on the surface where you can stay numb. "Come sit down with us? Or do you already have a seat?" I ask him.

"It's not a fucking concert, Martin," he says and laughs, coming to sit down next to my mom.

Even though its masking deep sadness, Silvin's twisted laughter is the only inkling of happiness in the whole church. The ceiling is practically dripping with grief. The kind of sad that just bleeds into you and never washes away. It shows on you. The weight of everything you're carrying just flows through your blood and sits right on top of your shoulders.

Silvin sighs and leans back into the wooden pew heavily, trying to give it some of the weight inside of him. His dark eyes stare ahead, lost in some memory that refuses to go away, denying him any chance of peace. He's too young to look so old. He's aged drastically since we all called him "Baby Face" in our best Southern accents. He's from Mississippi and had looked about fifteen during our first deployment, but now he looks older than me.

Baby Face has grown up a lot since he had chunks of what looked like raw tuna thump against his face as they fell from the sky. It took my brain another explosion to digest the horror of realizing the plague of chunks falling from the sky were pieces of human flesh, not fish. I was standing so close that a finger with a wedding band on it landed against the toe of my combat boot. Johnson's face had changed when he turned to look and realized that his battle buddy Cox was no longer standing there. I saw something in his eyes, the smallest gleam burning out as he lifted his weapon from his waist and kept on moving. He never mentioned Cox again, and after that he sat in silence as Cox's pregnant widow cried at his funeral.

Come to think of it, this funeral feels eerily similar.

I look around for a clock. Isn't it almost time to start? I want to get this over with before I actually have to think about what we're doing here. Funerals are all the same, at least in the military. Outside of it, I haven't been to one since I was a kid. Since I left for basic training, I've been to at least ten funerals. That's ten times that I've sat silently in a wooden pew and scanned the faces of soldiers staring ahead, the straight line of their lips well practiced. Ten funeral homes full of shuffling kids who didn't understand life, let alone death, crawling at their parents' feet. Ten times that sobs broke out in the crowd. Luckily, only half of the deceased soldiers were married with families, so that meant only five sobbing wives whose lives were ripped apart and changed forever.

I often wonder when the calls would stop coming. After how many years will we stop gathering like this? Will it continue until we're all old and gray? Will Silvin come to my funeral or will I go to his? I always come, as does Johnson, whom I spot out of the corner of my eye. Stanson, too, who is holding his newborn son. He's still in the Army, but even the few of us who are no longer active duty still come. I flew to Washington state a few months ago for a guy I barely knew but whom Mendoza loved.

There are more people today than usual. Then again, this dead soldier was liked more than most of us. I couldn't think about his name, or say it in my head. I didn't want to do that to myself, or to my mom, whom I'd picked up in Riverdale and brought with me to Atlanta. She always liked him. Everyone did.

"Who's that lady there?" My mom coughs, her finger pointing at a woman I don't recognize.

"No clue, Ma," I whisper to her.

Silvin's haunted eyes are closed now. I look away from him.

"I'm sure I know that woman—" she insists.

A man in a suit walks onstage. Must be time.

I cut her off. "Ma. They're about to start."

I scan the pews for Karina; she must be here by now. She said she was coming right at the beginning so she wouldn't stay the whole time. Next to me, my mom coughs again. She's been doing that more and more lately. She's had this cough for about two years now, maybe more. Sometimes it goes away and she's rewarded for quitting smoking. Other times it's wet and she gripes about how she might as well light up a Marlboro. I've argued with her half my life, since I was ten and I heard her doctor tell her she was going to lose a lung if she didn't quit. I look down at her as she rubs the tissue along her lips, coughing deeper. Her tired eyes close for a second before she goes back to staring blankly at the flower-covered stage. The casket is closed, of course. No one wants these children to see the barely recognizable body.

Fuck, I have to stop. I've spent god knows how many hours with medical professionals tasked with fixing me, so you'd think I'd be better at keeping those thoughts out. They never work, the techniques they teach us. The darkness is still there, unmovable.

Maybe I should tell the government to get a refund on my therapy? They paid for it, as they should, but did it work? Clearly not. Not for Silvin, not for me, not for the body in the casket onstage.

Count down, they recommended when my mind got this way.

Count down and think of something that brings you joy or peace. Feel your feet on the ground, know you're safe now, they repeated.

I think of *her* when I need peace. I have since I met her. It only lasts so long until reality sets in and I want to punish myself for the fact that she's not in my life anymore, and I walk deeper into the darkness.

I don't get the chance to finish my self-therapy session.

"We're going to begin if everyone can take their seats now." The funeral director's voice is soft and unaffected. He probably does this a few times a week.

The room quiets and the funeral begins.

After the service we stay sitting while some line up for a last good-bye. Silvin catches my eye and points upward, like he's trying to tell me something. As I look up, someone taps me on the shoulder. I'd be lying if I didn't admit that I briefly hope it's Karina. Even though I'm sure it's not.

And of course, it's not. It's Gloria, standing behind me in a black dress with white flowers stitched across the top. I think I've seen her in that dress at all ten funerals. This has been a wild fucking ride already, from meeting Karina at the coffee shop yesterday to seeing Silvin again, to losing the bid on a hell of a deal on a four-plex apartment just outside Fort Benning—and now seeing Gloria, who always reminds me of her husband. I've been failing to come to terms with the situation with him. It's proven to be a lot harder than anything I've done in my entire life.

"Hey, Gloria." I get up from the pew and hug her.

Gloria hugs me and pulls back, then hugs me again.

"How are you? I've been worried about you. You never answer my calls anymore." She makes a face. "Asshole," she whispers, looking me straight in the eyes.

"I've been swamped with work. You know I hate the phone."

"The kids miss you, okay? And they ask about you a lot."

The kids. Acid born of guilt burns my throat.

"I miss them too." I look at her feet, where the littlest one usually clings. "I'll call more, I'm a shitbag." I smile at her and she nods, letting me off the hook a little.

"You are a total shitbag," she agrees, a smile on her face. "Uncle Shitbag still needs to call them once in a while." She looks up and down my face. "I didn't even recognize you at first because of this." She touches her palms to the stubble on my jaw.

"Yeah. I'm a free man now and decided to start acting like one."

"I'm glad. It's good to see you. Even if it's here of all places. And you—" She looks at my mom and, without breaking her conversation with the woman she recognized from earlier, my mom hugs and kisses her on the cheek.

"Karina looks great." Gloria purses her lips and stares into my eyes. "She always does but she looks . . ."

I look away as she pauses.

"She looks happy. That's what it is." She smiles.

Gloria always loved Karina, and I've heard through the grapevine that they still hang out; the gossip reaches me even though I've moved far away from post.

Happy?

She couldn't have seemed further from happy yesterday, but maybe I only get the cold, detached Karina now. It's not like I don't deserve that.

I quickly scan the church for Karina's hair. It's brown again. That color that's "right between chestnut and chocolate," she told me once. It was her go-to color when she felt like she had her shit together. Controlling and changing her hair color was one of her rituals. She had many little things she did to exercise control while disguising it as luck.

"Yeah. I'm glad she is," I tell Gloria. "I saw her yesterday."

She doesn't have to tell me that she already knows. It's easy to gather from how unaffected she is.

"Anyway, the kids with you?" I change the subject. She gives me another eye roll and shakes her head.

"No. My mom's with them back at Benning. I figured they've been to enough of these for a while."

"Haven't we all?"

"That's for damn sure."

A woman approaches us and moves to hug Gloria. She seems to know her, and they start talking. My mom is still in deep conversation, so I look for Karina again. How is it possible that I haven't seen her yet? The church isn't that big. Then again, she's good at blending in, hiding in the midst of a crowd. It's one of her "things."

My mom's voice cuts through the hushed greetings and condolences being shared around me while I'm lost in my own head.

"Mikael, where is it your sister is wanting to go to college again?" she asks, confusion in her eyes despite the hundreds of conversations we've had about it.

"MIT," I tell the woman talking to her, whom I now recognize as Lawson's mom. I know she's a better person than her son, but that's not exactly hard to accomplish. After spending my last few years in the Army with him in my platoon and two deployments to Afghanistan later, I know Lawson better than even his own mother does. War brings people closer than anything can, except death. They go hand in hand in my world.

"That's it. MIT. She's the smartest in her whole class this year, and last. Two more years to wait, but they would be crazy not to accept her." My mom's black hair is falling out of the clip thing she always wears. The curls I helped her put in her hair this morning are fallen now. I reach down to push her hair back from her face.

The memory of Karina laughing at me as I burned my fingertips on a hot curling iron fills my mind. I knew she had to be the most thoughtful, selfless person I would ever meet when she offered to teach me how to curl my mom's hair after we noticed the burns on her hands. Some mornings Mom's hands would shake so badly that she couldn't do it herself, but she was too stubborn to ask for help.

I don't travel home as often as I should, but my mom loves to have me curl her hair when I do. She says it will make me a good father one day. Karina said the same, with a look in her eyes like she could see the future. Turns out she couldn't, and neither can my mom, because she still hopes for grandchildren from me to pass on the family name. Not fucking happening. There's no chance I'd ever punish the world with another me.

I sigh and grab my phone from my pocket, checking it out of habit while glancing around the room. It's emptier now, so Karina will be easier to find. Eventually I'll either know for sure that she's not here or she'll appear from whatever corner of the room she's hiding in. That's if she didn't slip out, and knowing her, there's a high likelihood—

"I'm right here, Dory."

Karina's soft voice sends both shock and relief throughout my body.

"There you are. Everyone keeps talking about you, and here you are," Ma says.

Karina's brows draw together, and she shakes her head. "Gossip as always."

Her lips curl into a smile and she puts her arm around my mom's shoulders and squeezes.

Karina's fingers go to Ma's hair, and she unfastens the clip. Her delicate hands twist Ma's hair then clip it back exactly how she likes it and a hell of a lot better than I can do. Man, they've come a long way since the beginning. It drives me fucking crazy with guilt that because of everything that happened, my mom doesn't have Karina in her life anymore. Unlike Gloria, who could drive to see Karina ten minutes away, my mom will never even sit behind a wheel again. Not safely, at least. The laundry list of mistakes I've made over the last several years just keeps growing. Even though now we are living separate lives, I've done too many unforgivable things to her.

"Do you want to go outside?" she asks Ma. "It's getting a little stuffy in here." The green of her eyes catches on the stained glass church window.

My mom follows Karina and they both look back at me standing still.

"Well?" they say in unison.

"I'll go with you." I look at Karina.

She stares back at me, her lips parting slightly, but she doesn't say anything.

As we turn, my phone vibrates in my hand. I go to answer it and catch Karina's eyes. She's staring daggers at my phone, one of her worst enemies. She expects me to answer it, like I always do, so I ignore the call and keep my eyes on her. She licks her lips and her eyes give away that she's surprised and that she sees this as a win. It was just one of my contractors anyway.

"Shall we?" I ask her, digging in my position of at least trying to stay on her game board. She nods and leads us out of the church as the bells from its tower ring through the air.

"It was so nice of you to come, Karina. That woman wasn't very nice to you," my mom tells Karina as we walk out into the fresh air.

"She was nicer toward the end, right before they got stationed in Texas. I hadn't gotten to that part of the story." Karina smiles, holding my mom's hand.

I knew Toni wasn't Karina's favorite person, but she still came to Tharpe's funeral. It's fucking awful, another death caused by the lack of mental health care when it comes to PTSD, but we all seem pretty numb to it now.

"Either way, I feel so bad for her and the kids. And we had some nice memories together." Karina's eyes touch mine as I think back to the memories she's referring to. They feel like another lifetime ago.

"All this loss. It's too much," my ma says, her voice trembling.

I hated bringing my ma to another funeral, but she insisted on coming since Tharpe was in my platoon and she assumed we were close. He and Mendoza had been much closer than we were, but I didn't want to fight with her over a funeral of all things, and she's a stubborn woman. The funeral felt empty without Mendoza, but he couldn't come, not because of his physical condition, but his mental. He's trying like hell every single day to stay afloat, and another funeral sure as hell wouldn't help that. That and he didn't want any more attention on him and his body as he learned to walk again. He's recovering and I'm damn proud of him.

"Your brother isn't here, right?" my ma asks Karina as we walk down the steps of the church.

She shakes her head, her focus on my ma, and I can tell she's purposely not looking at me.

"Elodie said to tell you hi by the way. She's sorry they couldn't be here, but Donavan is sick and they don't have a babysitter. Plus I think she's scared to travel without my brother, and the Army denied his request to come since they're technically not family."

The arcane rules of the military frustrating everything once again.

"How do you know Elodie?" I ask my ma out of curiosity. I never talk about my Army life with her, but apparently Karina has.

"I met her when they came to visit last year," my ma tells me. Karina's smug expression tells me she's enjoying my surprise.

"Really?"

"Yeah, really. We all went out to eat and had a nice time. You should have come," my ma scolds me.

"I wasn't invited," I said, looking at Karina.

The two women share a look. "I wonder why."

"What is this, you two are ganging up on me?" I can't help but be slightly thrilled that they have gotten so close. Even if Karina doesn't allow me in her life, at least she has my ma and my ma has her.

"Yep. So just take it." Karina sticks her tongue out at me while my ma isn't looking.

A wave of relief, happiness, and familiarity washes over me.

"Let's get some food?" my ma suggests. "Mikael, you can drive us, right?"

I nod, happy to have a little more time with Karina, even if her and my ma are planning on giving me shit the whole time. I'll gladly take it.

We end up at a small Cajun spot outside Midtown that I've been to a few times. I think Karina will love it, and her expression while reading the menu confirms it. Over the meal I let the two of them chat, my ma mixing up names and places while Karina listens to stories I know she's already heard. Watching them makes me fantasize about a different life. One where Karina is my wife and we're living in Atlanta, her owning a spa and me flipping houses. Going to lunch with my ma is a regular thing in my fantasy world, and I wake up every day to Karina's beautiful face and forgiving soul.

The meal goes by too fast, and I consider telling the server to slow the hell down and not give us the bill yet, but I'm too late. I try to take everything in, knowing I likely won't see Karina again for a while, if ever, though she's warmer toward me now than she was at the coffee shop; the façade of anger and her pretending to be a stranger has faded and her mask is slipping more and more by the minute.

"Should we get coffee somewhere?" I suggest, trying to prolong our time together.

"I'm tired, but you can drop me off at your house before you take Karina back to her car," my ma suggests. It's the opposite way, but I'm sure as hell not going to point that out.

I look at Karina for her consent, not wanting to pressure her to be around me, but hoping like hell she will agree.

"Sure. I'm not in the mood for coffee, but you can take me back to my car after we drop her off. Plus, I want to see your house anyway. Your ma showed me pictures but I'm dying to see it in person."

I nod, trying to remember if I made my bed or put away the dishes in the sink. I had no clue that Karina would end up in my house today, or ever, but I wasn't going to let some dishes get in the way of that happening. We drive to my house in near silence, and I hold my breath as we pull up. Karina's eyes widen as the three of us get out of my truck, she and I both going to either side of my ma to help her out and up the porch.

My ma hugs Karina, telling her she's going to wash up and will call her tomorrow. I wonder how long Karina's staying in Atlanta but decide to wait to ask.

"Do you want a tour?" I hesitate, unsure if it's a good idea or not. My ma has been around us the last couple of hours, acting as a buffer so we didn't have to worry about how awkward it would be if we were alone.

"I would, actually," she agrees, her eyes on the double-sided staircase that took me months to remodel.

"It's stunning." Her voice trails off as we walk through the sitting room and into the kitchen.

I wonder if she's going to notice that I designed my entire home for her. Every decision I made was based around what I knew she liked, from the color of the aged wooden floors, to the vaulted ceilings, to the tile in the bathroom and the shade of beige I chose for my bedsheets.

"This is my dream home," she finally says as we finish the nearly silent tour.

My heart is racing, burning, and turning in my chest. "I know," I admit.

Confusion flashes across her face. "Why did you—if you knew I would never come here, why did you do that?"

"Do you want the truth or some excuse to make you less uncomfortable?"

She huffs, stepping closer to me. "I'm not uncomfortable."

I take that as a slight opening, a tiny sign that her dislike of me has gotten smaller during our time apart.

"I hoped you would see it someday. If you ever needed me, or somewhere to go, or stopped by, I wanted you to know that this house could be yours. I desperately wanted to believe that you would be here someday, even like this." I wave my hand into the space between us.

As she studies my face, I do the same, trying to read her mind the way I usually could. "I don't know what to say," she finally says.

In an attempt to lighten the mood for her sake, I say, "That's a first."

Her hand moves to her hip and she glares at me, no anger in her skeptical eyes.

"Was this your plan? To use your ma against me and get me to come to your house to forgive you?" Her tone is light, airy, and almost playful. I'm confused but roll with it.

"No, but if it's working, I'll take credit for it." I lean against the wall, giving her a little more space even though that's the last thing I want.

"Have you really been waiting for me, Kael?" Her voice is quiet, unsure, and wavering.

"Every second of every day."

Her breath catches in her throat and she uses her arm to hold her body upright against the opposite wall. "I have something to tell you. I was going to tell you sooner but—"

I interrupt her. My chest aches as if I'm diving off a twenty-story building; my lungs feel as if they will collapse if she tells me she loves someone else. I'd rather not know. I can't take it.

"I don't want to know. I'm sorry, Karina, but the only thing that makes me able to get out of bed every morning and fight with the shadow of my past is the chance that you'll be by my side someday. Please don't take that away from me, even if that means lying to my face right now. I can't stand it. The idea of you with someone else, I literally cannot handle it, Kare."

Her eyes widen and she looks around the empty kitchen. "What . . . that isn't what . . ."

Her chest moves up and down and she places her hand over her heart to catch her breath.

"I'm moving to Riverdale." Her words don't make any sense as they come out.

"What are you talking about?" I ask for clarity. There's no way in hell she just said what I think I heard.

"It sounds crazy, but I'm moving to Riverdale. I begged your ma not to tell you because I wanted to be the one. Again, I know you're going to have a million questions and I don't really have all the answers, but Mali is retiring and decided to close the shop, Elodie and my brother are in Kansas and I sure as hell don't want to move there, and my dad and Estelle are going on a road trip in their RV for at least a year. I don't have anyone at Benning anymore except Gloria, but she's obviously so busy with Mendoza's recovery and the kids."

"You're moving in with my ma? Is that what you're saying?" I press my fingers to my forehead. I knew they kept in contact, but of course my ma, being my ma, never so much as mentioned this to me.

Karina nods, her hands now resting on her chest in a fist. "Your sister is leaving soon and no one will be there to take care of her. As you know, her memory is fading by the day, and I looked online for jobs, there's a few in the next town. The pay isn't great but if I sell my house I can live off that and maybe get training to be an actual caretaker for her, that way I would get paid for it, and I could help other people too. You know I love to take care—"

I wrap my arms around her, a little squeak coming from her as I pull her to my chest. I'm not a man of many or the perfect words, and am at a loss for what to say because *thank you* just isn't enough. Not even close to enough. Her body relaxes in my arms, and I feel her hands press against my back as she embraces me. Years of loss, of longing, of fucking near-death pain evaporate as she melts into me.

"Thank you, it's not enough, but thank you," I say, my eyes wet with gratitude.

I had been so worried about how I was going to convince my ma to move to Atlanta to live with me. Every time I brought it up, she cussed me out. She loves her neighborhood, her church, her home, and wants to live there until her last breath. I know that, but I still tried to convince her and had planned on trying until she gave in. I even bought the old abandoned house next to hers in case she refused.

The land . . . I could tear that house down and build a new one. Karina could help me design it while she figured out the next step in her life.

"Are you upset at all? I'm not trying to cross the line or invade your life," she tells me, her breath warm against my chest.

"Not even close to upset. Grateful, not upset, and those are lines you created, so please cross them." I beg her to erase them.

"I don't know what will happen in the future, but this choice feels right. I never imagined I would sell my house, but I can barely stand it anymore. It used to feel like the only thing I had that was mine, but lately it's been feeling like the only thing tying me to that damn town."

I'm surprised to hear her disdain for that house since she always put so much emotional value on it, rightfully so, but I couldn't be happier that she finally wants to leave Benning.

"Well, I'm happy for you, neighbor." I rub my hand down her hair as she lifts her head up, away from my chest to look at me.

"What do you mean, 'neighbor'?"

I grin at her, knowing there's a chance that this might make her change her mind, but taking the risk.

"I bought the house next door almost a year ago. I'm going to tear it down and we can rebuild it together, if you're down and need a hobby. There isn't shit to do in Riverdale so you'll be bored anyway," I tell her, as if I didn't just come up with this plan two minutes ago.

Her smile answers my plea, and I genuinely can't believe this is how our story is continuing. I guess some people do deserve second chances, and I am determined to make sure I earn mine.

ACKNOWLEDGMENTS

So many people breathe life into every book you hold, and I find it almost impossible to thank everyone here, but this is my feeble attempt.

This series has been a labor of love that has taken me through parts of my past, and there were so many times when I felt like throwing my laptop into the Pacific Ocean. :P But fortunately, I didn't, so thank you for taking the time and energy and using your hard-earned money to support me and my works. Whether you're new to my books or have supported me since my Wattpad days, your encouragement doesn't go unnoticed.

Flavia Viotti—my agent, my second mother, my friend, my partner in so many ways. My life has changed for the better since you came into it, and there aren't enough words to express how or why. From having nine hundred bottles of wine in Europe to all the *secret* things we're working on, there's no one else I'd rather do things with than you. Here's to many, many more years and projects to come.

Kristin Dwyer—this is our eleventh book together! You're my day one, and there are only so many times you can stand reading this in each book (ha-ha) but thank you for encouraging me and always being there for me to vent, plot, and drive through the Florida swamps in the rain with.

Vilma Gonzalez—thank you for reminding me how valuable and life-changing female friendships can be. You've been here for me throughout this entire series, giving me pep talks and distracting me with BTS videos when I needed them the most. :P You're the definition of a girl's girl, and I purple you for lifeeeee.

Erin and Douglas—you two make Frayed Pages go round, and your work and dedication to growing this little dream of mine are so appreciated. We've been through so much together and ily both. It hasn't been the smoothest, but I'm lucky to be doing it with you. <3

Anne Messitte—you've been the biggest cheerleader of Kael and Karina's story for years now, and it means so much to me. I've loved getting to know you, not just as an editor but as an incredible woman and mentor. Thank you for everything.

Deanna McFadden—thank you for always working around my chaos. Your willingness to think outside the box and support me as an author and my wild process has made this book. You're such a kind, therapeutic human, and I really appreciate you.

Maeve O'Regan—you're always such a light to work with! Tiny airports and Logan's Roadhouse will never be the same. :P Thanks for everything!

To the dedicated team at Wattpad WEBTOON Studios who have helped me grow Frayed Pages x Wattpad Books—you've been here since I was a baby author, and it means so much to me that ten years later you're still part of my career. Tina McIntyre, Delaney Anderson, Lesley Worrell, Amy Brosey, Rebecca Mills, Shannon Whibbs, Patrick McCormick, and Neil Erickson. Aron Levitz, you're basically grandfathered into every book I produce, and I love that for us. *pretend there's a unicorn emoji here*

To all my publishers around the world, the editors, marketing and sales teams, and cover designers, your work behind the scenes is what makes these books possible. Thank you so, so much!

ABOUT THE AUTHOR

Anna Todd (writer/producer/influencer) is the *New York Times* best-selling author of the After series, The Brightest Stars trilogy, *The Spring Girls*, and the After graphic novels. The After series has been released in thirty-five languages and has sold over twelve million copies worldwide, becoming a number one best-seller in several countries. Always an avid reader, Todd began writing stories on her phone through Wattpad, with After becoming the platform's most-read series with over two billion reads. She has served as a producer and screenwriter on the film adaptations of *After* and *After We Collided*, and in 2017, she founded the entertainment company Frayed Pages Media to produce innovative and creative work across film, television, and publishing. A native of Ohio, she lives with her family in Los Angeles.

@annatodd

@imaginator1D

ANNA TODD'S
BRIGHTEST STARS TRILOGY

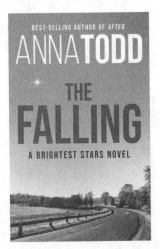

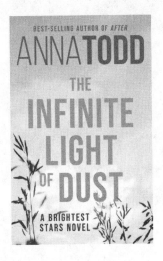